# PEACE,

**THIS IMMERSIVE SUSPENSE** novel from Talley captures the chaotic rhythm of San Francisco's Haight-Ashbury district in late 1969 . . . a dazzling tie-dye tapestry that brings a well-covered corner of American history to vivid life. It's a trip.
   **PUBLISHERS WEEKLY**

**A FRESH TAKE** on a nostalgically remembered era. . . . Murder mixed with psychedelia makes for an agreeable high.
   **KIRKUS REVIEWS**

**THE HOT BREATH** noirs of David Goodis crossed with William Burroughs' jittery kaleidoscopes are in evidence in Max Talley's thoroughly engrossing *Peace, Love and Haight*. The novel deftly captures the defeated promises of a time and place—yet is timeless.
   **GARY PHILLIPS**, author, *Ash Dark as Night*

**THIS AIN'T YOUR** grandparents' *Maltese Falcon* or your parents' *Inherent Vice*—rather, Max Talley weaves that DNA into a vintage 60s thrill ride and populates it with scary folk and a unique protagonist in Freddie Dorn.
   **CHRISTOPHER CHAMBERS**, author, *Scavenger, Standalone,* and *Streetwhys*

**WHO SAYS TIME TRAVEL** isn't possible? Max Talley's *Peace, Love and Haight* is a fun, fast and suspenseful trip back to San Francisco in the groovy, hip, and sometimes even dangerous summer of 1969.
   **GAR ANTHONY HAYWOOD**, bestselling author, *In Things Unseen*

**IT'S THE HAIGHT** in the late 60s. Fredrick Dorn, art dealer and reluctant snitch, battles a motley crew of mobsters, dealers, musicians, and other off-the-wall strangers, all intent on murder—his.
   **JOHN REED**, author, *The Kingfisher's Call*

**TALLEY UNLEASHES** a searing, incisive tale about the demise of the 1960s in which utopian notions of peace, free love, and community have been eclipsed by treachery, paranoia, and sex cults. . . . Talley unleashes a Gonzo-like journey through this vortex without making us feel dizzy or hopeless. He accomplishes this through a sophisticated sense of restraint and deft use of language.
   **SERGE F. KOVALESKI**, former investigative journalist, *The New York Times*

THE YEAR IS 1969. Love and peace have turned to fear and anger. Art gallery manager, Frederick Dorn, wants to clean up Haight Street, bring some normal back. What can one man do but go undercover for the cops. Max Talley takes us on a wild ride through the death of the Sixties with a brutal wit, vivid characters, and yes, a glimmer of hope.

    MELODIE JOHNSON HOWE, Edgar-nominated author, *Mother Shadow* and *City of Mirrors*

IT'S 1969 ON HAIGHT STREET, and all that's left of the Summer of Love is dregs. Gallery owner Frederick Dorn, haunted and hopeful, cynic and idealist, just wants make the street a little safer, even if that means dealing with the devil in the form of drug pushers, cops, and the Mafia. Hip, tense, and wildly propulsive, *Peace, Love and Haight* is an outstanding thriller, frightening to funny and back again in lightning leaps. As soon as you finish it, you'll want to start again.

    CYNTHIA WEINER, author, *A Gorgeous Excitement*

IMAGINE AN ELMORE LEONARD novel with an almost Brueghelian cast of crooked cops, predatory pushers, hopped-up hookers, teen-aged Jezebels, and horndog Jesus freaks. . . . Protagonist Freddie Dorn is learning street-life the hard way. Naturally, when a drug deal goes wrong in Baghdad-by-the-Bay, someone must go over the rail of the Golden Gate Bridge, no? Well, it's not going to be Freddie Dorn. He's getting smarter every day. Max Talley's novel is a rollicking tale, filled with suspense and gnarly humor.

    BARNABY CONRAD III, author, *Jacques Villeglé and the Streets of Paris*

MAX TALLEY'S NEW NOVEL is a fast-moving, gritty noir, with great dialogue, suspense, and characters that are larger than life. The dicey sixties in San Francisco reimagined.

    LEONARD TOURNEY, author, *Catesby's Ghost*

# Peace Love & Haight

# Peace Love & Haight

*A Psychedelic Thriller*

## Max Talley

THREE ROOMS PRESS
New York, NY

*Peace, Love and Haight*
A Psychedlic Thriller by Max Talley

© 2025 by Max Talley

All rights reserved. No part of this book may be reproduced in any form or by any electronic or mechanical means, including information storage and retrieval systems, without permission in writing from the publisher, except by a reviewer, who may quote brief passages in a review. For permissions, please write to address below or email editor@threeroomspress.com. Any members of educational institutions wishing to photocopy or electronically reproduce part or all of the work for classroom use, or publishers who would like to obtain permission to include the work in an anthology, should send their inquiries to Three Rooms Press, 243 Bleecker Street, #3, New York, NY 10014.

This is a work of fiction. Names, characters, businesses, places, events, and incidents are either the products of the author's imaginations or used in a fictitious manner. Any resemblance to actual persons, living or dead, or actual events is purely coincidental.

NO AI TRAINING: Without in any way limiting the author's [and publisher's] exclusive rights under copyright, any use of this publication to "train" generative artificial intelligence (AI) technologies to generate text is expressly prohibited. The author reserves all rights to license uses of this work for generative AI training and development of machine learning language models.

ISBN 978-1-953103-66-6 (trade paperback)
ISBN 978-1-953103-67-3 (Epub)
Library of Congress Control Number: 2025937098

TRP-122

First Edition
Pub Date: October 14, 2025

BISAC category code
FIC022090 FICTION / Mystery & Detective / Private Investigators
FIC022060 FICTION / Mystery & Detective / Historical
FIC022100 FICTION / Mystery & Detective / Amateur Sleuth
FIC031010 FICTION / Thrillers / Crime

COVER AND INTERIOR DESIGN:
KG Design International: www.katgeorges.com

DISTRIBUTED IN THE U.S. AND INTERNATIONALLY BY:
Ingram/Publishers Group West: www.pgw.com

Three Rooms Press
New York, NY
www.threeroomspress.com
info@threeroomspress.com

> "There was madness in any direction, at any hour. If not across the Bay, then up the Golden Gate or down to Los Altos or La Honda . . . You could strike sparks anywhere. There was a fantastic universal sense that whatever we were doing was right, that we were winning . . ."
>
> —Hunter S. Thompson, *Hell's Angels*—

*This book is dedicated to
all those who protested against
the vile and vainglorious back then
and for all those protesting
again now.*

# Peace Love & Haight

## CHAPTER ONE
# Who Scared You?

HAIGHT STREET WAS THRONGED WITH YOUNG hippies and middle-aged freaks that fateful day, the air thick from tobacco, incense, auto exhaust, and fried food smells. Some blue-nosed straights gawked on the sidelines as a discordant blend of noise echoed off storefronts. A balding man in a toga who resembled Allen Ginsberg shouted out poetry, while a dude in American flag pants blew on a harmonica, a young woman with ratty brown hair in her eyes played a recorder, and a painted face guy in army fatigues blasted trumpet victory calls. A seething madness, like a stalled parade stretching for blocks, and as Dorn veered out into car traffic then pressed through bodies blocking sidewalk travel, he reminded himself, this was freedom. No one living there, no one camped there wore suits or formal dresses or carried briefcases to some bullshit nine-to-five job. They had escaped Squaresville to find their utopia—BLISS!—but the masses just kept coming.

When the plain clothes cop first approached Frederick Dorn at his San Francisco art gallery, his instant response was, "No, hell, no." Become a fucking narc? Unthinkable. But that was back in December of 1967.

Eighteen months later, any lingering afterglow of the Summer of Love had most definitely ended. The Mafia moved into the

Haight, bringing cheap speed and strong heroin. A number of Dorn's friends either died or became sallow addicts. He even got robbed right outside his gallery by a deadbeat junkie desperate for another fix, so he bought a .38 revolver for protection. Dorn's ex-girlfriend Ramona's tragic overdose brought him to a decision. *Maybe I can work with the man to bust dealers ruining the neighborhood. I won't finger any users, just nail the scum bags at the top.*

"Detective Rodriguez?" he said. "It's Freddie Dorn. You asked for my help a while back."

"I remember," Victor Rodriguez replied on the phone, "but thought you forgot, Dorn."

"There's a neighborhood dealer named Rat-Man. Are you interested?"

"We're very interested in shutting Rathkin down." Rodriguez coughed. "Come in to talk."

Rat-Man Rathkin, purveyor of mass quantities of bad drugs. His experimental batch of Orange Marmalade caused a local dude to run into traffic and get hit by a trolley car; it also sent a fifteen-year-old girl to the psych ward in a straitjacket. Dorn's best buddy Van Monk had his brains permanently fried by a single dose of OM.

Dorn walked Haight Street in July 1969, a day after calling the station. Right in front of his gallery, a filthy man clutched a guitar with broken strings, one hand extended.

"You need food?" Dorn asked. "The Diggers serve free lunch in the park." He pointed.

The squatting, bearded man shook his head. "Need trips." He flapped his arms like a bird.

"Sorry, don't do that anymore."

"What are you, a Hollywood hippie?" The man spit on the ground.

Dorn had been called a capitalist pig just for wanting to make a living and pay his rent. "No, man," he said. "Find Lamb Chops in the Panhandle. He gives out samples." Dorn hoped to spur the guy away from his business, from scaring off customers. He knelt down to deposit three quarters in the guitar case.

Dorn finally reached the Park Station on the eastern edge of Golden Gate Park. He wore a floppy hat with giant sunglasses to make him unrecognizable to friends, but it also made him conspicuous to straights. Inside, the scent of body odor and desperation mingled freely.

"Detective Rodriguez?"

The desk sergeant squinted at him with suspicion. "He expecting you?"

"Yes." Dorn shuffled past benches holding delirious hippies, two Black Panthers, a chanting Hare Krishna member in robes, and a disoriented grandmotherly woman. He peered in the open offices until he found the sole Hispanic cop. "Detective?"

"Dorn? Come in." Rodriguez chewed on a sandwich. "So, can you help us nail Rathkin?"

Dorn stared at the scuffed floor, feeling uncomfortable, trapped. "I won't be a police informer, but Rat-Man needs to get busted. Too many casualties from his drugs."

Rodriguez flexed a police smile. "That's all we want," he insisted. "A little community cooperation. We both live and work in the Haight. You came to San Francisco from the Midwest a few years ago for the peace and love."

Dorn nodded, not overjoyed to hear the law's take on his life choices.

"You smoked some Mary Jane, maybe shot the acid—"

"Nobody shoots LSD."

"What I mean is, you're no teenager. Pushing thirty, probably. You didn't come for the crazies roaming Haight Street now." Rodriguez sighed. "Working together, we could make our neighborhood safer for families, for small business owners like yourself." He looked up. "Here comes my partner."

A six foot three man built like a longshoreman lumbered into the room, showing a walrus mustache under a ratty longhair wig, pink sunglasses, a paisley shirt tied above his beer belly, and stupid bell bottoms encasing biker boots. A scar snaked across a bulging forehead. His whole garish appearance screamed: NARC!

Dorn had heard about a violent undercover cop, dubbed Hippie Frankenstein by locals.

"He's why I need you." Rodriguez chuckled. "Detective Flannery doesn't quite blend in."

Flannery scowled. "You want to hire this loser, a scrawny freak?"

Rodriguez rubbed his hands together. "He'd be an adjunct, a temporary hire. Not official."

"I don't need insults from Hippie Frankenstein here," Dorn said.

Flannery glowered, moving closer.

"He's my responsibility." Rodriguez stepped between them. "Let's go speak to the Captain." As they walked the hallway, Rodriguez whispered to Dorn, "You'll report to me. Flannery has a hair-trigger temper. Former Green Beret."

It took a half hour. The captain didn't like the idea at all, but somehow Rodriguez convinced him. Dorn promised to contact them when he got a line on Rat-Man's whereabouts.

Dorn's real life nightmare began the next day when a dude named Vince Napoli visited United Hallucinations Gallery. Due to his brown suit with a fat purple tie, Dorn assumed he was Mob.

Vince approached him. "You know Rat-Man, Jay Rathkin."

"Do I *know* him?"

"I'm not asking, Dorn. Word is you do."

"He's a dealer." Dorn wished Detective Rodriguez would appear to make the thug go away. "He sells stepped-on pills to desperate local kids. They end up in the hospital, or dead."

"Heard you were his friend." Vince's expression relaxed. "In Roman times there was a tradition. A guy who had done wrong would take care of the problem, the problem being himself, by himself. Know what I'm saying?"

"I tell you, I'm not his friend."

Vince glanced at two hippie girls enraptured by a framed Jimi Hendrix Fillmore poster, the guitarist appearing all stone temple godly. "It would be beneficial if Rat-Man got my message, to retire—permanently."

"I'll try to get word to him."

"By tomorrow," Vince said. "Or we send janitors to clean up his mess. You don't take us for ten large and walk." He gave the gallery a sneering once-over and left.

Leon came out of the gallery's office, working a pick through his afro. "Yo, Dorn. That dude was a serious gangster."

He didn't reply. Leon tried to sell him bogus joints last spring. Catnip or something. Instead of scolding, Dorn offered him a custodial job, watching the gallery when he was away, to sweep and mop up. Surprised when Leon accepted.

"My man Vernon saw you talking to detectives at the Park Station." Leon frowned, his eyes slits, wary. "That's low rent."

Dorn pondered what he could reveal. "Do you know who Rat-Man is?"

"That honky shithead dealer. Sells his lame product in the projects. We call it rat poison. Hides in Oakland somewhere."

"I made a one-time arrangement to take the bastard down," Dorn said, "for the good of the community. Then I'm done." He wanted to believe that.

Leon nodded, his mouth twisting. "Sounds for real, Dorn, but I'll be watching. Rather be dealing weed on the street than working for a jive-ass narc."

Dorn felt as if he'd been scolded by his boss, not an assistant. "Okay, cover for me here."

Paranoia sank in after Vince's visit. Dorn had to deliver Rat-Man to Detective Rodriguez before the Mob offed him. Police wanted to sweat names out of the dealer; they needed Rathkin alive. *Find Van Monk.*

Dorn crossed town to 245 Hyde Street and entered Wally Heider's recording studio. Downstairs in Studio A, his buddy played on a session with the Mind Magnets. Dorn sat by engineer Bill Halverson to watch Van Monk nail his keyboard part.

"Hey, Freddie," Van Monk shouted afterward. "I just saw you, man."

"What? Where?"

Van Monk led him outside then lit a joint. "I saw you when I flashed forward to the 1990s." They perched on the stoop of the Black Hawk jazz club across the street.

Dorn didn't question it, that was his freak. But Rat-Man's poisoned drugs were behind the delusions. *Humor the guy.* "Sure, brother."

Van Monk passed the joint. Throaty saxophone honks emanated from an afternoon soundcheck downstairs in the Black Hawk's basement.

Dorn coughed, slapping his chest.

"Go easy, that's Crosby weed."

"Far out." Dorn laughed smoke. "You hear anything on Rat-Man? Where he's living?"

Van Monk tensed up. "At a derelict house in Oakland. Don't know the address." He pushed a tangle of brown hair from his eyes. "I'm all about peace and love, but if I ever see Rat-Man, I might kill him."

Bill Halverson signaled from the studio's doorway.

"Got to finish my session, but if you find that piece of . . ." Van Monk's voice took on a pleading tone. "You have to tell me."

"Dig it, man." Dorn couldn't involve Van Monk in it. Too risky. He needed Rathkin alive and alone—to answer a personal question. Dorn took a last hit then tamped out the joint.

WHILE LOCKING UP THE GALLERY THE next day, Leon approached Dorn. "Word is that Rat-Man lives near Racine Street and 63rd." He swiveled his head around. "Am I the shit, or what?"

"House number?"

Leon scowled. "A Victorian inside a locked iron gate. You can find it." He pointed two fingers at his eyes.

"I might need you to come along."

"Might?" Leon lit a filtered Newport. "It's South Berkeley, North Oakland. One street is university professors and students, the next has a whole lot of people like me. But not as mellow. Black Panthers, community activists, and residents who don't take kindly to a white dude out for a scenic stroll."

"Okay, I definitely need you."

"We're talking overtime. Double wages, right?" Leon grinned.

They chugged over the Bay Bridge in Dorn's orange Volvo and parked on Shattuck Avenue. As a fevered reddish sun sank into San Francisco Bay, they walked north on 63rd Street. Mostly two-story Victorians, small stucco cottages, and square brick apartment houses where young residents sat outside in the cooling air and watched them with wary eyes.

By the juncture with Racine Street, Dorn found an archway entrance of a darkened house.

"Why you stopping?" Leon glanced back at the apartment bloc they passed. "Not safe."

Dorn pointed at two ramshackle Victorians with peeling paint on Racine Street. Both had metal gates surrounding them. "I'll scope them out. Can you cruise up and down 63rd? Run interference."

Leon sniffed. "If I see a crew coming for you, I'll whistle loud, then you'll see my black ass sprinting downhill."

Dorn patrolled Racine, watching lights turning on in homes. He studied each of the two Victorians. One was lit up downstairs and upstairs, while the other showed a dim yellowy glow from the second floor. He walked by its gate, noticing trash in the garden, broken bottles, and a riot of weeds. A rat's lair. He moved back to the archway on the corner of 63rd.

A bedraggled older man clutching a paper bag shuffled over. "What you doing here after dark? You don't look local."

Leon returned in a hurry. "Move along, brother, this fool's with me."

The man waved his bagged bottle at them, cursed, then staggered away uphill.

"Don't look south," Leon said. "There's a Buick idling down there. Think they're watching you."

"Damn, Detective Rodriguez followed us over."

"Nope, these are hard-faced white dudes in tacky suits."

"Shit, it's Vince." Dorn thought a moment. "Go make a distraction, then meet me behind that green Victorian."

"I want a paid day-off next week."

"Fine."

Dorn saw Leon at the edge of an alley by the apartment bloc, near invisible in the new dark. Further downhill, the Buick sat rumbling. Just when Dorn thought nothing would happen, Leon threw a bottle that exploded against the Buick's windshield. Two thugs jumped out angry. Then several young men in the courtyard and entrance of the apartment complex massed around them, holding clubs and broken bottles. "Get the fuck out of here," said a shirtless, bald man wielding a baseball bat. "We're Oakland, not you."

Dorn sprinted toward the Victorian on Racine and Leon met him there minutes later.

"Beautiful, Leon. I think you started a race riot and a turf war."

He chuckled. "Mafia goons are hated in this neighborhood." He squinted. "They took off, but they'll be cruising the streets looking for you." He and Leon scaled the lowest section of rear fencing then thumped down into the garden.

"Watch out," Dorn said. Shards of glass and puddles of foul liquid glinted in the ragged grass. A length of rusty barbed wire lay unspooled, perhaps meant to line the top of the iron gate.

Leon climbed the porch steps but his foot broke through a rotted slat.

"Might as well announce ourselves with a bullhorn." Dorn clambered up over the side and crept along the porch. He tried each window until he found one that slid upward. They both entered a dark kitchen. Lights flashed on to reveal a smiling Rathkin holding a pistol.

"Come to steal my stash?" he asked. "Neighborhood thieves have tried." He gestured toward Leon. "But Freddie Dorn? Damn, you're a long way from the Haight."

"No one wants your poison drugs." Leon waved dismissively.

"Dude, turn out the light," Dorn said. "Two guys in a Buick are outside looking for you. They have guns. Serious thugs."

He pondered the information. "You came clear out to Oakland to warn me? Why?"

"They visited my gallery today, threatened me. Mentioned ten grand you owed them." Dorn leaned against a table. "Are they mobsters or dirty cops?"

Rat-Man stiffened. "I don't know, maybe you brought them." He switched off the lights. "I'll check, but I'm not buying your story yet." He herded them into the living room. "Sit." A beat-up sofa showed spring coils rising from its torn fabric. The dealer peered through the window drapes with binoculars. "Shit, there is a Buick," he finally said. "Cruised by twice, its headlights off." Rat-Man squatted down and eyed Dorn. "But why would *you* help me?"

"Because you're a fellow freak," Dorn said. "It's us against the man, and whoever those fuckheads are. But more because they think I'm involved too. Ripping off their pills. You need to make good or we're both screwed." He stopped talking when a loud rattling sounded outside.

"They're trying the front gate. Probably have bolt cutters." Rat-Man pulled his dark greasy hair back and grabbed a fringed suede jacket. "We'll take my escape route." He vanished upstairs then reappeared, clutching a bulging garbage bag and a locked strongbox. "Grab that flashlight. Come on."

They descended through a trapdoor from the pantry down into musty darkness. The basement had a door leading to a long slim passageway. Dorn pointed the flashlight with its weak beam, as furry brown things scuttled away in the shadows. "Is that why they call you Rat-Man?"

The dealer grimaced at Leon. "Rathkin to you."

The dank passage eventually led to a junction; a fetid sewer smell became overwhelming.

Rat-Man tapped metal with a dinging sound. "Follow me."

He handed the garbage bag to Dorn then scaled a rusty ladder that ran to the ceiling. Once at the top, he grunted while lifting something. A circle of moonlight lit the blackness below. Dorn and Leon pulled themselves out of the dank tunnel onto a deserted side street and Rat-Man sealed the manhole cover back in place. "My car is parked a block farther."

Dorn handed him back the bag of pills. "This is where we split up."

"You both owe me for saving you from those goons," Rat-Man said before hustling away.

Leon looked outraged. They took a long, circuitous route downhill to the Volvo. When Dorn returned to United Hallucinations, his office phone rang almost immediately.

"Any luck finding Rathkin?" Detective Rodriguez asked.

"Uh, no . . . but he's definitely in Oakland."

The cop sighed. "We already knew that. Found his station wagon earlier and towed it. If he picks it up, we nab him."

"He won't," Dorn said. "Good night." Feeling wound up, he paced the darkened gallery. Should he call Ali? No, that wouldn't help. She wanted her space.

Early afternoon, he'd smoked a bowl of hash with Moon Girl in the Panhandle. A woman of love beads, shawls, and patched-up jeans, who was quite lovely.

"Freddie, you seem tense about something," she'd told him. "Come over later tonight and I'll give you a body massage." Then a mysterious, intoxicating smile.

Dorn's clock showed nine-thirty; he called. Some dude answered, raspy and coughing.

"Moon Girl went to see Quicksilver and the Dead at the Fillmore. Be back in five hours."

Dorn tried to wait up, but dozed off by one a.m.

CHAPTER TWO

# On the Bridge

Near closing time at United Hallucinations the next day, the phone rang, Rat-Man's voice shaky. "Freddie, meet me on the Golden Gate Bridge at midnight."

Dorn acted reluctant. "For real? What now?"

"A hundred-pound shit-hammer came down after you left. My house was ransacked, my car got stolen. Heavy people are after me. They left a message: I have to check out tonight." Rat-Man's breathing sounded labored. "Anyway, you're in my will and the reading is on the bridge."

"Ask someone else."

"Dude, you saved me last night," Rat-Man blurted out. "You're my best friend."

"You have no friends."

"That's harsh." He coughed. "My other buds are doing time. I'm relying on you, Freddie."

"Fuck, okay." After disconnecting, Dorn contacted Rodriguez. He had to juggle the interests of the cops and the Mob with his own in this matter.

"No, I don't know Rathkin's location. Sounded like a pay phone. I'll call before I meet him." Dorn paused. "But here's the deal, you need to bust us both."

"Rough you up?" Rodriguez asked.

"Maybe just a little."

"But why the charade?"

"So you don't blow my cover. Whatever prison he lands in, if Rathkin gets word to the street that I set him up, I'm a dead man."

Afterward, Dorn relaxed at his desk while he could, then summoned his assistant.

"Nope, not coming with you there," Leon said. "Hell, no. I'm scared of heights."

"Yeah, I have to go alone." Dorn retrieved his revolver from a locked desk drawer.

"Do *not* take that. You'll kill him, or yourself." Leon pulled an Army knife from a sheath above his ankle. "Here."

Dorn held it in his hands. "Okay."

AGAINST BETTER JUDGMENT, DORN CLAMBERED OVER the closed security gate at the south end of the bridge and scuttled along the empty walkway for a hundred yards, then another, until he saw the hunched form of Rat-Man ahead. His legs dangled over the two-foot ledge. Dorn joined him, keeping one arm crooked around the railing like an anchor.

"Long time no see."

Dorn didn't reply. He sat on the iron lip. A ledge that existed inches from the public walkway in measurement, but miles away in sanity. He'd crossed the divide between a pedestrian taking in the view and a suicidal loner at the edge of his lifespan. Maybe someday the District would patrol the bridge, put up barricades to make it harder for the jumpers, but not in July 1969. Free love, free jazz, and free death.

"Thanks for coming," Rat-Man said, as if Dorn had driven up from the East Bay to a Marin party. "I needed a witness."

Rathkin reminded him of the Donovan song, "Season of the Witch." Hippies and beatniks striking it rich on the misery of gullible freaks.

By Rat-Man's side lay a six-foot duffel bag packed with something.

"You sure about this plan?" Dorn gripped his faded jacket tight for warmth.

"If I don't off myself tonight, the Mob will do it," Rat-Man said. "It's a control thing. Master of my own destiny." A thundering foghorn blat rose from the gray soup and vapors beneath their dangling feet. Occasionally the fog cleared to show glowing whitecaps riding the choppy swells on the bay below.

Dorn stared straight out at Alcatraz Island, because looking down made his stomach queasy, his head dizzy with electric fear and the whispery seduction to leap.

When the Mafia moved into the Haight last year, they only took notice of Rat-Man after fronting him five thousand Dexedrine capsules that he didn't pay them back for. The idiot lost the stash in a stolen car he ditched. The West Coast Mob didn't give warnings like in movies; they just got rid of you.

Dorn studied the splayed bag by Rathkin. "You asked me to come to witness this . . . theatrical absurdity?"

"One performance only. Death of the most famous dealer in San Francisco." Rat-Man outstretched his arms.

"Infamous, you mean. Van Monk should be here since you guys have serious unfinished business."

Rat-Man twitched. "Nobody would believe that crazy fool as a witness. He claims to be flashing forward in time." He sucked on a joint, an evil grin sandwiched between his charcoal stubble.

"You sold him the Orange Marmalade that's kept him tripping." Dorn wished he was inside one of the warm, lit-up houses jutting out on the Tiburon Peninsula.

"Hang on, man," Rat-Man said in an officious tone. "First off, I gave him the OM. A free sample. Also, Van Monk tried every new pill that hit the street. It's just a bullshit innuendo of a rumor of a myth that my product did that to him."

"How do you know? Have you eaten any?"

"Are you crazy? OM is like a cocktail of STP, DMT, and mescaline, cut with speed." Rat-Man exhaled. "Anyway, everyone's free, man, to take whatever they want." He pointed a finger. "And it's not very hip for you to be against freedom. Me, I just provide for others."

"Sure, Saint Rathkin." Dorn shivered. "Let's get this over with." It wasn't raining, but the air hung wet and cold against his face. He felt every wind gust buffeting him up there. "I don't believe an egotistical prick like you will ever jump."

Rat-Man laughed. "I took acid to destroy my ego, but it just expanded it."

"What's in the duffel bag?" Dorn sat uncomfortable, both arms crooked around the railing.

"My ticket to Mexico." Rat-Man tapped the bag gently. "A friend at Saint Francis Memorial owed me, provided a stiff. Dude OD'd yesterday. No positive ID." He pressed a finger to his nose and blew snot into the void. "After this guy's in the water for a while, he could be anyone." Rat-Man turned his head. "Are you getting the picture? Distraught dealer takes a mega-dose of drugs then jumps off the Golden Gate."

"Sounds outlandish, unbelievable."

"Man, we're in San Francisco in 1969. Anything is possible."

Somewhere, roughly 240,000 miles beyond Earth, astronauts approached the Moon to walk on it, so Dorn had to agree with the rat bastard.

"How's this work?" Dorn asked. A rotting sea smell wafted up from far below, among the wet echoes of waves slapping against steel bridge supports.

"You see me ready to jump, right? And you're going to watch a body in my clothes fall." Rat-Man smirked. "Then that's your truth, that's all you need to say. When the body is eventually found, it will back up your story."

"They'll identify him by his fingerprints—"

"Do you think my real name is Rathkin? Hell, no. Changed it when I left Jersey in '66. Whoever this guy is, that can be me. I move to Mexico and hide for a couple years like Owsley did, then I creep back up to LA. Start over."

"And the Mob will forget?"

"With your eyewitness account and the corpse, I will live to ninety, man." He unzipped the body bag but stopped. "There's more."

"Your last will?" Dorn shook his head. "What do I inherit? All the tainted drugs you couldn't sell?"

Rat-Man grunted. "Since I'll be officially dead, figured I'd come clean about Ramona."

"Ramona?" *That's why you're here, Dorn. Remember?*

Dorn had fallen for Ramona when he first came to the Haight. In the spirit of 1967, she soon shacked up with him. Things ended in early 1968 when Ramona told Dorn she was free, didn't belong to any one man. He had been devastated, but hid it. Not cool to be hung up on a single lady when you could be out digging women everywhere. But what if you loved one person more than the rest? Were you a square, bound in shackles like the Midwestern parents you escaped from? Would that eventually lead to marriage, cocktail parties, country clubs, and voting for Nixon?

A year later, Ramona got hooked on hard drugs. She drowned in her bathtub soon after while high on heroin. Ever since, Dorn had been curious about who turned her on to smack? Who first shot her up? There were only a few likely suspects.

Rat-Man stared at the bearded corpse's face. "Yeah, after Ramona split from your pad, I let her crash at my place in exchange for helping me sell blotter."

The weather on the bridge was a damp, bone-aching cold, but Dorn felt flushed and feverish. "So Ramona sold your acid, then moved out." Dorn sighed. "That's your confession?"

"I came into a batch of coke," Rat-Man said. "We snorted it together, but later I found out she was shooting it. That's when I told her to split." He looked at Dorn, then away.

"What about heroin?"

Rat-Man's forehead scrunched. "I don't do skag myself." He twitched. "But I keep product hidden under my bed. Came home after a weekend in La Honda to find my stash opened. Ramona had a key and I hadn't changed the locks yet. Junk does something to the brain." He swirled his index finger around. "Later, when I heard about her, the unfortunate event, I put two and two together." Rat-Man put his arm around Dorn. "I felt responsible even though it wasn't my fault, in any way, at all."

Dorn sat motionless, trying to meditate, trying not to think, but failing. Head throbbing.

"I know it don't matter that Ramona and I balled a few times. Just wanted to clear the air after her tragic incident."

Rat-Man peeled away the bag from the corpse. The bridge shook and a jolt surged through the iron girders beneath them. He grasped the railing.

"Earthquake." Dorn's heart constricted in his rib-cage. "Small ones happen every day. We don't feel them on the street, but they're noticeable up here." Dorn formed a fist. He hadn't struck anyone since grade school, had walked in peace marches, avoided Vietnam, and never ever considered hurting someone. But as Rat-Man said, anything was possible in San Francisco in 1969.

"Dude, you seem tense." Rathkin's ugly smile returned. "You and Van Monk always thought you were better. Scorned me, never socialized. Only came to score in desperate times. But see, we're all equal." He pressed his face close. "Free yourself, man. We both shared a fine chick." He punched Dorn's shoulder. "I congratulate you; now you congratulate me."

Dorn thumped him hard on the back. The bridge shuddered again—aftershock—while Rat-Man pitched forward, unbalanced, his hand flailing in the misty air.

"Hey, grab me." His voice rose an octave, and he reached back, but his fingers attached themselves to the body bag.

Dorn froze, watching himself watch a movie of real life occurring.

Rat-Man teetered forward, pulling the corpse off the ledge to trail after his plunge. He screamed "Freddie!" out into black space. Maybe a splash sounded, but more Rathkin's extended shriek merging with the seagulls' calls overhead. Then Dorn puked.

Twenty minutes later he felt steady enough to climb over the railing and walk back. By the tollbooths, traffic had decreased to the occasional car. At the end of the walkway, a large man came toward him. "Yo, peace and love, man."

*Hippie Frankenstein!* Dorn tried to run, but Flannery tackled him. "It's a groovy scene." The undercover cop punched his head. "Where's Rathkin?"

"Stop," Dorn said. "Rat-Man fell off the bridge. Don't need to play this scene anymore."

"Think you're far out? You're all fruitcakes or dealers or users." The Irishman straddled him and slugged him hard twice. Flannery's eyes glazed over—as if experiencing a Green Beret flashback. Fearing death, Dorn pulled Leon's knife from his boot; Flannery raised a blackjack high in the air.

Sirens wailed, coming closer, closer. Bright lights illuminated the darkness and a car door slammed. "Stop. Get off him," someone said. "Enough."

AFTERWARD, DORN CONVINCED HIMSELF THAT IT had been an accident from the earthquake, not his angry backslap that sent Rat-Man to his doom. Whether conviction or rationalization, neither was helped by Vince showing up two days later at Dorn's gallery. "Here you go." He handed Dorn five hundred in cash. "Your reward."

"For what?"

"We trailed you to the Fort Point Gate. Couldn't see shit in that pea soup fog, but we watched what that cop did to you after." Vince scratched at his mouth.

"Cop?" Dorn feigned ignorance. *How did Vince know?*

"His hippie wig fell off while he was pummeling you. We left when a squad car showed." Vince shook his head. "Thought you might be hospitalized."

"Spent a night in jail for suspicious activity. They let me go because . . . no evidence."

"Lucky you. Anyway, the first time you juice someone is the toughest." Vince unfolded the afternoon edition of the *San Francisco Examiner*.

*Two bodies found on the rocks by the south bridge abutment of the Golden Gate Bridge. Local drug dealer dies in dual suicide. Deaths caused by "impact trauma" according to the medical examiner.*

Vince gazed at Dorn. "I don't know who the other guy is, or care how it happened, just that you got it done. We'll never speak of this again, and we never had this conversation." He smiled. "Get some rest, Dorn. You're in bad shape. Go buy food with the money."

"Money?" Dorn pointed at the boarded-up shops along Haight Street, some with staved in windows. "I need protection from junkies and thieves out there, man."

"You got it." Vince shook his hand then left the gallery to duck into an idling Cadillac outside.

Dorn relaxed until the phone rang. "We would have preferred a conviction," Rodriguez said, "but you helped us eliminate a menace from the district. I think we could use you again."

"No way. Flannery nearly killed me. You arrived too late."

"He hates hippies. Anyway, not my problem anymore. Flannery's on a mandatory leave for assaulting an innocent bystander." Rodriguez breathed. "It wasn't personal though. He would have done that to any—"

"This isn't personal either." Dorn hung up to stagger through the gallery. He found ice in the refrigerator, put it in a baggie, then held it against his head as he reclined on the office chair.

"Was it worth it?" Leon asked, sweeping the empty gallery hallway.

"Didn't go as planned."

"No shit. You look like *Rosemary's Baby*."

"What?"

"You know, like hell. Whatever the pigs and gangsters are paying you, it isn't enough."

Dorn nodded, but even that motion hurt. "You can split now, Leon. I'll lock up soon."

"Okay, secret agent man."

Van Monk visited a half-hour later. "I wished that scumbag dead and then it happened. Like I have psychic powers. I feel guilty." So immersed in himself, he didn't even notice Dorn's bruised face. The radio played Crosby, Stills, and Nash, but their harmonies were already fading.

"We all hated the bastard." Dorn scrounged through his desk drawers for weed.

Van Monk frowned. "Rat-Man messed me up and I was planning revenge. Isn't that fucked up?" Van Monk knuckled his eyes. "Now it doesn't matter anymore."

"Season of the Witch" came on the radio and Dorn tried to keep it together.

Van Monk's mouth drooped. "Donovan was Ramona's favorite, right?"

"Yeah. The Summer of Love seems so long ago." Dorn switched to a jazz station, to Coltrane, the timeless flow of his searching saxophone, *A Love Supreme* amid this hate obscene.

Pale, strung-out teenagers shuffled by the gallery windows and a homeless Vietnam vet who had taken up residence in the alcove of a closed record store shouted obscenities at them.

"I had a future flash," Van Monk said. "A couple years from now, you tell me something heavy about what went down with Rat-Man. But I can't remember what it is now. Bummer."

"Yeah, bummer . . ."

CHAPTER THREE
# Bummer in the Summer

ALI ROSENBERG DESCENDED THE VICTORIAN'S STOOP stairs and let her sandals carry her north on Shrader toward Haight Street. Though near noon, last night's bay fog hadn't dissipated. The weather remained chilly so Ali wore a long, purple-gray suede coat she'd bought at the Blushing Peony boutique. It had a fur collar and was belted at the waist. With curly, dishwater blond hair falling to her shoulders, her Roger McGuinn rectangular sunglasses, and a rainbow-colored crochet handbag, the local dudes checked Ali out, smiling with approval. Women too.

Ali slipped into the I/Thou coffee shop and drank some organic tea. Just grooving on the scene, joining the ecstatic dance of evolved humanity, she thought. But Ali was lying to herself.

In early 1967, Ali moved up from LA to the Haight. Something magical was happening in San Francisco: a new life, a new world being built, one illuminated young mind at a time. She soon found an apartment two blocks from Haight. Perfect. Right in the nexus. Ali came to escape her messy divorce from Scott Coburn. A decent man at first, but after going to Vietnam in 1964, he kept re-upping every year, and she lost faith in their ghost marriage. Scott showed up twice a year on leave and rarely wrote to her in-between.

Everything seemed special and new at local dance halls when she arrived. Throbbing, pulsing, swaying to the rhythm at the Matrix. *Love, love, love!* The intense phosphorescent glow of people's skin under the multicolored light show, their ecstatic expressions frozen into time-delayed snapshots by the rapid stutter of strobe lights.

Since moving, she'd had a thing with Lenny Van Monk, then Frederick Dorn. Van Monk was a sweet soul, but drugs had fried his brains and recording sessions made him unavailable most nights. Their split was an easy one; he remained a good friend.

Had it been four or five months since she'd broken up with Freddie Dorn? Attractive to Ali because he seemed to have a plan, was always doing something, not floating or "just being, man," like so many in the Haight. Maybe Dorn reminded Ali of her father. That initial attraction had faded as she realized Freddie was neither mellow nor laid-back. He'd inherited some deep Protestant work ethic from his Kansas family background. He supported the art scene, but was all about making money. Of course you needed bread to live, but the point was to hide that, to act as if love and understanding was everything. Dorn had expanded his mind with drugs, but his stubborn personality remained.

Ali initiated their split, and then questioned it weeks after, months after. He had wanted to become serious, play house, eventually have kids. The disaster of her first marriage scared Ali away from such a commitment.

"Hey," a bearded man with a Viking helmet said to her. He sat slouched on the corner of Clayton with a sign: *Support your Local Poet*. "I'm hosting a reading tonight. Come by my pad."

"Groovy," Ali said. "A group of poets and artists?"

"No, just you and me."

"Another time, Saxon."

"Aw man, after midnight I'll tell you my mantra."

*Peace, love, serenity, bliss, cosmic joy.* Ali started to walk toward the 1700 block of Haight Street but Saxon grabbed her ankle.

"C'mon baby, don't you believe in free love, with me?"

"Get your greasy hand off me, you scurvy piece of shit." She kicked her leg free then rushed away, breathing hard. What had changed? *Peace, love, sunshine, eternal bliss, oh, fuck it.*

Crossing another street and passing The Psychedelic Shop, Ali recognized her trajectory. She had trekked five blocks out of her way hoping to casually encounter Dorn at work. *Just going for a walk, sampling the neighborhood vibe, and hey, what serendipity.* As the gallery loomed ahead, Ali felt nervous. She wanted to keep Dorn close, but not move in together, settle down or do any Midwest anachronistic jive. Instead of visiting United Hallucinations, she ducked inside Tonto's Expanding Headband Records and kept watch, blending with the rack browsers and teenage girls ogling Doors and Byrds album covers. When a break in traffic showed, Ali darted across Haight.

Two seedy men exited Dorn's gallery onto the street. One chewed a toothpick, the other wore a striped suit. Their hair was long, straight, and slicked back, but not hippie style.

"You looking for me, baby?" the uglier one said.

"No." Her stomach twitched as she caught a bad vibe. Art was expensive so she tried not to judge its buyers, but they seemed borderline thugs. Ali retreated to the record store. Minutes later, she mustered courage enough to wander outside, then a car pulled up and a Latino man with a mustache got out. The car, his clothes, and uptight manner all added up to a narc.

"Hey, man, you'll have to pay for that," came from behind.

Shit, she'd walked out holding a record, and it was the silly Herb Alpert one with a nude lady coated in whipped cream. Something her father would listen to.

"Sorry, I spaced." She handed it to the frizzy haired clerk. *What was wrong with her? Could Dorn help her?*

Ali's father called last night. "Scott is taking his month leave now," Abe Rosenberg said, "and plans to visit you in Frisco. He wants to try again with you back in Los Angeles, go to architectural school at Westwood. After he finishes his tour next year."

"Dad, please tell him not to. We're divorced. It's over." Ali had hung up the phone, her stomach in turmoil.

Ali wouldn't allow Scott to ruin her new life. She wandered outside, uncertain of what to do, moving one direction, then changing her mind and turning back. She collided with Dorn.

"I saw you come out of the record store and go back in," he said. "Were you looking for me?"

"No, no." She hugged him. "I went to buy an album but they didn't have it." She gazed at his suspicious face before turning away. "I thought about dropping by, but you're busy selling."

"You're always welcome. Never an interruption." Dorn touched her shoulder gently.

"Beautiful." Ali flashed back to their first meeting in 1967 at the Free Store. "I'm Alison, Ali Rosenberg." She'd used her maiden name since the divorce. "You sort of remind me of John Phillips from The Mamas & the Papas." Dorn had the lean wolfish face, a thin mustache drooping at the edges of his mouth. A little more hair and chin-length, but the same wiry height, with a serious expression and a slight sadness in his eyes—as if he'd witnessed too much, too quickly. "You could be his brother."

Ali lurched back to the present. "Great to run into you, Freddie. Got to go." She hesitated. "I love you." Dorn nodded with a cynical smile. She knew that he knew she said the same thing to her girlfriends, to Van Monk, to her housemates, and sometimes to brightly dressed strangers on the street. That was San Francisco. Love meant everything in general and nothing in specific.

DORN RECLINED IN HIS OFFICE OF the near-empty United Hallucinations Gallery on a Monday in late July. Daydreaming. Too early for business, the action still bubbling out on Haight. Protest songs were sung over strummed folk guitars, Buddhist chanting, incense, bongo drums, and street-jive. "Hare, Hare Krishna!" Leon mopped the main gallery's scuffed floor after a busy weekend. "Greasy Heart" by Jefferson Airplane played on the transistor radio, Jorma's fuzzed guitar piercing the music's sway with a pure acid tone. Dorn laughed at Grace Slick's caustic lyrics while he leafed through recent issues of *Dr. Strange,* reminding himself to contact the comic's artist Gene Colan. Seriously psychedelic art. Maybe Colan had some paintings Dorn could sell. But not now, something was weird in the air today. That quiet space just before the rain, before someone flipped the vibe switch from bliss to chaos.

He heard the hard stamp of square-heeled shoes charge into his gallery. The tense motion militaristic, not peaceful. Cops.

"Frederick Dorn, are you here?" It was Rodriguez.

Dorn slouched out of his office and signaled both men back.

"Freddie," Detective Rodriguez said. "This is my new partner, McKinley."

Dorn scoped the younger guy. Sandy hair, and one of those beefy, handsome but dumb faces. Looked like he had attended

Brown University through his family donating a library. When he grinned, Dorn hated him immediately.

"Detective," Dorn said. "I have a phone."

"This is an emergency." Rodriguez scratched his tight, frizzy hair. "Can we talk alone, without your boy?" Leon had stopped his cleaning and edged closer to listen.

"I'm no one's fucking boy." He slapped the mop down hard.

"Okay," Rodriguez said. "I mean, young man."

"Oink, oink," Leon said as he strolled the hallway.

McKinley flushed with rage and Dorn said, "What is it? Speak up."

"We have a 211 in progress. Need your assistance."

"Speak English, man."

"A bank robbery. Three guys sealed in, bank tellers with them." Rodriguez looked flustered. "If we rush the place, it's a blood bath. SFPD has enough bad press as it is."

"What the hell can I do?" Dorn paced, restless.

"We need to slip a civilian inside, so we can resolve this."

Dorn slammed a fist down on his desk. "I go take a bullet so you can play hero afterward? Fuck no."

Rodriguez restrained McKinley. "Dorn, you can do this without getting hurt. They won't mistake *you* for a cop. I'm begging."

Dorn raked a hand through his unwashed hair. "I don't volunteer for shit. It's going to cost you."

Rodriguez nodded. "The bank pays a reward to any citizen who helps foil a robbery."

"He needs an advance." Leon sidled back in. "$200 in cash."

"I don't have that much." Rodriguez held out his empty hands.

"A hundred then. Insurance policy. If Dorn don't make it back, it'll go to his family and kids."

Rodriguez turned. "You have children, Frederick?"

"Free love," Leon said to the cops. "Nobody knows how many kids these hippies have floating around out there."

Rodriguez and McKinley cursed their way through their pockets until they had stacked enough small bills onto the desk.

Dorn grabbed a paisley shirt and a headband from his closet. Alone in the kitchen area, he pulled a Ballantine beer out of the fridge, along with a tiny eyedropper bottle. At the gallery's door, Dorn spied their prowl car double-parked outside and locals gawking at it. "Bring me out like I'm a suspect. Otherwise, no deal."

McKinley cuffed Dorn's arms behind his back then pushed him up four steps and out onto Haight Street. When Rodriguez opened the car doors, McKinley pressed Dorn's head down to shove him into the backseat. "Get in, you damn punk."

Freaks on the sidewalk crowded around. "Fucking pigs, go home. We don't need the fuzz." Someone hurled a banana peel that smacked against the detective's head. "No police brutality," another yelled. A bottle broke against the car's hood and McKinley drew his .38.

"We're leaving." Rodriguez put his hand over his partner's gun. "Let it go." McKinley slid in next to Dorn, while Rodriguez revved the engine and jerked forward until the mob retreated. "Yeah, that idea worked really well." Rodriguez glared at Dorn in the rear-view-mirror. "I hope you have something better in mind for the bank."

"We need one more thing," Dorn said, joyous at the chaos he'd created. "Eye drops from an ophthalmologist."

"What?" McKinley frowned

"That's an eye doctor, junior."

"I fucking know what an ophthalmologist is." McKinley pressed his angry Irish face close.

"Detective, tell your partner to give me some oxygen back here." Rodriguez coughed. "Take off Dorn's handcuffs, McKinley." Then he drove west.

When he stood up straight, Dorn was over six feet tall, but a wiry guy. Not a fighter. He had survived to age twenty-nine—ancient by hippie standards—by thinking on his feet. Making decisions fast. Leave the party early, don't drink from a strange glass or eat any pill after midnight or you'll be taken away freaking out on a stretcher. He needed that common sense now.

Dorn heard music spilling over the edge of Golden Gate Park, a free outdoor concert. Exploratory psychedelic guitar rang out, but not Jerry Garcia or John Cipollina. It had more of an Afro-Cuban sound and a shit ton of percussion. "How am I getting in?"

"We have keys to a back door into a mail room."

Dorn frowned. "They're gonna hear me. Not cool. Should seem like I was back there all along, the mail clerk at work." The car stopped at the lights by Stanyan Boulevard, the music still pulsing. "I need a diversion." Dorn pointed north. "Get that band to jam really loud out front."

"How are we going to convince them to play at Irving and 12th Avenue?" Rodriguez swiveled his head.

"They're musicians. Offer to pay them." Dorn sighed. "Seven blocks. You guys can get them moved fast."

Rodriguez made calls on his police radio. "Yes, I'm serious we need this band." He finally disconnected, then faced Dorn and McKinley. "The robbers want an armored car to drive them to the airport so they can fly to South America."

"Seriously?" Dorn said.

"The leader is from Costa Rica, a half-assed revolutionary. Juan Cortez. They call him, 'El Bruto.'"

"The stupid, ugly one?"

"Well, it can mean the brute too. But he's a fool to pull this in my town." Rodriguez breathed heavily. "The others are just local punks. Anyway, we can stall them while waiting for their armored car ride. This plan better work, Dorn."

Rodriguez flashed his ID at the roadblocks on 11th Avenue where a crowd had begun to mass around National Bank. On the opposite side of Irving Street, a gaggle of newscasters and cameraman stood arguing with officers, trying to edge closer. Dorn watched Rodriguez turn right on Funston Avenue just beyond the bank to approach a side alley. Sawhorses blocked entry while three cops stood around chewing gum. Rodriguez showed his badge, and spoke with the officer in charge.

Stretching in the sunlight, Dorn put on his wild shirt then affixed the tie-dyed headband that looked like Salvador Dali vomited on it.

"Here." The main cop handed the eye drops to Rodriguez. "You're sending *that* guy in?"

The detective scanned the man's badge. "Roberts, your beat is this neighborhood," he said, glaring. "Funny that you never once brought Rat-Man Rathkin into the station."

Dorn laughed to himself. A percentage of the force were paid off to look the other way. Usually beat cops, men making small salaries and filled with a desire to live better.

"I'm wanted on crowd control." Roberts hurried off toward Irving.

Rodriguez pulled a puffy bulletproof vest from the trunk. "Need protection?"

"Nope. Peace and love win the day." Dorn didn't mention the snub-nose revolver tucked in an ankle-holster. Had worn it ever since Hippie Frankenstein beat the hell out of him. Bell bottoms helped disguise the bulge.

"Okay, let's go." Rodriguez led them down the alleyway. He gave Dorn the eye drops and a tiny plastic device. "Sends a signal to me. Press it twice to get you out the same door you're going in." Rodriguez paused. "Three times means hell is about to erupt, and then we'll come in blazing."

While they waited, Rodriguez said, "Stash this in your shoe." He gave Dorn a sheathed Exacto knife. Fifteen minutes later, the band's live music started. It grew louder as high, piercing guitar riffs started echoing off buildings and rattling windows. Waves of Hammond organ came crashing through the alley. "Is that what you needed?"

"Perfect."

The detective worked a key into both the door locks. Together, they edged the heavy door open, creaking and slow. "No alarm," Rodriguez whispered, "but it might send a signal to the clerks." They hesitated, crouched and tense, yet no one came. Rodriguez checked his watch. "It's almost 2:30. You've got an hour before a full assault happens."

"Even with hostages?"

"This bank keeps accounts for the department. Our station is a half mile east. You don't fuck with officers' salaries."

Dorn nodded then squeezed through the cracked door jammed against the doorstop.

"Prove me right about you," Rodriguez said, almost pleading. "If I get demoted, there's going to be some serious police brutality—in your gallery." The detective gave him a once-over. "Jesus, you look ridiculous."

CHAPTER FOUR
# The Revolution Will Not Be Televised

ONCE INSIDE, THE DOOR LOCKED BEHIND Dorn. Darkness. Air musty. He found the table leading to the wide mail slot where packages of money got handed through to the bank guard. Where the hell was that guy? Dorn snaked his head and shoulders through the passage to the connecting room, but his hips got jammed until he wiggled them through. He heard the bassy rumble of music throbbing outside, and discerned voices beyond the receiving room.

Using a shirttail, Dorn twisted the Ballantine's top off and carefully squeezed his lysergic dropper until ten drops fell into the beer. Pressing a thumb over the mouth, he slowly shook the bottle so it wouldn't foam up. Electric beer. Dorn sealed the cap back on with the flat of his palm. Next, he put an ophthalmologist drop in each eye. Blurred his vision slightly, but that was okay.

Dorn took a deep breath then unlocked the hallway door's twist lock. Turning the handle, he could hear people in the near distance: one man ranting loudly, others stamping around. He flashed to performing street-theater in 1967 with The Diggers across the Haight. Time to be an actor again. Grabbing a chair from the rear office, he hurled it down the hallway. Alarmed voices sounded. Dorn staggered toward a long-haired dude rushing at him with a rifle and an angry red face.

"Hey man, what's going on?" Dorn smiled, waving his beer in the air. "Is there a party?"

The blond, mustached man stared at him, still pointing the weapon. "Who the fuck are you? What are you doing?" Before Dorn could say anything, the robber prodded him forward with the rifle barrel to the front area of the bank—lit bright like a stage play.

A Hispanic man appeared, a cigar in his mouth, a beret, green military clothing, and a carbine slung over his shoulder. "What the hell do we have here?"

"Me? Who are *you*?"

"Our leader, Juan Cortez," the other man said. "El Bruto."

"The stupid one?" Dorn waved his fingers. "You see the traces?"

"El Bruto means the noble savage." Cortez scowled, placing a hand on his pistol. "This is my bank now. How did you get inside?" He slapped Dorn's face twice. "Answer me, idiot."

Dorn noticed the bank guard at the far end, hands bound by a rope and mouth gagged. "In my back office, man." He swayed to the live music leaking inside.

"You . . . work . . . here?"

"I'm the mail-room attendant," he announced loudly, so the bank tellers huddled together in one corner could hear him. "But I don't work. I just hang out back there for eight hours." He fluttered his hands around his head. "It's a gas."

The blond guy pointed. "El Bruto, look at his eyes. Shit, that guy's messed-up. He's tripping."

"Drugs?" Cortez turned to Dorn. "You take the mescaline while in the bank?"

Dorn slumped against the wall. "Daddy got me this gig. Wanted me out of the house. No experience, so they made-up a job for me. It's beautiful." He held the bottle up in toast.

"I'm really thirsty," the blond dude said to Cortez. "Can I have his beer, if you don't want it?" They all looked sweaty, uncomfortable.

"It's my beer, man." Dorn clutched it to his chest.

"Take it, Chad," Cortez said. "I no use drugs or drink. But just that bottle. No one gets drunk today. The armored car will be here in," he squinted at his watch, "thirty minutes."

Chad ripped the Ballantine from Dorn's grip, opened the top with a meaty hand and drank most of the beer down in a few gulps. Dorn hid a smile. Enough liquid LSD in there to make even a docile elephant go full Dumbo.

"This man really works here?" Cortez asked the captive female tellers. Thankfully, one nodded. "How do you get such a job? Who are you?"

"Winston Morgan." Dorn felt the bank humidity, air close with the windows sealed tight.

The third robber stepped away from guarding the front doors to hurry over. "Morgan, like J.P. Morgan?" He brandished a .45 automatic.

"Died long ago." Dorn adjusted his headband. "J.P. Morgan Jr. was my uncle." Even with blurred vision, he could see the tan sacks of cash piled at the center of the floor.

"What does all that mean, Hector?" Cortez asked. He took his carbine off one shoulder and slung it over the other.

Hector approached the leader to speak in his ear. Dorn heard "rich" and "hostage" and "ransom."

Cortez frowned at first, then grinned. "When our transport arrives, we are taking you with us, Win-ston."

"Where to?"

"Bogotá."

"Far out, man, beautiful. Never been to South America."

"Shut up, fool. This is no vacation." Cortez kicked Dorn then marched over to the captives. "And I'm taking along this *señora*, too." He gestured toward the most attractive teller, and bent over to squeeze her thigh exposed beneath a miniskirt. "You will be my queen."

The woman's face curdled. "Stop it," she said in a shriek. Live music vibrated the walls.

A gray-haired bank teller with glasses stood. "Leave her alone. Take me instead."

Cortez threw his head back, laughing. "Sit down, ma'am." He licked the teller's face he desired, his cow-like tongue stained by brown cigar spittle.

"Do you know that group outside?" Dorn tried to keep cool. "They're pretty groovy."

"Yes." Hector sighed. "I think they used to be called Santana Blues Band. They perform everywhere."

"Man, all that percussion and those minor chords. That's not blues," Dorn said. "Maybe if they played shorter songs, had more singing, those cats could actually make it big somewhere."

"Sit down, you fool."

TIME PASSED AND THE TENSION INSIDE grew, the humidity ridiculous, as air conditioning had been shut off. Chad was dosed to the gills, barely able to contain it. Dorn had diverted Hector to the back room with a story about having a water cooler there. After he left, Dorn pressed his signal device, and hopefully Rodriguez had nabbed him. Cortez stood glowering, in a foul mood.

"I am so thirsty." Making weird facial gestures, Chad began walking across the bank as if navigating a tightrope. Cortez scanned the street, likely for any sign of the armored car's arrival.

On the ground and sliding on his ass, Dorn eased around the bank guard. Name tag read: Myron Jennings. With the Exacto knife, he sliced the bonds tying the man's hands behind his back. Then Dorn formed a cannonball position on the ground as if in deep meditation.

"Where you going?" Cortez asked Chad. "Stay put." He moved a ways down the hallway and yelled, "Hector, what are you doing? Get back here." While El Bruto concentrated on that, Dorn slipped his snub-nose into the guard's pocket.

"Can you shoot?" he whispered. Jennings nodded. "When I make my move, concentrate on the younger dude." Jennings gave Dorn an *I'll-kill-the-motherfucker* look.

Cortez returned. "What's wrong with you, Chad?"

Chad performed tai chi and ballet moves on the empty floor. He snapped to attention then padded in his socks back to a young female hostage who had charmed him.

"Cortez?" Captain Nelson hollered. "Your vehicle will be here in ten minutes."

El Bruto shouted back, "Stop stalling me! It's been a half hour. Where is it?"

"It's coming," Nelson answered. "Major traffic on the Oakland Bridge. Listen, can we have a hostage?"

"A dead one unless you produce the car." Cortez began cursing in Spanish. He studied the prisoners, sizing them up.

"Don't do anything rash. It's almost here," Nelson shouted from outside. "And please take special care of the mail room boy." Nelson paused. "His family is very concerned."

"Win-ston is doing fine," Cortez replied. "Unless you try anything." The leader retreated, swiveling his neck this way and that. "Goddammit, where is Hector?" He marched down the hallway with his carbine pointing ahead.

Dorn acted. He ran toward the front bank doors bundling his arms together.

"Hey, what's he doing?" Chad said, a pistol dangling from his grip. Jennings pressed Dorn's snub-nose to the intoxicated man's skull. "Drop it or die, asshole."

When Dorn hit the door, the glass cracked but didn't break. He had seconds. Finding a metal ashtray can, he picked it up with both hands to ram it through the thick glass. Everything shattered and he fell partially outside.

"No, no," Cortez yelled. "I need Winston, my insurance policy." He came sprinting over, ignoring Chad, focused only on his Morgan family hostage.

Dorn felt dazed, small cuts on his arms and knee. He attempted to rise.

"Drop flat to the ground!" Captain Nelson barked. Dorn fell face first onto the pavement coated with glass shards.

Cortez must have reached the doorway, because Dorn heard a sharpshooter fire twice until the leader collapsed next to him, bloody and gasping for breath.

"Cease fire," Nelson ordered through the bullhorn. The raucous live music stopped, leaving only distorted police radio jabber as a phalanx of cops moved in from all sides on Irving Street. When the drugged Chad tried to flee across the bank floor in his socks, Jennings and the hostages piled on to bring him down. His body jerked as he cried out for mercy.

Detective Rodriguez came inside to inspect the carnage, while the hippie teller found bandages and gauze for Dorn's glass cuts in the bathroom. "I need to leave the back way," he told Rodriguez. "No press. Do *not* leak my name to the papers. I have to live in the neighborhood. Revolutionaries are sprouting everywhere and I don't need them gunning for me."

"Who do we say helped?"

"A good fucking Samaritan."

Two cops brought the wounded body of Cortez inside to wait until the ambulance arrived. The leader mumbled, almost hissing, his eyes glassy. For a second, Dorn felt a weird sympathy for the misguided crank. "El Bruto?" he said next to the man's face.

Cortez coughed up phlegm, then blood. "Winston . . . You were right about me."

"About what?"

"I am the stupid one." His mouth went slack and he blacked out.

Dorn met the bank manager, Edgar Wilkins loitering in the back alley. "I have your reward," Wilkins said. "$2,000. Would a check be acceptable?"

"Nope. Cash." Dorn felt blood course into his head. "And where the hell were you during the robbery?"

"I shut myself in the vault, following bank procedures." Wilkins sauntered off, muttering to himself.

"Your plan was crazy, absolutely nuts." Rodriguez rubbed his knuckles against his forehead. "Very unorthodox tactics. Too much risk. I'm not sure Captain Nelson will want to use you again."

"Good," Dorn replied. "I'm not a narc." He lifted a fist into the air. "Power to the people."

After Wilkins grudgingly paid him, Dorn wandered through the now loud and crowded bank, sunlight streaming in, reporters shoving microphones toward anyone lingering. Cops swarmed everywhere, plainclothes detectives questioning the tellers, attendants in white from the ambulance jammed up against the bank doors, a doctor saying, "Critical condition. Get this Cortez into the ICU immediately." Dorn walked past the bank guard and saluted.

Jennings shook his head. "So where you going now?"

"I need a nap. Like for a few weeks."

## CHAPTER FIVE
# Cinnamon Girl

THEY TOOK DORN OUT ON A stretcher, a sheet obscuring his face. When the ambulance dropped him and Rodriguez off at the Park Police Station, Dorn threw away his bloodstained second shirt before cleaning-up in the men's room. Drenching his hair under the sink faucet, he pulled it back and tied it into a short ponytail. "Goodbye," he told Rodriguez as he moved past his office.

The detective waved him in. "And your snub-nose?" He proffered the retrieved gun.

"You're going to bust me?"

Rodriguez shook his head. "But we should get you a concealed carry permit. You can do some target training too, on Sundays when the range is near empty."

"Yeah, okay. See you."

"Until we meet again."

"No, goodbye."

"You say goodbye, and I—"

"Do *not* quote The Beatles to me, man."

Dorn walked six blocks back to United Hallucinations. Inside his office, Leon sat reclining, feet on the desk, listening to news on the radio. Dorn pointed until he retracted his legs.

"I heard about a hippie hero who looked close to death," Leon said. "Knew it had to be you." He stood then strutted around Dorn. "Shit man, you actually helped stop the bank job." He grinned. "I won't tell a soul, because some folks think any radical who steals money from the man's bank is righteous." He frowned. "But I have family with accounts at National Bank. And I never heard shit about that Cortez fool being no hero to no one in Oakland."

"Yeah, he was a fraud. You'll see dudes in military green and berets talking nonsense while handing out pamphlets in the park."

"So anyway." Leon worked his index finger and thumb below his lower lip. "As your agent, I think I deserve fifteen percent of your reward."

"Reward?" Dorn sat, lying his head back.

"Don't try to bullshit the original bullshitter," Leon said. "Banks give rewards to anyone who foils a robbery or helps retrieve stolen funds. So what did you get?"

Dorn glanced out the window at legs moving by. "A thousand."

The small area of forehead showing beneath Leon's afro scrunched in thought. "That makes $150 you owe me."

Dorn laughed then put his legs up. "Let's pretend for a moment that you are my agent. How did you help me get that gig? Rodriguez approached me directly."

Leon slapped his head. "That ain't how it works. An agent gets a cut of any funds you make. I'm here looking out for you day in and day out."

Dorn opened his strongbox for the cash Rodriguez and McKinley had previously paid. "A hundred bucks."

"Done." Leon took it the moment Dorn's hand lifted from the box.

"Maybe you could earn your next commission."

"I'm on it." Leon hustled out of the office, counting the bills.

D**orn woke from his chair nap** when Leon announced he was going home. Dorn sat up. Patrolling the gallery, he straightened prints that hung askew, and studied the recent posters by Stanley Mouse and Rick Griffin. Damn, if he could get Griffin's original art from the Dead's new album *Aoxomoxoa*, he could sell that for a bundle. Dorn locked windows, turned off lights, and climbed up the few steps to Haight Street.

Dusk inhabited the neighborhood, long sharp shadows knifing the pavement while an orange glow glazed the painted tops of Victorians. This time of day always made him think of death. He felt the loneliness of having no real purpose in a world of people pretending to have a purpose. When Dorn shuffled toward Clayton Street, a street freak bustled out from a shuttered store's doorway, eyes wide and yellowy, hair stringy and matted. Probably in his thirties, but looked way older.

"I need money. Give it here." He waved a jagged implement. Scrap metal brandished as a weapon. The urchin vibrated with druggy confusion—too high or too straight.

Alone and tired, Dorn had been through enough hassles to last a month. Seeing a nearby trash can, he grabbed the steel cover by its handle then approached the assailant.

"You want to go right now, shithead?" Dorn slammed the man's shoulder, and his bravado crumbled.

"Whoa, man, I was just joking."

"Drop that knife or whatever it is."

The guy obeyed, shoulders trembling. He put up two fingers. "Peace and love." Then his eyes flashed. "Wait, are you that guy I heard about?"

Dorn decided to own it. "Yeah, what's your name?"

"Judd."

"Judd. I'm evicting you. A citizen's eviction. Don't want to see you or any of your junkie fuckhead friends in this area from now on. Move to Oakland or Vallejo, or better yet, Sacramento." Dorn clanged the lid against the trashcan like a drummer counting a song in. "You hear me?" The deadbeat nodded. "So get going—now!"

Dude scampered away, staring over his shoulder in fear.

Dorn exhaled, tried to relax, heart throbbing, unsure of what had possessed him. He veered south to visit Ali's place over on Waller to mellow out. She was his most recent ex, but they had some deeper friendship going. Ali tolerated Dorn in all his uptight, non-hippie ways.

He climbed the stoop outside her Victorian, painted purple, red, and green. The archway above the front door was emblazoned with peace symbols and stars. She lived on the first floor, so he scraped his shoes on the entryway mat, then knocked on her door. "It's Dorn," he said over the sound of Janis Joplin wailing.

"Freddie." She opened the door a crack. "I was thinking about you."

Ali had wavy, dirty blond hair, wore an Indian blouse with a crocheted shawl slung over, above a pair of faded jeans with patched knees. Metal frame round glasses gave her a thoughtful expression. When she took them off, only at night, in bed, her face was beautiful. Someone once described her as a Jewish Joni Mitchell. Not quite right, but somewhere in that galaxy.

"I figured that when you were outside my gallery," he said.

Her face colored as she glanced downward. "Come in. Do you want some herbal spinach tea or Ramen noodle soup?"

"Neither." He moved into the living room, squatting down on a pile of pillows she used for seats. "I feel a bit lost. Depressed."

"I remember." She squeezed a teabag around a spoon, before drinking from her mug. "Sunset. The day is dying, so you feel like a part of you is going with it too." She sniffed. "You're not even thirty and already haunted." She sat cross-legged facing him. "You don't do smack. I don't think you even trip anymore, so you'll likely live a long time. Why the fear?"

"It's more dangerous living in the Haight, living in San Francisco now." He stared at her. "Do you carry protection? I just almost got mugged."

"Really? Bummer." Ali thought a moment. "No weapons, but I bought this." She opened her fringed suede carry bag to remove a canister.

"Mace? Wow, I thought mainly cops used that."

"I got it from a friend of a friend." She frowned and rubbed her nose. "I like to go to the Panhandle or meditate in the park. People always hassle me, ask me for money or food. One dude got aggressive so I flashed it." Ali set it back in her bag.

When Dorn stretched his long legs out, Ali peered at one ankle. "What's that for?" She frown-stared at him. "A gun?"

Dorn had locked the snubnose in his desk, but left his ankle-holster on. "Yeah." He sighed. "Break-ins all over. Someone tried to rob my gallery." When she said nothing, he continued. "It's for defense. Either that or I move to Marin, like the Dead did. I'm not going to be victimized."

Ali sipped her tea. "Not the same as when we got here in '66."

"I guess that was too good to be true. Unlocked doors, everyone getting along, free concerts most days, only the undercover cops to fear. Not each other."

"Yeah, that's why I was thinking of you, Freddie." She scooted closer on her ass, an old technique when she wanted to give the third degree. "I've been hearing things."

"What? I don't know—"

"Friends have seen heavy people visiting your gallery. I saw some too. Like mobsters and cops." She stared downward and exhaled. "Not sure which is worse."

Dorn didn't want to lie, but couldn't reveal the exact truth either. "Look, I run a commercial gallery. I'll sell art to anyone who comes in. My rent isn't cheap."

"I know you're a businessman and that's cool. You can't give everything away for free, unless you were Rockefeller. It's just . . ."

"I don't know what you saw or heard, but cops questioned me after the robbery attempt, and there was another botched break-in while I was asleep." He played with his hair to avoid her steely gaze. "They asked me for details, to investigate." He extended his hands. "They haven't found shit, so that's why I bought a gun since I saw you last."

"And the gangsters?"

"They want freaky art to help score with chicks, I guess."

"That Rat-Man thing was crazy. I read he worked for the Mafia. What a way to die." She kicked at Dorn with her bare foot. "And you and Van Monk were tight with him."

"Not tight." Dorn wanted to change the subject. "We both scored from him. Then Van Monk got super messed up from some psychedelics Rat-Man got, stuff from military hospitals. Dude was toxic."

She folded herself up, serene. "Is the gallery owner a free spirit or a Midwestern businessman? Freak or square, freak or square?"

"I don't own, I lease." He rubbed his face. "It's been a long day, I'm going home." Dorn gripped the cabinet, pulling himself up. "What I told you last month. I still feel the same."

"I know." She jumped off the floor and hugged him tight. "I wanted to ask for a favor, but not now. Stay in touch, mystery man."

DORN WAS EXPLAINING THE RELEVANCE OF Robert Crumb's album cover art displayed on his gallery wall to a prospective buyer when Leon sidled up. "Gotta talk to you, man."

"In a moment." Dorn gave him the stink eye. "I'm dealing with a customer."

"It's important." Leon shifted his weight back and forth like he needed to piss badly.

"My office in five minutes." Dorn turned back to the businessman who wanted to be hip. "Someday people will be fighting over this piece."

The man's short hair had been combed forward into bangs, sideburns grown below his ears. Corporate guys who drank away their lunch hours at topless bars like Big Al's on North Beach, hoping that the dancers would find them groovy, rather than soulless plastic sellouts.

"Someday, maybe." The man's mouth curled downward. "It just seems a bit cartoony and tawdry for the price." He stared at it again. "I'll come back over the weekend with my lady friend. She understands hippie art more than me." With that, he wandered out.

"Number one rule," Dorn told Leon inside the office. "Never scare customers away."

"What, because I'm—"

"Because you interrupt my sales pitch and are rude," Dorn finished. "I can only keep you employed if I actually sell art."

"Yeah, yeah, yeah, but I got you a gig." Leon was animated, moving around the space, herky-jerky. "My cousin Vonda at Berkeley. Her roommate ran off to a place white people go when they want to live like bums and pretend to be poor."

"What? You mean a commune?"

"Damn straight. Bunch a messed-up freaks sleeping together in one house, eating beans, crapping outdoors, and digging gardens in the dirt."

Dorn thought about it. Communes were fairly new, a reaction to the crime and hard drugs in the cities. People heading out to the countryside, to farm, to be one with the land. Seeing the way the Haight had changed, it didn't sound so terrible an idea in 1969.

"Anyway," Leon continued, "Meredith's parents want her out of there."

Dorn yawned. "If she's eighteen, then she's an adult. Can do whatever she wants."

"Will you see her parents after work to hear them out?" Leon moved in close.

"What's your interest?" Dorn asked.

Leon rubbed his thumb against his index finger. "The parents are willing to pay big to get her free. And as your agent . . ."

"Yeah, I dig. Tell them to meet me here at six."

The Duncans arrived as Dorn was locking the windows in the main gallery. He led them into his office, then shook his head *no* before closing the door on Leon. Richard

Duncan looked late-forties, with a puzzled hangdog face and his brown hair beginning to recede. Dorn had witnessed similar expressions on fathers wandering the neighborhood searching for their runaway daughters. Nobody searched for runaway sons, except the draft board. It was like The Beatles "She's Leaving Home" in living, breathing parental form. Martha Duncan had a reddened Irish face—from crying or sun exposure or alcohol. Maybe all three.

"Please make yourself comfortable." He'd brought in chairs.

"We don't know Leon," Rich said, avoiding eye contact. "But his cousin Vonda is—"

"Yes, I know." Dorn perched on the edge of his desk, wearing a sports jacket he kept in the closet for gallery openings and when dealing with art buyers.

"Leon said you were a private third class," Martha said in a trembling voice. "I don't know what that means."

"A private eye," Richard guessed.

"A private third eye," Dorn corrected.

"Like a hepcat detective," Richard explained to Martha. "He can blend in with the nutjobs, the longhaired lowlifes, the hookers and scurvy dope dealers out there. No offense."

Dorn frowned, resting his chin on a hand. "Meredith is nineteen, right?" They grunted in assent. "As you know, I can go find your daughter at this commune, make sure she's healthy, but I can't force her as an adult to leave."

"The police told us the same," Richard said. "That's why we're here. She's being kept a prisoner against her will." He stood as if to convey seriousness. "She sounds like a zombie in phone calls, ever since going to West Wind in June. They're brainwashing her."

"Baba Gagi runs it." Martha crossed herself. "Who knows what that dirty foreigner is forcing her to do."

"Martha, please," Richard said. "Let's stick with the facts." He turned. "Gagi asked for two hundred dollars at first, but last time we spoke, he wanted a thousand or she wouldn't contact us again."

"Blackmail money?" Dorn asked. "What for?" Neither parent answered.

"I tried calling West Wind's number," Martha said. "They claimed no one named Meredith is staying there." She wiped her eyes then blew on a handkerchief.

"Could you visit their community in Fairfax?" Richard asked. "Then determine if our little girl is a captive, like we believe, or"—his mouth twisted—"a willing participant."

"I want to help . . ." Dorn's voice trailed off. "There is the matter of money. It'll take me a week staying there to be accepted by the commune. That means shutting down my gallery business and taking a loss."

The door cracked open silently behind the couple. Leon played with a yo-yo then gestured to signify that Rich and Martha were related to the Duncan Yo-Yo fortune.

Rich pulled out his wallet. "Is a hundred a day sufficient, with a five hundred bonus given if you bring our little girl safely back home?"

"Yes, that would be," Dorn said, while Leon did a quiet victory dance outside.

Rich laid seven hundred-dollar bills on the desk and asked, "When will you go?"

"Today's Friday. Need to work the gallery tomorrow. How's Sunday?"

Rich's face tightened as he put another Benjamin Franklin down on the pile. "Saturday would be much better."

"Done." Dorn drew up a primitive contract. He added if they didn't hear from him by the following weekend, to alert Detective Rodriguez at the Park Station. Somehow that made them feel better, that this lanky, long-haired, unofficial investigator had connections in the Department.

CHAPTER SIX
# The Golden Road
## (to Unlimited Devotion)

Dorn filled his Volvo with gas on Saturday, feeling vaguely depressed, trying to pinpoint it. Not something smoking a joint could ease. The death of idealism, the failed dream that the youth of America would inherit their country and save the planet. After Bobby Kennedy got assassinated last year, the fix was in. Especially apparent when Dorn saw Nixon's sweaty face, that perpetual five o'clock shadow on television. He campaigned as "the peace candidate." What a fucking joke. Clearly much worse than Humphrey or even Johnson—hounded out of office by war protesters. *"Hey, hey, LBJ, how many kids have you killed today?"*

Dorn told Ali, "Don't watch the evening news. It's a bummer. Thirty minutes of pain."

But you couldn't turn off or stanch the steady blood drip from Vietnam. Dorn felt guilty he hadn't spoken out more, attended more peace marches. Maybe Ali was right, he was a businessman disguised as a hippie. And now even worse, a borderline narc, a neighborhood crusader trying to make things better. Maybe a week at West Wind would mellow him out.

Dorn recalled what Meredith told her parents on their last phone call: "The divine spirit resides in close proximity to the Baba Gagi. So I will remain near him too." There was something about acid, about the drug scene in San Francisco that weakened the mind, made certain people more susceptible to bogus gurus and self-declared spiritual leaders.

Before noon, Dorn drove across the Golden Gate Bridge, motoring north on Highway 101. A swoop and span of girders and abutments, the great steel cables holding an impossible mass of metal together, hungry seagulls circling above wandering tourists. The bay was choppy below and—both east or west—the view magnificent. However, he'd never cross the bridge or hear its name now without thinking of that fateful night with Rat-Man.

"No sweat," Leon had recently insisted. "You just need to fill your brain with new bad memories to blot that old one out, man."

Dorn's car radio played Zager and Evans' "In the Year 2525," a hyper-strummed folk tune which kept modulating keys and getting more dire. Totally nuts. Yet Dorn felt a sense of rebirth, of hope as he drove Sir Francis Drake Boulevard through Marin County. Tall redwoods showed and sun broke the fog to glaze the spread of valleys and illuminate distant mountains. Perhaps anticipation trumped actuality, while expectation trumped clarity.

Three miles northwest of San Rafael, Dorn cruised through the small downtown of Fairfax, past Sherman's General Store, past the Fairfax Theater's art deco neon marquee. Eight miles beyond it, just before Samuel P. Taylor State Park, he spotted the wooden sign with bright orange paint stating: *West Wind – Divinity and Tranquility Center ahead.* Dorn turned through open metal gates that swung closed after he passed. Electric. He followed the pitted dirt road that took ten minutes to traverse its forested mile to a big clearing where a group of redwood cabins lay spaced around loamy gardens and crop fields.

Burnt golden hills sloped off in the distance as sunlight lay warm on his head in the drowsy afternoon. Something had cranked Dorn's odometer back to when he arrived at the Haight in late '66—to a brighter world filled with possibility. He parked where several cars, some dented, others old rust-buckets, sat by a main building. DayGlo paint above the doorway read: *Main Orifice & Head Quarters.* A porch held rocking chairs with dazed cats on a hammock.

Dorn smelled pine incense, heard wind chimes, and far-away mellow music—mandolins, banjos?—and laughter. As he walked in sandals toward the office, naked children ran by, their faces inscribed with peace symbols and hearts, while a bearded dude in a loincloth beat on hand drums, his face ecstatic as he pounded out of sync with a portable record player playing a Jefferson Airplane album. Dorn couldn't help but smile, inhaling the tang of eucalyptus trees somewhere nearby. Did he come to rescue someone's daughter or to join the circus himself?

A man at a reception desk smiled in expectation. "You called earlier. I'm Tarick. So good to see you again."

"Again?"

"We have all lived many times." Tarick tapped his fingers on the desk. "Don't you think you've visited us before?"

"Um, sure." Dorn sniffed the incense burning on a taper. "Is, uh, Lord Gagi here today?"

"Of course. He is here yesterday, today, and forever after. Baba meditates in his inner sanctum." Tarick moved from the desk. "Come, you must meet his Divine Holiness."

Inside a private office that reeked of curry, Dorn saw the spiritual leader sitting in the lotus position on a Persian rug, beaming with eyes closed. "Welcome, welcome," he said. "I have been waiting to meet a visitor today." Baba Gagi opened his eyes wide. "You would like to join us?"

"I came to feel the vibe," Dorn said. "Maybe check things out for a week."

"Of course, my son." Baba had long black hair streaked with gray. Though he seemed to be well into his fifties, his brown facial skin looked baby smooth. A white traditional smock hung about him like a tousled bedsheet. Sandals sprouted from either side beneath and Dorn noted his bare feet with long, curling toenails.

"We must interview you," Baba said. "Once accepted, you can stay here as long as you like." Baba laughed in high-pitched yips. Pictures hung on the walls of Baba and Donovan, one with Timothy Leary, and one where Baba sat by Rod McKuen in matching shifts at a public event. The photo with Tiny Tim should have given Dorn pause, but he let it pass.

"Please give our visitor a tour," Baba said. "We shall speak tonight, after dinner."

Tarick walked Dorn past the gardens, across a field, then down a gully to a large swimming hole. "Our commune is one with nature." He extended his open palm toward the pool where three women and two men—all naked—splashed and frolicked in the water.

Dorn gazed at their attractive bodies with admiration. The women looked carefree, none of the tensions of the city inhabiting their expressions. Was one of them Meredith? It seemed like summer camp for hippies. Everyone at West Wind appeared healthier than his urban friends, showing a radiant glow of physical activity, of purpose. Maybe Meredith found her tribe and Dorn would have a week of relaxation.

Tarick led Dorn to the male dormitory cabin, with small rooms and a central living room where additional people could sleep. "This would be your bunk for the week. But in exchange you must work the land, contribute to our society."

"Of course." Dorn nodded.

"Couples often live in a tepee." Tarick pointed out a window toward a few conical structures at the edge of gentle hillside near a welter of oak trees that eventually merged into redwood forest. Like some lost fairyland.

Afterward, they visited the greenhouse and a barn workshop. Beyond it, sat a small nurse's station with medical supplies. A zaftig woman haloed by an explosion of dark curls lay on a cot napping. In the kitchen, two women peeled potatoes and a black man cut lettuce leaves into a giant salad bowl set on a long slab table. That area connected to a spacious dining room.

"At present we have eighty members of our divine community," Tarick said. "But we hope to expand to two hundred."

"When you say 'divine,' do you mean praying?" Dorn despised organized religion.

"No church services. Every day is a holy blessing that we acknowledge in our own way, privately. People are free, as long as they contribute, and are not violent or thieves." Tarick paused. "No drug use, beyond natural-growing herbs. We forbid alcohol, except wine and our own homemade beer."

Tarick led Dorn to the bathhouse in which people bathed communally under four shower faucets. He opened the door wide despite clouds of steam billowing out. The man showering was wrinkled, ancient. "And that is the founder of West

Wind. We call him Elderberry." A large bar of communal soap that looked like polished gray stone hung from a rope.

Dorn retreated outside. "Does everyone change their names?"

"Yes." Tarick's frozen grin appeared frightening. "You become a new being when you join us, so your name and identity must change."

Even the two large outhouses with four seats in a row and only small plywood panel separations didn't dissuade Dorn from staying for dinner.

"We have nothing to hide here," Tarick said, "beyond our sadness for not arriving sooner."

IN THE COMMUNAL DINING ROOM, DORN ate dinner with Tarick, Baba, and four young women: Apricot, Dandelion, Vera, and Magnolia. They flirted with him, playing footsie, touching his hands, rubbing shoulders, and displaying their attributes under thin blouses and cut-off jeans. He sensed an act, a seduction to reel him in. And it was working. Lentil soups and fruity organic teas were served, a garden salad that tasted of dirt got passed around.

Afterward, some diners went onto the porch and danced to music coming from a cassette player. Dorn observed them while slumped in a rocking chair at the far end, content to just feel the cool night air wash over him. Women in blue jeans with patches, denim on denim on suede, crocheted belts holding up hip-huggers, girls moving barefoot or thrust forward on pumps, halters draw-stringed in the back, soft felt hats with floppy brims. Some women partnered with one another rather than dance with the barely swaying men. The dudes wore T-shirts and bell bottoms or striped pants that looked vaguely circus-like; they showed gold-rimmed spectacles and lambchop sideburns, headbands and symbols painted on faces.

*Astral Weeks* played, the music hypnotic and repetitive, a folk-gypsy-soul blend. Van Morrison attempting to go beyond language by singing with gasps and chokes, oohs and ahs, glottal noises, baby mewling, raspy growls of someone attempting to clear their throat.

Dorn then wandered the hallways inside. At least twenty-five members formed a seated circle in a connecting conference room. He watched from just outside as they clasped hands and with closed eyes began to chant "Baba-Gagi-Baba-Gagi-Baba-Gagi-Baba-Gah!" repeatedly, without pause. A hand gripped his upper arm.

"To my Truth Room." Baba led him to the rear of the main building where Tarick waited.

Dorn felt a bit stoned, light on his feet, and dizzy. He hadn't smoked anything but his thinking vibrated with a buzzed tingle.

"And now the questioning." Baba gestured toward a metal-frame bucket chair.

Dorn sat on it, noticing two guys who looked like Petaluma rednecks. They wore seedy mustaches and both chewed gum, T-shirt sleeves rolled-up to display biceps. "Who are they?"

"Hutch and Skeeter." Baba smiled. "Truth enablers."

Dorn figured them for muscle, Gagi's enforcers. "Okay . . ."

"They keep curious Fairfax locals from trespassing." Baba sat on a stack of plump pillows facing Dorn. "You will answer truthfully and quickly."

Dorn nodded. He wouldn't fudge. No one beyond Leon knew of his SFPD connections.

"Who are you, where are you from, where do you work?"

"Frederick Dorn, from San Francisco, I manage an art gallery. United Hallucinations."

"How did you hear about West Wind?" Baba moved his whole pillow construction closer.

"I think a cat named Blue Boy told me." Dorn was improvising, but like more recent Coltrane, he was blowing free jazz to a bebop audience. Baba nodded and Hutch walked toward Dorn, right hand holding a blackjack.

"Blue Boy?" Baba drew the words out. "Answer again and carefully." Skeeter roused, massaging a clenched fist. "Who told you—"

"Meredith Duncan said she was coming here in June," Dorn spat out. "I met her at a party in San Francisco and dug her. Wanted to see her again, plus check out communal living." The room went silent. Dorn wondered if any of the girls at dinner were Meredith. If so, his cover was blown and the weather forecast called for pain.

When Baba waved his hand, Hutch and Skeeter retreated to their window-sill positions. "That is a better answer." He smirked. "And did you notice her during dinner before?"

Dorn had only seen one childhood photo of her. He felt groggy and jerked his head to shake it off. "No," he said. "I looked around, but with all the people there, I didn't."

"Good." Baba scraped his curved fingernails together. "Meredith was not there. But she is with us—always."

His words had a sense of finality. Dorn would have to gauge the women's ages: those in their late twenties like him, the recent college graduates, and older teenagers like Meredith.

Tarick reentered, nodding at Baba. "His identity and job have been confirmed."

At present, Dorn just wanted to sleep, though it was only 8:30.

"Tell us about your family." Baba clawed at his beard with long, dirty fingernails.

Dorn figured Gagi and Tarick had some extortion-blackmail racket going on. His early mood of wonder during the day had darkened with night.

"I hate them," he said. "Rich Midwestern assholes who own a hardware chain. All they care about is making money." He pressed hands against his feverish brow. "I had to split, man. They weren't real. Totally plastic." It helped that beyond his folks being loaded—they weren't—the rest was basically true.

"Money, yes." Baba scooched over, his sweaty face nearly touching Dorn's. "And if you were to stay, would they be willing to make contributions to our society?" The wistful expression again. "Maintenance on this vast property can be quite a burden."

"Sure I'd call them, request funds, if I stay." Dorn stared at Baba. "I need a purpose, to find myself. Can you help me?" Dorn needed to lie down.

"Of course, my child." Baba eyed the others. "Please take Frederick to his dormitory. He requires a nice long rest."

Dorn attempted to stand, but lost balance and gripped the chair-back. He found himself being carried across the outdoor grounds. Hutch and Skeeter lifted him onto a stiff mattress atop a low cot next to bunk beds, then left. Dorn didn't even mind the dirty sheets that reeked of sex or the noisy music playing somewhere near. Not even the clove cigarette smoke. He conked out.

Dorn woke near two a.m. with a headache. The sound of male snoring came from the bunks as he tried to sit up. The dinner food or the tea had been drugged. If he wasn't careful, Dorn would become a zombie, and some other hepcat detective would be dispatched. But was there another like him in 1969?

Without city lights, the darkness outside seemed impenetrable. Dorn wore moccasins for stealth on the dirt walkways. The dormitory cabins formed an oval circle around a garden, and a hundred yards beyond it lay the main office building. He saw one yellowy light glowing at the west end, so he navigated around the east side to the gravel parking lot. He tucked into his Volvo then found a penlight in the glove compartment. Fortunately, he'd left his snubnose and ankle holster buried under the passenger seat. Apparently, Hutch and Skeeter had removed his wallet while conked out.

Dorn walked along the grass tracing the long driveway feeling restless. Bits of moon and sky showed under the canopy of trees, while tiny critters rustled in the bushes. He found a small barn with padlocked doors. Wedging them open slightly, he pointed the flashlight inside. A Mercedes-Benz, a Bentley, and a Rolls-Royce, all shiny and clean. Clearly, Baba Gagi liked to live well. The cars parked by the office were VW buses, Toyotas, old Jeeps, and rusted Volvos.

He hiked to the front gate on a reconnaissance mission. How easy was it to escape? Dorn sensed when he did leave West Wind, it would be in a hurry. When he got within twenty feet, bright motion sensor lights flashed on. Two men he hadn't met came at him, the mustached white one holding a bat, the Latino guy with curly hair rattling chains.

"You're trespassing. This is private property."

"No, I'm Dorn. Frederick," he said. "I just joined West Wind today, my brothers."

The snaggletoothed white dude checked a clipboard. "It's okay, Raul, he's on the list."

Raul lowered his chains. "They don't tell us shit, Garth." He glared at Dorn. "Anyway, there's a midnight curfew."

"Really?" Dorn extended his hands. "I couldn't sleep, needed to walk." He noticed the locked metal gates. "What's the deal? I thought this place was all about freedom."

Garth started to laugh then stifled it. "The sealed gates are for your protection," he said. "There are desperate local men who'd like to ball the young chicks inside." He laser-eyed Dorn. "Maybe rob the place afterward."

"Yeah," Raul added. "Cops used to park by the cabins to watch women with binoculars."

"I see," Dorn said. Anyone who wanted to leave was essentially trapped. "Well, I'll just walk the fence-line until I get back around to my cabin."

Garth tapped his bat against the ground. "Can't let you do that, friend." He grinned. "A mountain lion's been on the loose. Usually they don't attack, but this one's hungry and mean."

"Yeah, why do you think we carry weapons?" Raul slung the chains over his shoulder.

"I'll take the driveway then. Goodnight." Dorn strolled casually and heard them follow for a while, but when he eventually glanced behind, they were gone.

## CHAPTER SEVEN
# Wear Your Love Like Heaven

Dorn got shaken awake just after dawn by Tarick. He protested, rolling over. "We are farmers, basically," Tarick said. "Early to bed, early to rise, makes Baba's children wise." He yanked the sheets off Dorn. "Breakfast at seven, then you hit the fields at seven-thirty."

The extremely cold water in the communal showers woke him fast. All around were naked bodies, some hairy, some beautiful, others gnarled and swollen. If the sixties had taught Dorn anything, it was that the Love Generation's emphasis on nudity was not always erotic.

That thought was contradicted when a shapely woman with wavy sandy hair toweled him dry. He struggled to maintain eye contact. "Meredith?" he asked.

She looked puzzled. "I'm Ruby Tuesday."

"What was your original name?"

"That person is dead. She was the caterpillar, I'm the butterfly."

The breakfast was not to Dorn's taste. Beans and oatmeal, fruit, raisins, and nuts. But he guessed the overlords only drugged their dinners because they needed a vigorous workforce. Half gulag; half organic farm. The coffee and strong teas helped amp him up with caffeine. Tarick seemed to be the leader in the a.m. for apparently, Baba Gagi woke at noon in time for lunch.

After breakfast, Dorn shoveled fertilizer into a new garden plot. Dirty, sweaty work and the fertilizer smelled of ripe manure. The sun rose in the sky until he went shirtless, wearing open sandals. Dirt and soil eventually decorated him as well as the other guys he worked with. Unlike the thugs from the previous evening, these were hippie dudes in their twenties. Dorn hoped to remember all their adopted names: Skycloud, Caribou, and Bear Scat.

"What is your West Wind name?" Skycloud tried to appear and speak like an Indian, but was just a Californian with center-parted, long black hair, a deep tan, and a feathered headband.

"Haven't got one yet."

The three men studied Dorn. "You have to last a whole day first." Bear Scat scratched his prominent belly. "Not everyone does."

When they took a break at noon, Dandelion sprayed them with a garden hose to clean off the sweat and soil. Tarick brought them cucumber sandwiches festering with sprouts, and warm yak milk to wash it down.

A half hour after the meal, Dorn felt an energy surge, and watched the others lean into their shoveling, mucking, and carting wheelbarrows with renewed energy. An electric charge sparkled in his brain. Speed. Some methedrine in the lunch to keep everyone motivated, then they'd bring everyone down with tranquilizers at dinner. Ingenious. How long did it take for the brainwashing to kick-in? Every time groups outdoors or in the dorms chanted "Baba Gagi," he felt a part of himself slip away.

Dorn imagined he had a week before becoming a zombie too. He kept looking, but still couldn't pinpoint Meredith. No one in the community appeared under eighteen; kids only allowed as day guests by the office. Baba wanted to avoid charges of underage runaways.

While he and Caribou shoveled fertilizer from a wheelbarrow, Dorn asked, "Do you know Meredith? I met her back in the city, but haven't seen her yet."

Caribou stared at him, his dirty blond hair tied in a ponytail. "She's someone else now. I believe a plant name."

Well, that narrowed it down to twelve women.

"Questions weaken the soul," Caribou said, eyes magnified through his oval wire-rimmed glasses. "Baba says we must answer everything, but ask nothing. Only then can we evolve." He went back to work, but glanced over. "Be careful who you question. We are all tasked with watching each other." He smiled, suddenly boyish. "Don't worry, I was once new and stupid too. Asked too many questions, was punished. It's written in the scriptures."

"Can I read them?"

Caribou frowned. "Only Baba does, then he imparts their harsh wisdom to us."

DURING DINNER ON DORN'S THIRD EVENING at West Wind, Baba Gagi shuffled over to a podium. He basked in the applause, playing a hand in the air. "We welcome a guest member into the flock, Freddie Dorn. If he lasts the week, perhaps he shall stay permanently." Baba pointed him out. "Tonight is his christening. We shall refer to him as Moonflower. His initiation will occur later."

The men at his table slapped Dorn on the back; the young women appraised him with sly glances.

Dorn wondered why he'd been named after Datura, a mildly poisonous weed that could cause seizures, blackouts, and even comas? Did Baba suspect that he came to poison their well?

The meal continued until Baba offered him a chalice filled with liquid. "No thanks. I'm good," Dorn said.

Gagi looked stricken.

"No, you must drink it all," Tarick said. "This magic blend will keep you up tonight for your initiation." With them hovering and others looking on, Dorn swallowed down the thick, syrupy concoction. It tasted both sweet and sour, of mushrooms, roots, leaves, and dirt.

"Tarick, take him to the ceremony room." Baba smiled. The sixty followers in the dining area all applauded.

Tarick led Dorn around the sprawling building. The room resembled a yurt attached to the main structure. Candles and incense burned and the only furniture was a king-size mattress. "Remove your clothes and wear this, Moonflower." Tarick handed him a paisley velvet robe. "Meditate in a lotus position on the bed to await your spirit visitations." He bowed then left Dorn alone in the near darkness.

Whatever had been in the goblet made Dorn's temperature rise until he became feverish and flushed. He could feel hairs on his arms and legs, an acute awareness that verged on discomfort. He breathed in the musty incense then experienced hallucinations at the periphery of his vision. He thought of Ali, then of Deborah, his high school girlfriend.

The first visitation was by Dandelion. She peeled off her short dress and pressed against him. Dorn realized then the potion was an aphrodisiac causing painful arousal. Dandelion climbed him while he drifted off to somewhere else: Midwestern fields, darkened movie theaters, skinny dipping in a lake. When he came back to the room, Dandelion wiped sweat off his face before laughing as she departed. Apricot followed her, and Black Orchid followed after. Dorn went through the gyrations, realizing he was a numbed machine that could not release. The women rode him, twisted him around, and seemed to be worn out when they left.

The fourth woman looked unfamiliar, younger.

"Who are you?" Dorn asked.

"Jasmine." She undressed.

"Was your name Meredith before?"

Her face twitched as if with a bad memory. "Jasmine now. Before doesn't exist." She nestled close. Dorn gazed away. She was beautiful, but he'd been hired to save her.

"Meredith," he said, her face showing annoyance, "your parents sent me." He whispered, "They want to see you. Are you a prisoner?"

She began to tear up. "I love Baba Gagi, but I love my parents too. Once we have joined West Wind, there is no leaving." She stroked his leg.

"Stop, we're not doing anything." Dorn pulled the sheets over himself. "I need to get you out of here, but if you tell Tarick, I'm dead."

"You can't rescue me, Moonflower. I am one with the Baba—for eternity." She looked sad. "But I won't reveal your truth." Meredith scurried off.

Dorn hoped it had ended. He still felt blood pulsing in his head, but needed to walk off the drugs. All the women had been desirable, but they participated as slaves, directed by Baba to literally seduce him into the cult. He never argued with sex—good or bad—when it was offered, yet he felt he'd endured the night more than enjoyed it. He squinted in the candlelit chamber to find his clothes.

When the door opened again, an overhead light glowed on. It was Abzorba, an over six-foot, bearded man with a prominent belly. And he stood there naked. "I'm next, Moonflower."

"Sorry, I can't, I'm exhausted. I need to meditate in solitude." Dorn reached for the candle in its glass then threw it at the overhead light. Both shattered and the candle sparked onto the carpet.

"Fool, that could start a fire."

With Abzorba preoccupied, Dorn grabbed his clothes and forced the one window in the dark room open enough to wedge himself through.

Outside, Dorn bolted into the thin lip of forest around the driveway. He heard voices, people coming from the highway gate. Possibly Garth and Raul. Dorn slipped behind the main building and yawed west around the cabins, following the fence's perimeter line. He passed the gardens and reached the cornfield. All he could hear was the distant "Baba Gagi" chant that had spooled into his brain, haunting him before sleep, then again upon waking. Beyond the cornfield, the fencing rose, nearly ten feet high with barbed wire running along its crest. Dorn followed it, moving east through a copse of live oaks, manzanita, and ceanothus bushes, and below tall eucalyptus trees he contemplated climbing. A rustling sounded just ahead. When a gray fox darted by under the moonlight, Dorn exhaled before walking again. He tripped over something, perhaps a monster root rising from the ground, and plunged face-first onto the soil.

Dorn rose to an angry looking black man pointing a rifle. His extended leg had tripped him.

"I'm sorry," Dorn said. "Are you Baba's security? I belong here. My initiation was tonight and I needed air. I wasn't trying to—"

"Escape?" the man asked before laughing. "I don't work for that fraud. Hell, I don't work for no man but myself."

Caribou and Bear Scat had warned Dorn about Tyrone Jackson, the vet who'd been a smack addict, then homeless. Tyrone currently lived in a canvas pup tent by a shack and an outhouse on a saddle of land beyond Orchard Hill, just past the commune property. And he didn't like to socialize. He bought food in town or ate what he scavenged. Unfortunately, his vet status reminded Dorn that the distant war was ongoing, the draft still a menace.

"Are you Tyrone?"

"I sure as shit ain't Spiro Agnew."

"What are you doing inside the fencing?"

"Night reconnaissance. Fought for this fuckin' country in the jungles," he said. "I was a Lurp. Still am. Patrol deep into enemy territory." Tyrone rested his rifle butt on the ground. "There's a break in the upper fence less than one klick from here."

The night was humid and strange bird noises echoed in the trees, and though he'd never been, suddenly Dorn felt as if he'd strayed deep into Vietnam.

"Why the hell you roaming around the back country, son? You should be inside chanting that baby gaga bullshit with the other zombies."

"I'm not one of them."

"You damn sure look it."

"What exactly goes on here?"

"Man, I had brothers captured then brainwashed in Hanoi, but the North Vietnamese had nothing on this crew." Tyrone gripped Dorn's shoulder, forcing him down into a squat. "Thought I heard someone." He brought out infrared binoculars to scan the area. "Just a deer."

"What's Baba Gagi trying to do?"

"I only infiltrate to grab K-rations when I can," Tyrone replied. They both sank onto the moist night grass. "But from what I can piece together, they drug the food, break down resistance, keep you tired from working and chanting so you can't think no more." He paused. "What's your name?"

"Moonflower," he said. "I mean, Freddie Dorn."

"See, you're not sure." Tyrone nodded. "Some kind of sex angle too. They stage orgies so that younger Tarick guy can takes photos." Tyrone's brows formed a puzzled expression. "Can't figure out if it's a blackmail deal or it's a scam for old Baba to get more action than he saw in his whole damn life."

"Or maybe both," Dorn said. "Can you show me the fence break? Have to get out of here before I become a mindless follower."

"Before?" Tyrone's white teeth were illuminated by the moon. "Put your hands over your ears, tell me what you hear."

Dorn tried. "Nothing," he said, but in truth, "Baba-Gagi-Baba-Gagi-Baba-Gah!" repeated over and over. He was fucked.

HE DREAMED OF CONFLICT IN HIS cot, of being pulled back and forth by two giant men. Dorn woke to find Tarick jostling him, while an angry Baba Gagi slapped his face. "Get dressed and join us," Baba whispered then departed. Dawn was just coloring the sky and dudes in nearby bunks snored and farted with drowsy contentment.

Dorn threw on his clothes. Had they figured out his angle? Did Meredith squeal on him?

They walked out into the still chilly air to Baba's private residence, a cabin with a dome-like ceiling. Rustic on the outside, but lavishly decorated within: a fancy television, an Akai component stereo, a fish tank–sized shifting light cube, thick rugs and wall hangings, and a large sitar stood in the corner. Baba Gagi reclined on a rippling waterbed. Dorn had heard about them but never actually seen one.

"You!" Baba sat up to point his index finger with its sharp fingernail. "You left your pleasure ceremony last night. No one has ever done that. We arrange those specifically and you spurned your reward."

"I was with three or four women," Dorn replied. "That wore me out. I felt high and feverish. I needed to move around outside, get air."

"You shunned Abzorba." Tarick's tone scolding. "Disappeared for hours."

"I'm from a very religious family," Dorn said. "Felt guilty. Couldn't do it. My church taught me—"

"Forget Christianity. False idols." Baba rose, wobbling a little. "This is your new church. I have studied the ancient scrolls, been taught by the original Maharishi and the Grand Vizier."

Dorn forced a smile. "I want to read the texts too. Understand this cult of yours."

"Religion, not cult," Tarick said.

"No one else reads the holy scripts." Baba circled Dorn. "You must trust implicitly in me." He frowned. "Or you will wander the land beyond our gates, spouting madness. Shunned by society and our community." He made eye contact with Tarick, seeming to communicate wordlessly.

"Eat your breakfast." Tarick led Dorn outside. "A hearty one since we have a special work duty for you today."

Dorn's morning was spent washing the soap scummed walls and clearing hair-clogged drains of the showers, then after an isolated lunch, he cleaned the outhouses. They gave him a janitorial jumpsuit with a clothespin for his nose. A shovel and buckets were his main tools. By the end of the afternoon, he reeked of shit and urine and mud and decaying animals that died beneath the pits.

Dorn had plenty of time to think. Tarick must have photographed his pleasure ceremony antics, to threaten to send to his parents. They punished him because Dorn didn't weaken from the drug effects to accept Abzorba. Men were undoubtedly blackmailed on this angle; women perhaps by photos of group sex.

After he got cleaned up, the commune members were drifting into the dining area. Dorn found his Volvo and luckily, he still had the keys. The engine started, but the gas had been drained, the fuel needle hugging empty. *Fuckers!* He unlocked the glove compartment. Dorn took both Leon's knife and his snubnose in its holster then hid them beneath the porch outside his cabin, making sure no one saw. By the time he got to dinner, most commune members were either chanting in the library or free-form dancing to droning music in the performance space.

He ate a lukewarm plate of mystery stew with mushroom gravy alone at a small table tucked near the kitchen entrance. Baba must have retreated to his cabin with a young lovely; the annoying Tarick remained thankfully absent, perhaps doing the books in the back office. They sold food, crafts, and stinky organic soap at a farmer's market in Fairfax once a week, but clearly the bulk of revenue flowed in from elsewhere.

"Moonflower?" Jasmine hovered by his table. She checked behind her. "I need to talk."

"It's okay." Dorn slurped down his stew. "Baba and Tarick aren't around."

"They have eyes, ears everywhere." Jasmine's face went pale. "They won't let me call my parents anymore. I'm freaking out." Her body shook. "Sure they're square, but my mother is like my sister. Just a really uptight older sister who bosses me around."

"I dig," Dorn said.

"Baba is mad because you and I didn't ball last night."

"What?" That confirmed to Dorn the sex was being filmed.

"If a girl is rejected during the pleasure ceremony, she must prove herself in a group session."

"An orgy?"

She shuddered. "Yes, and with security guys too. I'm freaking about it." Jasmine looked anguished. "I took an oath to Baba, to live and be part of this community, but I want to see my parents. After that, I'll spend the rest of my life here."

"What?" Dorn said. "You're just nineteen. That could be seventy years. Jesus, and you'll have to make it with Gagi."

"Once we're established here, they stop imposing flesh demands. Anyway, that's my trip, my burden." She gazed around, wary. "You wanted to get me out, right? Well, how about Friday?" She sighed, rubbing at her eyes. "My group session is this weekend. They want to debase me so I'll never want to face my parents again. I'm scared."

"Go back to your chores," Dorn said. "I'll come by your cabin at one a.m. tomorrow night when everyone's asleep." Her face showed confusion, doubt. "Trust me," he continued. "It won't be easy or pretty, but we'll reach San Francisco by dawn Friday."

Jasmine kissed his cheek then scurried away toward the chanting room.

Dorn walked out on the porch to smoke a cigarette. He only inhaled cancer sticks when nervous. Fifty feet away, on the hood of a car in the darkness, sat Hutch. Dorn pretended not to notice, but knew the shit-bird was watching him.

After tamping out the butt, Dorn walked the pathway skirting the main building's west wing. He heard Hutch follow at a distance. Reaching the building's corner, he turned north, and shielded by the structure, ran as fast as he could. Dorn bolted around the other wing to head back east. The first floor was raised a few feet with a crawl space showing in between the high summer grass. Slats of white wood crisscrossed each other, but he found a few splintered pieces. He edged himself into the damp and dank underneath. Above he could hear "Baba" chanting, footsteps tromping about, and Dorn tried not to imagine what lived down there: possums, raccoons, rattlesnakes, and black widows. Every time he felt a twig touch his neck he practically jumped out of his skin. *Stay mellow, dude.*

Just beyond, he heard Hutch, the susurration of grass brushing ankles. The thug stopped; he walked back a couple of steps. Dorn felt on the verge of being discovered. He groped around the darkness to find a rock but his movements must have scared local wildlife. Two rabbits darted from the crawl space out into the grassy area. Hutch cursed quietly then set off east again—in pursuit of nothingness.

Dorn crawled out and took the perimeter route until he looped around to the break in fencing. By climbing a gnarled oak tree, he could leap beyond the property line without tangling in barbed wire. Using the moonlight and small penlight, he made his way through a jumble of brush toward the open fields that sloped up a hill. Dorn didn't expect to go unnoticed.

Tyrone blocked his path, a carbine held in his right hand and a huge Army knife in the other. "Is that you again?"

"Of course it is."

"All you honky hippies look alike to me," Tyrone said. "High and stupid." He sheathed his knife then slung the rifle over his shoulder. "This is my property. I don't recollect inviting you over for dinner."

"I thought your property started atop Orchard Hill."

"You gonna argue about land with an armed man?"

"No," Dorn said. "I need your help. I'm taking a girl out of here late tomorrow night."

Tyrone sat down on a stump. "So you fell for some chick, decided maybe you don't want every dude in the commune sharing her. What happened to free love?" He laughed in a snarl.

"Not sure I ever believed in that." Dorn wanted to rest too, but saw nothing to sit on, and Tyrone did not seem one to share his stump.

"So you're a fake hippie," Tyrone said. "You ain't the first. San Francisco is bursting with bogus gurus and leaders, with militant radicals who don't know their heads from their asses."

"I was sent." Dorn squatted down on his haunches. "This girl's parents want her back, think she's being held here."

"Sure she is." Tyrone stood. "Trouble is, most of them zombies want to stay. Like willing prisoners. I saw that shit in 'Nam." He looked beyond Dorn, then over his shoulder. "So you expect Tyrone to save your ass?"

Dorn rose too, his knees cricking. "No, I just need a big distraction after one a.m. tomorrow night."

"You talking zero-one-hundred hours?"

"Exactly. If you can divert attention to back here, maybe the girl and I stand a chance."

"You said her parents sent you . . ." Tyrone's voice trailed off. "Sounds like they must be paying you."

"There's a small remuneration involved."

"Hell, when you start talking like a cracker bank manager, I know there is." He stared off into space, the wash of stars vivid so far away from city lights. "I'd say a good distraction costs about a hundred, don't you?"

"Definitely." Dorn needed to get back before Hutch or anyone said he was missing. Another day of outhouse duty would kill him.

"Damn, that was easy. I should have asked for more."

"That's all I got," Dorn lied. "Doing this as a kind of favor. If I could, I'd burn this place down—for free."

"Communes are neutral," Tyrone said. "The management is the problem."

Dorn trekked back. Laying down on his cot, he feigned sleep. Hutch eventually came by to check on him, then departed.

CHAPTER EIGHT
## Shaman's Blues

AT BREAKFAST, TARICK AND BABA GAGI insisted Dorn join the crew selling goods at the Fairfax farmer's market. He sensed their eagerness for more money. Maybe some parents had refused to make "donations" to West Wind's upkeep. Dorn finished his omelet, cognizant this quiet moment would be the best moment of the long day ahead.

"Listen, Moonflower," Tarick said. "You're going to manage a table at the market. Don't wander off." He smiled fierce. "I won't be there, but my eyes will."

Dorn had noticed Bear Scat watching him closely. Informers got rewarded with the best day shifts, like picking grapes in the vineyard or preparing food in the kitchen. The whole commune seemed swathed in paranoia: fear of discovery and the resultant punishment.

"I know about your night walkabouts." Tarick glared at him from the opposite bench. "Curious folks who wander the grounds are often thieves. You rarely join the communal chants."

Dorn met his gaze, unflinching. "Baba-Gagi-Baba-Gagi-Baba-Gah," he chanted. "I hear that all the time. Why should I join the others when it's already inside?" He tapped his head.

Tarick nodded slowly. "Remember, we don't put pieces together into jigsaw puzzles here, but rather break you into little bits. Then we rebuild you into a better person." Tarick left.

They drove into Fairfax in VW buses. Caribou and Bear Scat in charge, though Garth from the front gate drove the lead bus. Dorn noticed the fuel gauge at near empty for the VW he rode shotgun in. Just enough to get to town and back. Ruby Tuesday, Dandelion, and several plant-named women traveled in the back with the produce and goods, but no Jasmine.

Fairfax had that hippie, rustic western town feel. Shaded by stands of towering redwoods, the main street held a general store, funky clothing shops, restaurants, and two bars. Contemplation was hip, so residents gave the aura of blissfully escaping the crowds and traffic of nearby San Francisco and the madness of America at the end of a tumultuous decade.

They set up both tables and booths from two waiting pickup trucks at the western edge of town. The commune sold potatoes, corn, beans, sprouts, wheatgrass, herbal medicines, honey, rancid home-brewed ale, organic soap, old underwear, tie-dyed shirts, and sandals.

Dorn worked the beer and honey table with gusto, calling out to people wandering by. He knew any leftover crap beer would be served at West Wind's dinner, so did his best to unload it, offering samples. If someone cringed after swallowing, he explained the initial taste was strong but the aftertaste would be mellower. "It grows on you, man, like a Frank Zappa album."

Garth and Bear Scat hovered nearby. Utilizing his art gallery charm abilities, Dorn sold more honey jars and beer than anyone expected. As he succeeded, both observers gave him more latitude, then concentrated on tables where sales were less brisk. Nobody wanted their manure fertilizer facial rub.

Finally, at 2 p.m., they allowed Dorn a half-hour lunch. He walked Main Street until certain no one was following him, then ducked into the cool dark of Nave's Bar & Grill. A couple of burly mountain women worked there, but customers seemed to be mostly young men. Some shared pitchers of beer, others played games of darts. The long-haired rednecks that Dorn sought.

His confidence built-up by hours of selling, he bought a Ballantine then joined one of their tables. "I'm visiting for the day from West Wind."

"Ha," said a mustached guy. "You a vegetable too? They come in every week looking hypnotized."

"No siree," Dorn said. "I'm from the city. Just visiting the commune." He leaned forward to make eye contact with each man. "Hell, I've gotten more action in a week than in my whole life. I'm so chafed, I begged the leaders to give me a break today." He slurped the head off his beer. "I'm pushing thirty, friends. I can only have sex three times a night. But the ladies want more. What can I do?" He scratched his ear. "I'm surprised you fellows haven't visited."

A bearded guy smiled. "I'm Kenny," he said. "I heard rumors of orgies and went up there a month ago." His face twisted with the memory. "Found a locked gate manned by guards waving guns."

Dorn cocked his head. "At what time?"

"Maybe 11:30," Kenny said.

"The magic hour is one a.m.," Dorn said. "Guards go on a break."

"What about the gate?"

"It's a thin fence with a chain lock." Dorn grinned. "Anyone have a beat-up pickup truck? You could ram that gate open easily." He downed his mug. "Well, no matter. You probably have plenty of eager women right here in town." The men's faces drooped. "Back to work now. Anyway, weeknights are your best bet. They expect intruders on weekends." Being Thursday, Dorn figured they'd come soon, rather than wait until Monday. They wouldn't get anywhere near the women's dormitory, but could cause a ruckus at the front gate.

After visiting the men's room, Dorn spotted a pay phone outside. *What if the locals didn't show tonight?* He found a dime to call Park Station.

"Yeah, what do you want, Dorn?" Detective Rodriguez said. "I'm busy."

"Could you help me out here in Fairfax after midnight tonight?"

"Are you out of your mind? Marin County, on short notice? It's out of my jurisdiction."

Dorn explained the Baba Gagi set-up, the drugged hippies basically imprisoned within locked gates patrolled by armed thugs. And the daughter he hoped to spring tonight to return to the Duncan family.

"*The* Duncans? What the hell have you gotten mixed-up in, Dorn?"

"Listen, you may need my help in the future. All I'm asking for is a little off duty reciprocation. Back-up if things get out of hand."

"Jesus Christ." Rodriguez cursed but didn't hang-up. "Can't go up there myself, but I have an idea . . ."

Dorn waited.

"I could send Detective Flannery up."

"Hippie Frankenstein?"

"Flannery got another ten-day suspension for roughing up two gay men in the Castro District." Rodriguez's voice lowered. "If he just happened to be traveling through Marin as a private citizen, Flan could break that cult compound wide open."

"He'd agree?"

"If I tell him helping out a prominent local family would help in reinstating him as a detective. He hates walking a beat."

"Do *not* mention me." Dorn rubbed his chipped tooth with a finger. "Just tell him to open the front gates of West Wind at one a.m. Bring bolt cutters for the chain lock." Dorn noticed Garth wandering through the dim bar to find him. "Got to split now, they're watching me."

"I'd tell you to be careful, but you never—"

Dorn hung up. Entering the barroom, he pulled up his zipper while smiling at Garth.

ONCE DORN FINISHED DINNER AT WEST Wind with Caribou, Elderberry, Magnolia, and Apricot, he moved onto the porch. *Would anything happen? Would everything happen?* He had summoned the four horsemen of the apocalypse, but wasn't sure they'd accept the party invite. Nervous, he requested a cigarette but was only offered a moist banana peel to smoke.

Tarick joined him, putting an arm around Dorn's shoulder. "Congratulations," he said, beaming. "You sold more beer and honey than anyone ever has. You will lead the farmer's market crew every week, inspire our lazy followers to sell."

Dorn nodded, hoping that was all.

"Join us to spectate in the speak-your-truth ceremony." Tarick showed the reptilian smile again. "Get a taste of what to expect for yourself tomorrow night."

The post-regressive therapy sessions took place in a carpeted room with two chairs at center. Baba Gagi presided while Tarick fumbled with a Teac reel-to-reel tape machine set into a bookshelf.

"Our newest member, Angelsea, shall take a Share Chair." Baba pointed to a young freckled woman with long reddish hair. "Harmony wishes to speak her truth to you, Angelsea. But first, share your innermost feelings about her."

Harmony, a dark-haired, Irish-looking woman took another chair facing Angelsea.

"I like Harmony," Angelsea said. "She's very pretty and has been kind to me as a newcomer."

"No, no." Baba's face curdled. "Mere pleasantries. We are here to grow. Be honest. What bugs you about Harmony? What do you absolutely detest?" His voice became whiny, rising in pitch.

The ten people circled around on the floor stared at Angelsea expectantly.

"Tell me, tell me your truth." Harmony seemed happy, the center of attention.

"Well," Angelsea said. "You always watch me, tell me what to do. I appreciated it at first, but need space to work on my own trip. I love you, but you're suffocating me. I can't breathe."

Harmony looked stricken as the others applauded in a robotic manner.

"Delightful," Baba said. "Now, Harmony, share your deepest feelings about Angelsea."

"I was next in line to be with Matthew, to be his soulmate," Harmony said. "Then Angelsea came, walked around topless.

You bewitched him. So even though I love you as a sister, I hate you, hate you, you bitch!" Harmony stood to shout the last words in Angelsea's face. She trembled, pulling her legs up onto the seat.

"Lovely, lovely," Baba said in a sing-song tone of delight. "Remember, Harmony, the love in our souls is the highest, purest form. Under this definition, Matthew loves you, loves me, loves Angelsea equally. The only difference is that Matthew and Angelsea are having physical love, deep probing sex, animalistic coupling. They pleasure each other's bodies in the morning, afternoon, and during the evenings too." His eyes bulged. "We cannot be jealous of such urges. They are chemical, hormonal, no?" The spectators clapped in their weird clipped rhythm. "We will all share each other's partners, no?"

Harmony wiped away her tears then forced a smile.

Dorn felt his stomach tighten. Free love and total honesty hadn't worked in the Haight, and he couldn't imagine a positive outcome in the claustrophobic world of West Wind.

At eleven, when he returned to his cabin to feign sleep, most others were already sleeping. Caribou sat in the lotus position on the deck outside, burning incense and chanting. Dorn had avoided drinking anything at supper, sipping tea from his bota bag instead. He secretly made a sandwich in the kitchen before the meal got prepared. By working the commune members from dawn to dark and then drugging their dinners, Baba and Tarick insured most would conk out early. Those who did remain awake would be left in a fuggy, listless state—unable to either break out or visit Fairfax for boozy adventures.

Dorn lay back but continued to sip tea to stay caffeinated. At midnight, Caribou mounted his top bunk. A call and response of snoring soon sounded. Fifteen minutes later, the security team made their rounds outside, approaching the cabin door then slicing the darkness with flashlight beams.

"Smells terrible in there," Hutch told Skeeter. "Like foot fungus."

"Let's go to the girls' cabin," Skeeter said. "Some chicks sleep naked. No sheets or nothing." The sound of their boots crunching on the pebbled pathway faded.

Dorn checked his pocketed watch in the dark. Only a square, a fake hippie actually wore a wristwatch in San Francisco in 1969. Because time was a concept, man, not reality. However, Dorn had to meet buyers at specific times. He was a businessman, not a freak who could just stare at the sun's position in the sky to make a vague guess.

Under a thin sheet, he lay fully dressed, knife nearby and snubnose in ankle holster. *Must have spaced out, dozed off.* He woke with a start at ten to one. Dorn grabbed his knapsack, then slid his boots on outside on the landing. Besides nightbird songs, he sensed nothing. No footfalls, cigarette smoke, muffled conversations. Checking in both directions, he crossed the oval of gardens toward the female dorm, hoping Jasmine was awake. Once confident that Hutch and Skeeter were not present, Dorn took off his boots to creep inside.

"Meredith," he whispered to her sleeping form on a lower bunk. "Jasmine."

She awoke on the verge of crying out. Dorn cupped his hand around her mouth. "It's me, remember? We're leaving now." He gazed around. A woman tossed and turned, but no one sat up.

Jasmine rose and slowly dressed, oblivious of Dorn. He turned away.

"What about my stuff?"

"Bring one carry bag," Dorn whispered. "You'll be back, right?" He hoped she wouldn't. No attachments. Toss it; burn it. Jasmine nodded. "Do you have a knife, any weapons?"

"Just this." She held a canister of mace.

"Aim at chest level," he said. "Not directly into the eyes."

Outside the cabin, Dorn kept an arm hooked through hers. They stayed off pathways, circling the office complex in the tangle of brush. From the building's southwestern corner, he could see the Volvo about fifty yards away under the outdoor lamp's yellowy glow. The sound of men talking on the porch began to drift over. Likely Hutch and Skeeter. Damn, it was 1:15. He motioned Jasmine to sit on the grass. "We wait."

A grinding metallic noise came from the south, of clanging and repeated brute impact. Alarmed voices shouted in the distance, from the direction of the gate. Hutch and Skeeter raced up the driveway road toward the ruckus. Had the townies actually tried to ram the gate?

"Ready?" he asked Jasmine.

They darted toward the Volvo; Dorn revved the engine. The needle sat at empty, but he usually got seven miles on fumes. Enough to get close to Fairfax. He rolled down the front windows so they could hear the commotion and rumbled onto the driveway. Halfway to the gate, Dorn saw someone running toward them.

"Watch out!" Jasmine said.

Dorn recognized the mustached guy brandishing a bat so he sped up. Garth gave no quarter, swinging the bat around on a rope loop. At 40 mph, Dorn slammed into the security guard, throwing him into the brush. Jasmine screamed. Dorn skidded to a halt in a flat patch on the roadside. "It's us or them. You want out of here, right?"

"You're not about peace and love," she said. "You're a weekend hippie."

Dorn snorted. "Some of us have to work during the week." They heard banging and more arguing ahead so he turned the ignition off. "We'd better travel on foot." He unholstered his gun.

Garth staggered out from the bushes, forehead bloody, limping along, but still holding the bat. Dorn didn't want to shoot him. Escape was the plan, not murder. Instead, while Garth attempted to get closer to Dorn, Jasmine maced his chest and face. Garth shrieked in pain, dropped the bat to claw at his eyes. "I'm blind, you bastard bitches."

Dorn and Jasmine kept off the driveway in high grass under gnarled oak trees. The main gate area was lit up by headlights. A townie pickup truck had dented the gate, pushed the wire inward, but stalled there. Insults went back and forth. Raul swung his chains at a local yokel who tried to mount the staved-in section while Skeeter was on the ground, wrestling and punching another townie who'd gotten inside. Hutch stood over to the left by another section of fencing, holding a pistol defensively. "Stay back!"

A tall, muscled man tore a hole open with wire-cutters then charged inside like a linebacker. Hippie Frankenstein. Hutch fired his .38 into the cop's chest, throwing Flannery back against the fencing for a moment. Must have worn a vest, expecting trouble. Using the massive pliers, Flannery gripped Hutch's pistol and squeezed the gun barrel closed, then tossed it off into the darkness.

Dorn slammed the butt of his pistol against Skeeter's head. He slumped, gripping his skull in the dirt. Luckily, Flannery didn't recognize Dorn in the dark. The cop handcuffed Hutch's arms behind his back, before turning his attention to the chain locked entry gates. He swiftly snapped links, pulled the chain off, and told the locals in their pickup truck to reverse. Then he wedged the bent gate southward to open it a bit.

Suddenly, Garth came lurching into the action. He swung the bat blindly, first hitting Skeeter as he attempted to rise, then impacting the back of Flannery's head. The cop collapsed. Raul came at Dorn, swearing in Spanish. When he struck Dorn's left shoulder with his bundle of chains, it hurt like hell. The next hit, knocked the snubnose from his hand. *Fuck.* A single headlight pierced the darkness as the roar of a motorcycle came from the commune. It rumbled up into the middle of their struggle, all engine hum and gas stink.

"I will repel this invasion," Baba Gagi cried, his voice shrill. He got off the bike behind Tarick. Jasmine stood hunched, frozen in fear. The tide had turned. The locals cowered outside the gates, while Flannery lay groggy, near unconsciousness. Dorn was unarmed and outnumbered. He had blown it. Abject defeat.

A flash of green and orange flares lit up the sky overhead. When a series of explosions sounded nearby, the ground shook. The combatants turned to stare northward as a distorted megaphone voice yelled out codes and military jargon. Dorn saw fear contort Baba's face. More flares sparked in the sky, while the percussion of a machine gun rattled in the distance. Tarick abandoned Baba Gagi to speed back to the compound.

Raul crumpled to the ground, his body enduring a fit. "I'm having flashbacks." Both hands covered his ears. "Not going back to Cambodia again. I've had it, man, I'm done."

Tyrone was raising holy hell in the back country. Crawling on his knees, Dorn felt around for a weapon. Cold metal. A loose stanchion that had been part of a barrier. Garth should have been history from the car impact and being maced but continued to shamble about like an unstoppable woodland zombie. Dorn crouched in place. When the blinded man stumbled by him, Dorn swung the metal stanchion into his kneecap. Garth groaned and went down, without a weapon, just a flailing fool.

Flannery pulled himself back up to wrestle Baba to the ground, both soon tangled in the leader's flowing white robe. Blood came when the cop hammered Baba's nose repeatedly with his fist. In return, the cult leader raked Flannery's face with his long fingernails.

Dorn tugged Jasmine's hand. "Come on." They raced back to the Volvo. More explosions sounded as the night sky lit up with more flares. Did Tyrone have a mortar? He certainly took his war maneuvers seriously.

"It's like an invasion," Jasmine said, wide-eyed. "It's freaking me out. Are you with the FBI?"

"No," Dorn said. "I'm just doing your parents a favor."

"By destroying our commune, our serenity?"

He squeezed her wrist. "West Wind isn't about peace. Tarick and Baba have a mind control thing going on, a sex cult. They blackmail families, got money from your mom and dad."

"My parents are paying Baba? For what?"

"They recorded and filmed everything. Photographs of the pleasure ceremonies, recording the Truth sessions." Dorn pushed her into the passenger seat.

"That's disgusting." Jasmine seemed awake but also in shock. "I can't believe it."

It took a few tries before the car's ignition turned over. Dorn let it warm up; he couldn't afford for it to stall. Just ride it out until it died in a few miles, then run, run, run.

He motored off the grass and built up speed. As they approached the gates, Dorn switched on his bright lights then honked the horn. Raul ran off toward the woods while Flannery and Baba rolled away into the scrub brush.

"The gate," Jasmine said.

"It's unlocked," were Dorn's last words. The Volvo smacked into the cracked gate that had jammed on the humped dirt, and with a growl of acceleration pushed it wide open. The pickup truck had retreated enough so Dorn could squeeze around it. The townies watched them in shock.

"Do you think that dented your car?" Jasmine asked.

Dorn didn't want to dwell on it. He concentrated, merged onto Saint Francis Drake and motored east. The fuel ran out a half mile before Fairfax, the glow of pole lights on Main Street in the distance. He coasted off the highway.

They walked arm-in-arm like weary battle survivors into town. A Lincoln soon drove up with Rodriguez at the wheel and the Duncans jumped out to embrace Jasmine.

"Darling," Martha said. "You look filthy and smell awful, but you're all right."

"Everything will go back to normal," Richard assured her. "We got you membership in the tennis club and at the polo grounds."

Dorn wondered if he had saved Jasmine or just commuted her prison sentence?

A few locals, still awake at two a.m., wandered about to watch from the sidewalks. When the town sheriff arrived with lights strobing, Rodriguez showed his ID, then talked to him and his partner in hushed tones. An ambulance joined the sheriff and they all sped off toward West Wind.

"Good job, Dorn. I think." Rodriguez gave Dorn his five-gallon red gas can. Then the detective ushered the Duncan family into his Lincoln and drove southeast toward San Francisco.

Dorn felt no sense of victory. He hiked bone-tired to his stalled Volvo with the gas, hoping to be asleep at home before dawn.

CHAPTER NINE
# You Set the Scene

A WEEK LATER, DORN SAT UNCOMFORTABLY in an examination room at the Haight Street Free Clinic. He could hear wailing from the outer hallway. Freaks who took too much of something sat on the floor while interns tried to calm them down. You had to be really far gone to want to enter this crowded madhouse. In 1969, more drugs flowed through the Haight than in any previous year, and while it had been mainly pot and acid before, now mescaline, psilocybin, STP, DMT, coke, heroin, and speed had all joined the party.

A man chanted in a baritone voice, then unleashed pained howls. Dorn felt lucky to know Director David Smith, an art collector, who gave him a private room to wait in.

Dr. Janssen, one of the volunteer physicians, soon entered looking harried and was trailed by a very young Hispanic nurse.

"Doctor," Dorn said. "Could I consult with you in private?"

Janssen gave a knowing smile to the woman, who waited just outside.

"You said extreme itching, rashes, and pain urinating." Janssen squinted at a clipboard.

"Exactly." Dorn made eye contact then looked away. "Am I dying? Is it going to fall off?"

"Jesus, Dorn," Janssen replied. "You're no teenager. You've got to know by now that free love comes with consequences."

"What?" It couldn't be that. He'd been so careful, dating one woman at a time, at other times going solo—feeling desperately lonely.

"Have you attended any orgies lately?" Janssen asked. "Gone home with any runaway girls you met in Golden Gate Park?"

"No, I never do that—" Dorn suddenly remembered the initiation ceremony at West Wind. How many women had he been with that night? At least three. "You think it's . . .?"

Janssen motioned him to lower his pants. "The big G." He sighed. "Pull them back up." He wrote on a pad. "Okay, Juana is going to give you a quick shot."

"No problem." Dorn rolled up his sleeve. He just wanted to get this over with, to stop scratching his crotch like the aged winos loitering in abandoned storefronts by his gallery.

"Not in your arm. Turn around and drop them again." Janssen let out a percussive laugh. "Bend over the examination table."

Dorn obeyed, feeling embarrassed, but Juana probably saw a dozen asses a day. His would just blur into a never-ending nightmare of hippie butt cheeks to haunt her. Poor girl. The needle was enormous, the syringe packed with penicillin or whatever the fuck they used.

"Just relax. Over in a minute," Janssen said. "I've got someone down the hall who's trying to claw his eyes out. Got to run."

One minute, Dorn thought. How bad can that be? The needle pierced his buttock and immediately he felt liquid fire coursing into him, along with an electrical jolt. *Sixty, fifty-nine, fifty-eight* . . . He lost count around thirty, then his face fell forward onto the papered leather of the examination table.

Dorn got home, took a bath, blazed a joint, and stretched out on his bed—watching the light box atop the stereo shift colors. After a long day, he just wanted to drift off to sleep, fully dressed, uncaring. That was the point of living in the Haight. Make up your own rules: go naked by day, sleep clothed at night. God bless and go fuck yourself, America.

Just as Dorn sank into a half-dream state, knocking sounded. He ignored it. The knocking turned to pounding. "Dorn. Freddie, I need you." Ali's voice.

Dorn sat up in bed to shake his groggy buzz away. Standing barefoot, he saw his reflection. A mess. Red-eyed, hair tangled, shirt half-unbuttoned. *Who cares?* he thought. *No reason to impress her.* He opened the door.

Ali pushed in, body humming with electric anxiety. "Freddie, he's coming up to San Francisco. He's coming to the Haight tomorrow to see me." She gazed at his dishevelment. "Did I wake you?"

"Yes, you sincerely did." Dorn walked to his kitchen sink piled with soaking dirty dishes and rinsed his face. "Gah." The soapy water stung his eyes. "What are you talking about, Ali? Who's *he*?" Dorn felt fully justified in being annoyed.

"Scott Coburn," she said. "My ex-husband."

Dorn noticed Ali looked frightened, older-looking, as if she hadn't slept for days. "Wait, I thought he died in Laos, was out of the picture like two years ago."

Ali sat down on a coffee table, cupping her face in her hands. "We got divorced in 1967. He went missing for several months. Viet Cong kept him as a prisoner but Green Berets found their village and freed him." She was almost gasping as she spoke. "I never told you that part." She gazed up. "He told my parents that he doesn't accept our divorce. Is driving up here to convince me to remarry him, to have kids."

"So tell him no." Dorn wanted to go back to sleep, not hold her hand.

"He isn't rational, went crazy in 'Nam." She reached out to grip Dorn's wrists. "I need your help. Will you pretend to be my old man, living with me? If he sees that, he'll give up and go away." Her eyes began tearing. "He's on leave, has to ship back to the jungle in two weeks."

It sounded horrible, playing make-believe house with Ali. Phony, humiliating, and possibly forcing Dorn into a conflict with a Green Beret who could snap his neck for breakfast. He stared at Ali in silence, then said, "Okay."

Ali embraced him. "Thank you, thank you." Her hands caressed his back.

Dorn pulled away from the clench. "I want to crash now, not hear about your psycho ex-husband." Ali flashed a peace sign and left smiling.

CHAPTER TEN
## Alcoholics Hieronymus Meets Truman Peyote

AFTER SHUTTERING UNITED HALLUCINATIONS THE NEXT night, Dorn met Ali at the Bard Theater on Fulton Street. Better to be among a group of friends if Scott Coburn showed, he figured. The Bard's owner was an older Italian dude, Giorgio, who planned to renovate the space into a small boutique rock club, but for the summer he'd allowed Dustin Blazer to use his theater for happenings, jam sessions, and meditation, as long as no property damage accrued.

Dustin hung out in the back office writing manically, hoping to get his articles published in *Rolling Stone*. Thirty, with thinning black hair on top and mutton chop sideburns jutting forward on his face, Dustin worked construction jobs during the day then followed the freak parade at night. He could be a sweetheart or confrontational, depending on his mercurial moods.

"Hey, man," Dustin said, when Dorn and Ali entered the theater through the side roll-up garage door. "Traveling together again?"

Ali wrapped an arm around Dorn. "I can't escape this guy."

Dorn forced a laugh.

Mingo worked with tools in the corner. A giant, heavyset Latino, he'd landed in the Haight after getting a dishonorable discharge from the Navy. With his bushy black hair combed forward Beatles-style, he mumbled and grunted mostly, but possessed a good heart under his gruff exterior. The others valued his protection. "No one messes with Mingo," Dustin often said.

Joanna did tai chi poses onstage. She named herself after a Dylan song and was theatrical as shit, always searching for magic everywhere. Signs of the occult, tarot cards, psychic readings, and deciphering hidden messages in rock lyrics. That was her trip. Joanna looked extra beautiful when wrapped in scarves or a headdress.

"I was a bird in a past life," she told Ali as she danced and leaped about. "I dream of flying whenever I sleep

Mingo, wearing a welder's mask, busied himself by spray-painting a Ford Country Squire station wagon in primary Day-Glo colors.

"Mingo wants to discover America, you know, like the Pranksters did," Moon Girl said, in-between blowing bubbles from a soap pan.

"In that car?" Dustin smiled wide. "I think America will discover Mingo first." He passed a joint to Joanna, who paused to study it. Everything held significance to her.

No one ever knew when Dustin was high. He acted the same manic way no matter what. Drugs could not override his locomotion. When focused, he hammered away on a black manual Smith Corona typewriter. "Same one as in the *Don't Look Back* film," Dustin once said. "Bobby Neuwirth gave it to a friend who sold it to me."

"Where's the scene tonight?" Dorn asked, as he cranked down the garage door.

"Don't know, but I need to talk to you, alone." Dustin pointed toward the backstage.

"Are you gonna get heavy?" Ali lifted up her pink-lens glasses.

"Never," Dustin replied. "Just guy talk. No need to trouble your little chick mind—"

"Screw you, you chauvinist." Ali made her way over to Joanna.

Dorn walked with Dustin through layers of stage curtains into the office.

"What's this about? I don't owe you a cent, Blazer."

Dustin scowled then shoved Dorn against a wall. "I hear you're a fucking narc now." He stepped back, hands clenched into fists. "Are you here to get info on me and squeal to the pigs?"

Dorn restrained himself. "Total bullshit, man." He raised his fists in a defensive boxing stance, then bounced his weight from foot to foot. "Yeah, I helped take down Rat-Man. He messed-up Van Monk, got smack to Ramona. Remember how that ended? Because I do. He sold bad trips to teenage runaways." Dorn stopped moving. "I don't remember you ever loving Rathkin. What changed?"

Dustin laughed. "Put down your gloves, Muhammad Ali, you're scaring me." He hooked one thumb into his vest and put on a bowler hat. "I wouldn't cross the street to piss on Rat-Man if my pants were on fire. It's the precedent you set. First you finger a shithead, but maybe next time it's my dealer, then a user." Dustin edged forward. "Like me."

Dorn grabbed a chair and held it up, ready to swing. "Wrong, Blazer. I'd never turn in friends. You know things are worse in the Haight. Poisoned drugs, too much dope money, street people with nothing, bikers, robberies, rapes, kidnappings, the Mafia."

"Before getting here, I lived in Detroit and Cleveland." Dustin glanced at Dorn, then at the wood chair he gripped. "I get what you're saying, but the Haight is mellow in comparison."

"Comparison?" Dorn said. "This was supposed to be a utopia, man."

"Yeah, we all had that dream in '67, but it ended after the Summer of Love. Guess you missed the hippie funeral." Dustin perched on a high stool. "Drop the damn chair."

"On your fucking head if you touch me again." He kept it aloft, though it was uncomfortable. Blazer could lull you into lowering defenses, roll a friendly joint, then pounce.

Dustin rubbed his mouth. "Locals have seen suspicious people visiting your gallery, plainclothes cops too. That ain't right. I mean, I get it. You want to pull out the bad weeds from the garden, return things to the beautiful way it was. That's poetic, sort of stupidly heroic." Dustin gazed at the ceiling, expression wistful. "But you can't put the evil genie back in the bottle, so you're walking a tightrope. Crocodiles if you fall one way, and a snake pit on the other side."

"Yeah, but you could help me. Save the district."

"Help the pigs? They've busted me for drunk and disorderly, for holding just five joints." Dustin sank his head into a hand. "Why would you work with them? If you'd come to me first, said, 'Hey, let's deep six Rat-Man,' I would have dunked him in the Bay myself." Dustin appeared hunched, almost infirm.

"I didn't do that. He fell off the Golden Gate Bridge." Dorn watched Blazer. When the dude acted listless or weary, it was usually jive.

"That's what the newspapers said, but is that the universal truth? I mean, we came out here to cut through the lies with the help of Owsley. To find peace and love and brotherhood—" Dustin sprang from the stool.

Dorn brought the chair down on his head, breaking wood struts, busting the frame. The thing a flimsy piece of shit. Dustin grabbed at his skull, reeling, but soon launched onto Dorn and they landed on the floor, swinging, clawing, and kneeing each other. Maybe it was a minute, but it felt like eternity until Dorn found himself levitating. He opened his eyes to see Mingo between them. The man built like a defensive tackle held them up by their collars, arm's length apart.

"You want to kill someone?" Mingo said. "Start with me."

"We were fooling around, Mingo," Dustin said. "Let me go, brother. Just joking."

"Jesus Christ." Ali pushed into the room. "You guys are friends, supposed to be evolved. What is it this time?" she asked. Mingo let them loose but remained on guard.

"We were fighting over you." Dustin smiled at Ali. "I got jealous seeing you two back together."

"Dorn?" Ali peered at him, mouth soured. "Is he for real?"

"Never." Dorn straightened his clothes. "Let's go. I don't need a lecture from him." He glared at Dustin. "Remember, judge not lest ye be judged."

"Yeah, quote the Bible, you hypocrite." Dustin wagged a finger. "You know what Bobby Dylan said about businessmen drinking his wine. That's you, man."

"I'm happy to drink Dylan's wine," Dorn said. "He's got money, so it wouldn't be your Mad Dog or Muscatel crap."

Suddenly, the Chinese gong rang loudly from out onstage, and they both ceased arguing. To strike the gong meant whatever just happened had ended, a signal to the collective unconsciousness, to the hive mind assembled in the theater: they must move on posthaste to the next beautiful thing.

Dorn and Ali walked out of the office hand in hand, then descended from the stage to join the others listening to music.

*Disraeli Gears* by Cream played on a portable turntable with built-in speakers. Jack Bruce sang about purple fishes while Joanna hummed along. Soon, the percussion of Dustin's fevered typing added another layer of agitation to the whole scene. Moon Girl did a slow-motion dance on the lip of the stage, trailing her fingers by her eyes in delight. Van Monk showed up during her dance, talking to himself.

Dustin explained earlier. "Last year, Moon Girl was Van Monk's old lady. She wanted to be free. No boundaries, no hang-ups. He can dig that, but his soul hasn't adapted yet." Dorn understood, doing his pretend couple routine with Ali.

Free love was complicated. Everyone in the Haight espoused it, claimed to believe in it, but deep down had not evolved to its implications. Easy to say in the abstract—no one belongs to anyone—but when it becomes personal, all kinds of heavy shit from centuries of social patterning comes rising up like a volcanic eruption of puke.

That night proceeded much as any other. Constant music, joss sticks burning, lights playing off the film screen at the back of the stage, joints passed around, and gossip about touring bands gigging nearby. Until a strange man with a bronzed, leathery face entered the theater.

"Hey, Ali," he shouted. "Your husband has returned from across the globe to see you."

Dustin rushed from backstage in the theater to leap off the stage. "You're married?" He approached Ali with a comical *what-the-fuck* expression. "Seriously?"

"No, we divorced, two years ago." Ali nodded. "This is Scott."

Dorn felt uncomfortable. The gun at his ankle—useless. This was psychological warfare.

Ali's cheeks burned with blood. "He's on leave from Vietnam."

Scott showed longer hair than a military crew-cut, but three inches was narc length. His headband with a single bird feather rising from it signified a tourist shop buy for weekend hippies. He wore a flowery shirt under a furry vest, blue jeans, and buckled biker boots. Scott shook Dustin's hand, grinning. "I'm here to join you all, to plug into my bliss."

Ali gripped Dorn tight. "How did you find us?"

Scott's eyes sensed the vibe between her and Dorn. "I asked around Hippie Hill. At the Print Mint they said you guys were on Fulton Street near the Park, so I ended up here."

Mingo put down his paint-sprayer before ambling over. He grunted then tapped Dustin's shoulder, his eyes wide and hungry-looking. "Sunshine?"

Dustin handed him some acid.

Mingo swallowed it, fastened his welding mask, and went back to work. In a tuneless caveman voice he sang along with the "Na, na, na, nah-na-nah-na" ending of "Hey Jude."

"Hey, I bought some stuff too." Scott held several microdots in his palm.

Dustin moved close to him, completely unthreatened by a Green Beret. "Are you going to be mellow about the situation?"

Scott's head twitched. "What situation?"

"Ali is no longer *your* old lady. She's with Dorn now, and could be with me next week if that's her thing. I mean, it's up to her. Nobody is anyone's possession. That's why we live here, dig?" Dustin stood with his muscled arms akimbo. "Dig?" His upper-torso angled forward, almost challenging Scott to swing. But he didn't.

Ali looked embarrassed to have her private life discussed publicly.

Scott stared at the cement floor. "Yeah, I dig. I got turned on in 'Nam. Saw how everything is interconnected. Imagine going on a night patrol on acid, knowing it could be your last trip on Planet Earth. Literally."

"That's heavy," Dustin said. "I can relate, but we've renounced violence. If you dose tonight, are you going to get all Saigon paranoid, start attacking people?"

"Here in the States I'm just following Jesus—peace and love." Scott opened his vest to show he was unarmed.

Dustin's forehead scrunched. "Can't argue with that."

Scott placed his drugs on an empty plate and the others came over to study them.

"Should I?" Ali whispered, but before Dorn could answer, she swallowed one.

Using a fingernail, Dorn cut a piece of a microdot to put on his tongue. Then he walked toward the stage and discreetly spit it out. As Ali's protector, he needed to keep vigil on her chemical ride.

"Not for me," Dustin said. "Work to do." He faded the overhead track lights to a muted glow, then carried his typewriter to the dressing room backstage to not mess with their vibes.

Joanna turned on the automatic slide-projector a Dutch guy who did light shows at the Avalon loaned them. It projected melting gel images, Marvel Comics, Salvador Dali paintings, fireworks photos, 1940s movie stars, and fiery red sunsets onto a movie screen hanging on the rear wall above the stage. Time passed. Moon Girl lit more sticks of incense and waved them around, while Mingo put a Ravi Shankar record on. Sitars made buzzing insect sounds that droned throughout the theater, causing metal parts and aluminum ashtrays to hum with sympathetic vibrations. "Ommmm!" Mingo chanted loudly. With his welder's mask still strapped to his head, he resembled a robot creature from a fifties sci-fi film.

"That stuff is weak, or it's bogus." Scott looked annoyed. "I wanted serenity, tranquility, and peace."

"Wait, what?" Dorn asked.

"They offered me acid but I asked for something stronger." He grinned reptilian. "So they gave me STP. It's great, right?" Scott downed another microdot with a gulp of his beer. "Here Dorn, that tiny bit you took won't do shit." He offered two doses.

"No, I don't really trip anymore."

"Christ, what kind of a fairy are you shacking up with, Ali?" Scott sneered. "I'm over there fighting the Commies so they don't come to America and make you eat fish slop and rice." He gripped Ali by the hips. "Go wild, with me!"

Dorn interceded but Scott elbowed him away. "Fade, man, fade."

Ali slapped Scott, breaking his embrace. "What the hell is wrong with you? You crash our zen scene and bring all your macho bullshit?"

Dustin rushed between them. "Brother Scott, go breathe in the corner, or fucking split, man."

Scott wandered off, cursing under his breath.

Dustin led Dorn backstage. "STP is bad news. A disaster when it hit the neighborhood two years ago."

"Yeah, we better watch him," Dorn said. "This could get ugly." They both sat close, their fisticuffs forgotten amid a larger threat. "I need something to keep me going tonight, but clear."

Dustin handed him a tablet.

"Caffeine?"

"White cross, a diet pill. Basically the same thing."

Back in the theater, Joanna's face beamed as she waited. "This is so exciting, like we're pioneers, or astronauts."

## CHAPTER ELEVEN
# Something in the Air

The STP hit Ali hard, uncoiling and winding in spirals through her brain. Bard Theater's space expanded into a canyon as she studied shadows in corners, then watched the dirty velvet stage curtains flutter in the breeze coming from an air vent somewhere. She'd never noticed dust particles float at the edges of the light cast by the slide projector before.

Dorn removed his batik scarf to tenderly wipe perspiration off her face. "It's okay," he said softly. "It came on strong, but it'll mellow out. Just ride the wave. Don't slip under."

Scott paced the theater and from what Ali could see, her ex-husband had problems with his jaws. He flexed a wide frightening smile, then contracted it, over and over. "Serenity, Tranquility, and Peace," he shouted. Mingo clapped loudly, his pupils so dilated, they eclipsed and blotted out his irises. Solid black marbles in an egg-white sea.

"Saturday afternoon," Moon Girl sang softly along with the Jefferson Airplane album.

"I have to get some air," Scott announced. "I'm suffocating from all your bad vibes in here." He threw off his vest and bolted outside.

Ali leaned against a wall. "I need air too, I feel overheated. I just didn't—"

"Didn't want to go with Scott," Dorn finished, leaning close. He suddenly resembled a doctor examining a patient. "You're really flushed. We'll travel together. Safer that way." He scrambled up on stage to turn the music down. "Hey, people, let's take a stroll, groove on the street energy."

Dustin appeared, glancing at each of them to gauge their experience. "I'll keep watch on the castle, my lovely glowing friends."

Moon Girl decided to stay, and Ali caught the vibe that she wanted to make Dustin. If that was her thing, then that was beautiful. Joanna joined when they strolled outside into the electric atmosphere of Fulton Street, the foggy night air a cooling balm. "I thought I was in ancient Egypt," she said, "and Dustin turned into a Pharaoh."

They laughed together because Ali knew they could each picture Dustin in that costume.

"The garage became a temple," Joanna continued, "of columns and geometric architecture. Years passed and it was a tomb." Her face looked elderly for an instant then she bent over to vomit into the gutter.

"Hey, let's have none of that," a street urchin said from a doorway.

The quintet turned south toward Haight Street. Luckily, they blended in with the general youth insanity of people in bizarre clothing walking in the middle of traffic while cars honked at them. Freaks with brightly painted faces ran by, hooting and laughing, or making weird moaning, droning sounds. Thunderclap Newman played from an upstairs window where unseen revelers sang along joyously.

"Something *is* in the air." Dorn took Ali's hand. "Acid energy, all over the Haight tonight."

"Is that good or bad?" Ali's voice sounded squeaky like a little girl.

"Neither," he replied. "It just is."

They turned east at Ashbury and Hayes, over to Masonic, bisecting the Panhandle. The energy intensified the closer they got to the nexus. A man in a bowler hat filled his mouth with booze then lit an acetylene torch. He blew out the alcohol and ignited it into a flash of blue flame.

Ali hallucinated a Chinese dragon belching fire, the street filled with costumed people, a parade. She slipped out of Dorn's grip, as their sweaty hands felt weird pressed together. It made her imagine harbor seals mating underwater. She realized procreation was just a shared bodily function, but a bodily function nonetheless, just like swallowing food, or peeing, or . . .

"Shit, it's like Chinese New Year." Van Monk pointed.

For a second, Ali felt better. Someone else existed on the same plane, her same visual trip.

"I keep getting higher." Worry had etched into Joanna's features. "We're never coming down."

Mingo placed a giant hand on Joanna's head to gently stroke her hair. "We'll be normal in a few hours."

They bought orange juice, along with plastic containers holding chunks of cantaloupe, watermelon, and honeydew, to eat sitting on a bench by a bus stop on Masonic. The sounds of commotion came, first vague, then rising in stridency, of glass breaking and yelling slowly boiling up from the west somewhere. They followed it over to Haight Street where a figure seemed to be flying. Ali stared in disbelief.

A shirtless man wearing plastic devil horns and a face darkened with makeup was jumping from parked car to parked car, coming east in their direction. The large man kicked a side mirror, sending shards of glass spraying everywhere. A small crowd followed behind, some egging him on, others yelling, "Get a grip, man. Cool it." When a spectator grabbed at his foot, he booted him in the face. Then Ali recognized Scott. He leaped off a Chevrolet's roof to land hard, indenting the hood of a Buick. Catching sight of Ali, he ran toward her.

When Dorn tried a football block from high school, Scott rammed into him. Momentarily stunned, the Green Beret threw him into the gutter. Ali rushed over to help Dorn up. "I'm sorry."

"This is the end!" Scott sang. He returned to his jumping game until he reached the last car on their side of Masonic Avenue. Then he bowed to his street audience and, without looking behind, attempted a backflip. Instead, Scott slammed against a sightseeing tour bus crossing Haight Street. The bus honked as he was cast down hard to the curb.

After the driver emerged to shake his head with disgust, he contacted his dispatcher, let off a few senior citizens—who'd gotten more than they expected from the "See Hippie-Land" tour—and rumbled away.

"Someone call the Haight-Ashbury Free Clinic," Van Monk shouted. A station wagon refitted as an ambulance arrived within five minutes. Scott remained conscious, but blood trickled from ugly cuts on his forehead and scalp.

He reached an unsteady hand upward. "I did it all for you, Ali."

"I can't handle this." Ali held her face in her fingers, body quaking.

Joanna burst into tears. "This is a bad sign. Our whole trip is cursed."

"Mingo, stay with Scott until he gets bandaged," Dorn said. "I'll take Ali to my place to cool out. We'll meet you back at the Bard Theater."

AT TWO A.M. IN DORN'S APARTMENT, Ali took a long bath, hallucinating Viking ships and deep sea fish-creatures, then imagined a natural birthing of a child. She blacked out and came to, naked in an empty tub like a beached sea mammal. The clock read four. Ten hours since dosing and Ali still felt frighteningly high.

Dorn peered in. "I drained the tub so you wouldn't drown." He handed her a towel, leaving her alone to get dressed.

"I'm sorry I involved you, Freddie," she said. "A few years ago, Scott went crazy in a pool hall in Westwood. It took four cops to bring him down."

"Thanks for telling me that now."

"So tired. I need to sleep, but can't," she said through the door. "Can we lie down?"

Dorn and Ali tossed and turned on his mattress. She became enmeshed in Byzantine visions: castles with jutting turrets, royal conspiracies plotted, and traitors executed before her eyes. At first, she witnessed it from afar, but she got cast into the midst of their squabbles, their Medieval battles. Ali fought a knight who pretended to help, but really wanted to behead her.

She awoke with a start, alone on the floor of Dorn's bedroom, the place trashed. Sheets torn and blankets strewn to far corners of the room. Close to noon and hallucinations continued. Her spine ached.

Dorn studied her from outside the window.

"Why are you out there?" Ali's voice was hoarse.

"You started hitting things. I finally left." His face showed concern. "Going to the gallery. I'll meet you later. Clean yourself up."

In the bathroom, she looked horrible: witch hair, red eyes with dark circles under them, scratches on her arms. *Did I lose it completely?* Ali took a long hot shower, even using deodorant soap, but still tripping hard at two p.m., twenty hours after she took STP. Maybe Joanna had been right. They would never come down. She watched cartoons on television until Bugs Bunny merged into a news report on Vietnam. Ali felt her insides churn. *Scott, why did you have to come back to make things worse?*

The screen flashed a dark-haired man with jowls, a five o'clock shadow, and a strange blocky hairline. Nixon. Part used car dealer, part insurance company embezzler. "Peace negotiations," "troop reduction," and "Vietnamization." Every word he spoke seemed a lie. Ali switched channels to see ferret-faced Governor Reagan bragging about sending police officers into Berkeley to quash protests and how he'd punish the radicals. *Enough!* She turned off the set and straightened up Dorn's bedroom. Had this extended trip ended whatever their casual but intimate friendship was?

WHEN DORN RETURNED AT SIX, THEY both strolled down the slope of Central Avenue to Haight Street, then turned west toward the stores. Most faces they encountered looked strained. Ali grokked that many neighborhood people were crashing after bad hallucinogens. With Owsley hiding in Mexico, quality control had vanished. They shambled about, bodies incredibly weary, frazzled zombies waiting for the after-effects to subside. Others laughed, sang songs or blew on harmonicas—the lucky ones who were still riding the high.

United Hallucinations Gallery loomed ahead. They heard a commotion, people shouting. Ali's first instinct: *Duck into the gallery and hide.* Too late.

A naked man in the middle of the street ran in their direction, his flaccid member flapping wildly. With head bandaged in white gauze, he resembled a mummy. Ali folded into Dorn, started trembling, shuddering. But then the apparition called out, "Alison!"

She panicked and bolted back east. Dorn followed.

"Ali, it's me. Your war hero." Men in scrubs pursued him, but he stayed ahead. "Wait, I won't hurt you."

Scott had escaped from the Haight-Ashbury Free Clinic. He stopped to catch his breath, then began peeling off the bandages wrapped around his face. "I copped some more acid and feel much better now." Scott removed enough gauze to show the ugly stitched scars on his forehead and swollen black and blue eyes. "They couldn't hold me, the Phantom of the Opera."

Ali scrambled from Masonic back to Central while Dorn trailed after. *Why did she involve him? Dorn couldn't protect her against this level of brute psycho shit without using his gun.*

"Don't run away. I love you, baby!" Scott yelled. "Love me, this is who I am. Your forever husband."

Ali heard sirens, police squawking through car-mounted loudspeakers. She overshot Central, landing inside Buena Vista Park. There were two children, maybe three or four years old, walking, falling, playing on the grass. The kids' hippie parents lay huddled together motionless on a picnic blanket. Ali knelt down by the blanket, to feel a positive vibe amid the tension boiling up a block behind her. Dorn joined her. She noted the children's unwashed hair. The girl's face—what Ali assumed was a girl—had dirt smeared over it. Then the young boy, mumbling nonsense gibberish, looked straight up at her.

"Play with us?" His expression showed disorientation. The parents smiled. Ali studied the four sets of eyes. The whole family were stoned: pot, acid, pills.

"No, no, no!" she said, recoiling. *Total freedom, total chaos.*

Scott could be heard shouting nearby as the men pounced on him, the wailing sirens louder and shriller, their pitch higher and higher, to merge with Ali screaming.

Her screaming continued until the ambulance with Dorn riding shotgun carried her away, him saying, *don't give her an antipsychotic,* until the men in white injected something into the crotch of her left arm, until the frazzled chief doctor shouted above the noise of all the drugged people in San Francisco General Hospital losing it, until the startled women in folded napkin hats obeyed his orders and strapped her down to the bed, and finally then, after all had been destroyed or lost, Ali slept for a long, long time.

THE ARMY BAILED SCOTT OUT OF jail and sent him right back, of course. They relied on borderline crazy men to fight their illogical war. Soldiers routinely lost it in battle, or at base camp, in Saigon bars, in transit, and also back in the States. Ali recovered in two days.

Dorn helped her get home from the clinic. Ali laughed about it, before the hilarity turned to tears. Dorn just sat with her, repeating, "It's going to be okay," because he probably wanted it to be for her and wished that for himself, even though some psychological Rubicon had been crossed and ahead lay only turmoil, drama, and further confusion.

"Don't ever let me trip again, Dorn. Promise me."

"Yeah, no. I mean, yeah, never. Of course, it's a promise."

She watched Dorn heat up lentil soup then make her an organic salad. When she eventually woke after dozing off on the couch, the room was dark and a blanket had been wrapped around her. He must have strolled back to United Hallucinations.

## CHAPTER TWELVE
## Ball of Confusion

LEON WALKED THE PANHANDLE WITH VONETTA and tried to act cool, not blurt out whatever mad thoughts bubbled into his mind. He felt relieved she was nineteen, totally legal, and a year younger than him, but she came from a conservative religious family, and Jesus, he really wanted to corrupt her. No doubt about it, she had long legs and a God-given ass. Leon hadn't been to a church in six, maybe seven years, except at a funeral for his grandfather.

He stared at her processed dark hair pressed neatly to her head. "I wish you'd spend some time with me at the gallery."

She looked at him funny. "I already saw the place you worked at when the owner was gone."

"Owner? Oh, you mean Dorn." Leon forced a laugh. "I basically run the place, you know, the manager."

"You're the manager?" She stopped mid-stride.

"Not like an official title, but it's understood."

Vonetta shook her head. "You don't have to pretend to be someone you're not. My folks taught me the importance of honesty and character."

"Yeah, sure." Leon hated when parents or ethics came up, because he didn't have the first and didn't want the second. "I meant I want you to stay with me there at night sometime . . ."

She smiled shyly, staring at the grassy ground where pale hippies stretched out on worn blankets. One or two soul brothers and sisters picnicked in the distance. "You know I'm old-fashioned," she said, "but if we *were* to socialize at night, why not where you're staying?"

Leon lived in his uncle and aunt's small Oakland apartment. They had the bedroom while he crashed in their living room. He could not make it with a super fly lady there. Watch television and hold dinner conversations, yes, but this was 1969. Free love had never been very free for a young brother, and by 1970 he might not be able to afford it anymore. "Yeah, I have my pad in Oakland." His face must have curdled.

"But what?"

"It's totally mine, but see, I let my uncle and aunt stay there too." Leon grinned as he stroked her shoulder. "I don't want them living out on the street. That would hurt me, baby."

Vonetta's eyes turned to slits. "Le-on. Let's talk about this later." She waved to a girlfriend approaching. "I've got a ride home from Natalie."

"I'm trying to be honest with you, girl."

"Try harder." She kissed his cheek then rushed off to embrace her friend; they walked off arm and arm. Leon sank down to sit on the grass, wondering if he could cop a joint nearby.

"Leon Mitchell?" A young dude in tan slacks and a short sleeve, collared shirt squatted on his haunches nearby. He looked maybe twenty-four and very earnest, like a camp counselor. "May I have a word with you?"

Leon flashed his palms at him. "Look, Mister Narc, you've got the wrong guy. I ain't stoned and I'm not holding neither."

"Not a bust." The man blew air through his nose, a contemptuous laugh. "Take a walk with me for a minute. I have a proposition for you."

"Proposition? Sorry, I don't dig men that way, especially honkies."

"A business opportunity. Money." The guy reached a hand out to lift Leon up.

He stared at him, winced, then stood. *When a white man wants to give me something, that's bad news, man.*

The young guy kept talking nonstop as they strolled. When he asked questions, Leon just said, "Nope" or "No way, I can't do that, Mister Narc."

"Call me Buddy or Bud." He paused to lean on the iron gate at the corner of Oak and Cole. "I've been assigned to watch officers at Park Station. Detective Rodriguez and Frederick Dorn, your boss—"

"Partner, my partner."

"The guy who owns United Hallucinations, who hires you," the cop continued. "They both have something going on. Could be harmless, but it might be a dirty money thing or a drug deal."

"No way, man."

"If it isn't, that's Jim-dandy." The cop set his sunglasses atop his tennis club hair. "I'll pay you $20 for any tip you give me about Dorn's phone calls, his whereabouts, who he meets with." He stared away. "Up to $40 a day. You live with your relatives, right? That extra cash could impress a young girl, buy you both a hotel room."

"Just shut up about her and that."

"I'm not asking you to betray your boss. Just give me a daily report on where Dorn goes, who drops in to the gallery, and especially any phone or in-person conversations he has with Detective Rodriguez." The cop pulled a twenty from his wallet. "Take this just to think about it."

*I can't turn on Dorn, I can't rat on Dorn. But isn't he working with the fuzz too?* Leon folded the bill into his pocket. "Buddy, I've thought about it." Leon's guts congealed. "Okay."

The delighted cop extended a hand. Dorn recalled his grandfather telling him, "When the devil smiles and shakes your hand, don't look him in the eye. Helps you keep a tiny little piece of your soul."

CHAPTER THIRTEEN
# Boardwalk Shuffle

DORN WANDERED THROUGH THE FLATS NEIGHBORHOOD of Santa Cruz at dusk, wary and wasted—more by life and car travel than any particular drug inhabiting him. Seagull screams came from up high. Where Dorn roamed was a bit unsavory, the illuminated sprawl of a county fair by the sea looming just ahead: The Boardwalk.

"Window pane, microdots," a filthy dude said to Dorn, his teeth exceptionally distressed. To achieve that at twenty-five took dedication, a negligence that could only be dreamed of in Irish pubs.

"I'm high on Jesus," Dorn replied. Religion a potent deterrent to street dealers.

"Jesus did peyote," the young guy insisted. "Mushrooms too." Dorn kept moving.

He approached the entrance. The thronged crowd a mix of Norman Rockwell families on vacation, displaced hippies moved south from San Francisco, and the dark-eyed hustlers and two-bit cons who flocked to the flashing lights with their promise of rubes to fleece—the eternal Americana of the traveling carnival anchored at the western edge of the continent. Thankfully, people ignored Dorn, a lone man traipsing along beset by a cumbersome carry bag. He needed to find his mystery contact fast, ensure the guy was legit, make the handoff, and split.

VINCE NAPOLI HAD DROPPED IN TO United Hallucinations Gallery two days ago. The mobster stood in Dorn's office as if he owned it, while Leon watched as he pretended to sweep the hallway.

"I assumed our business was finished," Dorn said. "I did what you wanted, and you've kept the street trash outside from breaking my windows or pissing in my alcove."

"I need you to do this other thing for me." Vince fingered his tie, which seemed to be strangling his stout neck. "See, my associates think you might be a narc." He shook his head. "Police would never hire a scrawny hippie like you. I told them you're a dirty detective-for-hire. Whoever pays you, you'll take the job. Whether it's us, or crooked cops, or even the spades out in Oakland. Am I right?"

He wasn't but Dorn nodded. He saw Leon in the hallway lift his broom up in the air like a bat, but thankfully didn't swing it.

"Just make a delivery, be my bag-man." Vince leaned against the office doorway then turned to grin at Leon. "You'll get paid a little, but better for you, you'll prove to my superiors that you're our friend, not a question mark." He sighed. "You don't want those fellows to have doubts. Thinking hurts them, makes them tense."

Dorn studied the bag set at Vince's feet. "I don't know. What's inside? Money, drugs?"

"The less you know the better." Vince rubbed his hands together. "It could be clothing." He half-smiled. "How's your blond girlfriend doing? Alison? You want us to keep an eye on her too, so no punks hassle her?"

"No, that's not necessary." Dorn didn't want anyone else hurt by his foolish choices. Not Leon, not Van Monk, and especially not Ali. "Okay, one last time," Dorn said. "If your associates aren't convinced that I work only for me, then I'll buy a machine gun and a big insurance policy."

"Funny guy." Vince approached then squeezed Dorn's cheek. "Hey, I'm your biggest fan after what you did to you-know-who on the bridge."

"So what neighborhood in the city am I going to?"

"City?" Vince laughed. "Down to Santa Cruz."

"That's like eighty miles away."

"You'll get $50 for gas and food, and a motel room is already booked for the night after tomorrow."

"I'll deliver the package, but then I'm getting the hell out of there."

"It's a free country, but think of it as a paid vacation. Take in the fun at The Boardwalk. Probably some good-looking girls down there if you give them a bath." When Dorn didn't reply, Vince continued, "And guys too. Can't tell hippies apart. Hell, I don't care who you stick your *pisello* into."

DORN DRIFTED PAST THE FLATS AREA, a little wary of loitering street-corner men. Just out of sight, the Monterey Bay rammed up against wood pilings, the docks, and low sea walls. Beyond that, the coast curved north toward the pristine cottages of West Cliff Drive, but here it remained seedy. Bad drug deals and car thefts lay just outside the glowing corona of carnival tourism.

Dorn kept walking.

The Boardwalk. Ferlinghetti's *Coney Island of the Mind*—transported three thousand miles away. Any similarities baked into the original design at the birth of the century, though served locally with a flatter, blander accent: less Italian, Jewish, or Bowery-inflected. *Hip, hipster, hooray! Going, going, gone daddy gone.*

Dorn carried a bulging leather bag whose weight caused him to switch hands every five minutes. Locked beforehand and further sealed by a strap. Felt like bunched cash when it banged against his knees, since gold was heavy as fuck and weapons would jut through the soft leather.

Ridiculous that he'd gone through with this, was anywhere beyond his tight Haight Street orbit. Another bullshit favor that would earn him . . . nothing really. Some breathing room before the next request. Two young men separated from the inky shadows across the avenue and darted toward him, one closing in. Under the streetlamp, neither showed the telltale mustache.

Dorn pressed the gun forward inside his jacket pocket until they could both see the barrel's outline. "Back off, cowboy," he then gazed at the other punk, "and the horseshit you rode in on." They both retreated into one of the dark alleyways that ran between the shabby single-room cottages of the Flats. Mexican drug dealers and white trash dope addicts lived there under squalid conditions.

He exhaled before continuing on. After their pretend togetherness act, Ali went off camping with girlfriends to recover from her STP freakout. "I need to just be, man," she'd told him. "A nature high. Groove with the eternal now and take a high dive into the universal always."

"Yeah, beautiful," he'd replied. "I can dig it." Because what else could you say to that kind of hippie wisdom without sacrificing your cool?

The wetness of the air, the rank odor of molting seaweed mixed with salt, affected Dorn, chilling his skin through to the bones. You could hide from the Pacific Ocean in San Francisco's downtown or in the Haight, forget it even existed. Not in Santa Cruz.

He climbed the few steps from the street, entered the big doors, and crossed through the game rooms that lined the east side of the Boardwalk. "Three throws for a quarter!" Families herded around pinball games or manned steering wheels for car seats that lunged ahead into screen-approximations of a race track, while college kids yelled in anguished competition as they played foosball. Weird carnival organ music bled in from outside mixing together with crooner seaside ballads from long ago times. "Everybody come dance tonight, bring your sweetheart to the boardwalk on the beach." Ancient Rudy Vallee shit.

Dorn picked up his pace, past the curio shops and barkers repeating their spiel, beyond long rows of Skee-Ball games lined with dedicated throwers eager for stuffed animal nirvana, past Break-a-Plate, Dime Toss, Balloon Bust, Ring Toss, Milk Bottle, "Knock 'em down and win your prize. Step right up, little lady. Winners every hour." Dorn suffered this gauntlet of noise, of aimless visitors careening into one another, lost yet giddy on a sugar high of atomic intensity. He moved by the gawkers and the hawkers, the locals and the yokels determined to catch his attention. Dorn felt a hand tugging the bag amid the thickening crowd, and he yanked it up high as if keeping a baby above rising flood waters.

A man with long sideburns and a toothpick extruding from his liver lips acted startled. "I thought that was my briefcase," he said with a pained smile.

"Where are you from?" Dorn asked.

"Castroville." He pointed. "Just round the bay."

"Wrong answer. Now beat it."

They stood in an alcove between game booths and food stands, people rushing by, indifferent.

"Curious to see what you were carrying that was so heavy." The man's mouth went ugly and he flashed a knife, keeping it tucked in close. Almost invisible.

Dorn glanced around. No security patrolling, or any figures of authority, just barkers in dated costumes—tugging on their suspenders and sporting straw boaters. A few kids played nearby, but mainly just them, two men frozen in their moment of private drama. No rules, no charts, just brute improvisation. Dorn pulled out his pistol and stabbed the barrel into the hood's chest. "Lose the blade—now!" The jerk's face paled and he obeyed. "Turn around and fucking run, or I'll drop you." Even Dorn was surprised by his brutal tone, a hard-case mobster borrowing his larynx.

The pickpocket thief, who probably worked the length of the Boardwalk, had frozen, head trembling slightly. Dorn slapped his jaw lightly with gun metal to wake the fool.

He rushed across the esplanade and out an exit to Beach Street.

Dorn paused, heart pounding. Shooting someone was the last thing he wanted, leading to discovery, capture, and arrest. He may have imagined himself a hippie shamus, a private third eye, but he was working as a Mob whore for Vince, not with Detective Rodriguez and the SFPD tonight. Dorn was a delivery man, a stooge, and likely a patsy too. To any officer of the law, a low-rent criminal carrying a pregnant bag of dirty money.

He kept moving, reminding himself that Santa Cruz faced south. Made it warmer, more like Southern California than the Bay Area, but messed up compass directions. He now headed east to where the arcade ended and the outdoor rides began, the smell of the sea mingling with Coppertone lotion, with cotton candy, and sugar-glazed confections. Girls in miniskirts draped over concession counters, tanned legs rising toward . . . *Jesus Christ, stay focused, Dorn.* Sky-high screams came from near then far, of riders careening this way and that on the Rock-O-Plane, Sky Glider, the Flying Cages, and of course The Giant Dipper—that rickety old roller coaster visitors flocked to because, lordy lordy, it sounded and looked and felt so unsafe.

Dorn strolled the boardwalk planks, past the audience watching musicians on the bandstand play hits by Jan & Dean and the Beach Boys, their nasal songs already sounding ancient, quaint in the 1969 of Hendrix and The Doors. But it encapsulated the Boardwalk, a manufactured time capsule of some ersatz late fifties Americana—before J.F.K.'s assassination, Civil Rights, Vietnam. The walkway soon spread wide to encapsulate the carnival rides. He lingered in the shadows beneath and behind Ali Baba's Flying Carpet, the designated meeting point.

Dorn puffed cigarette after cigarette waiting. He hated nicotine, but was antsy, nervous. Eager faces stared at him, some clearly dope dealers, others troublemakers looking for wounded sparrows to pounce on. Those drunk or dazed tourists who'd paused to get their bearings or to puke behind the rides after drinking too much of the pissy, no-name beer that flowed out of taps at various stands. Dorn waved the curious types by with agitation, and frowned then pantomimed a "no" to hustlers who fluttered their eyes and puckered their lips.

Finally, a short dude in his thirties with a bushy mustache and a porkpie hat sidled over, real casual. He fit the basic description. "Hey, I'm the guy."

Dorn remained wary. "I know a lot of guys. Where you from?"

"San Francisco." He grinned. "Live on a Sausalito houseboat."

*Mustache, houseboat.* That was what Vince had told Dorn. The whole thing felt suspicious, but he didn't have the time or energy to deduce who were the authentic scumbags and who were just wannabe schmucks. So he nodded. "Let's go behind those closed food booths."

"Sure, sure," the stranger said. "Whatever works, works."

They navigated the small alleyway, Dorn's feet sloshing through puddles and crushing discarded plastic cups. He tried not to imagine the nefarious goings-on of such dank, shadowy spaces. Confident that no one cruising the Boardwalk could see them, Dorn halted. "So this is it? I just hand you the bag then walk?"

The other guy's face became pinched. "Yeah, we're not trading. You're giving me what's owed and that's the end of it." He picked at his teeth with his pinky. *Something weird about his mustache.* "Best you leave first so we aren't seen together."

Though tired of lugging the bag around, Dorn hesitated.

"Jesus, come on. Let's not get caught here," the dude said. "I saw cops patrolling the boardwalk earlier." He looked over his shoulder.

Dorn wanted only to get to his hotel room or even drive north home. "Okay." He dropped the bag to the ground and slid it over to the stranger with his foot. "I don't plan to get it from behind." He removed his pistol. Keeping the gun pointed at the smiling stranger, Dorn backed out of the alleyway and dashed over to his original spot under Ali Baba's Flying Carpet. Music blared from the platform where a few aloft children screamed, but it wasn't a scary ride. Just took you high up to give a view over the coastline and across to the Monterey Peninsula twinkling in the distance.

"Hey," a man shouted, approaching in a rush. "Where were you? Where's the bag?"

"What?" Dorn studied the medium-sized man with a bushy mustache and hat. "Fuck."

"You gave it away?"

"Yeah, to another clown with a porkpie and a mustache." Dorn sucked in air. "And how do I know you're the real guy?"

"Because Vince and Antonio sent me here to meet a tall, skinny hippie near thirty with longish hair. Bjorn or something, right?"

"Uh, yeah. How was I supposed to know who was who?"

"I'm Tony, Vince's second cousin." The thug glowered. "Was he five-ten like me?"

"No, shorter." Dorn chewed on his teeth.

"Did he say where he was from?"

"A Sausalito houseboat."

"Did he mention Waldo Harbor?"

"No."

"That was part of the code." Tony glanced in every direction. "You damn fool. We have to find it or I'm in big trouble, and you're dead."

"I just left him over there." Dorn sprinted toward the shuttered concession stands and the flunky trailed after him. He cautiously tilted his head into the alleyway but it lay empty. Dorn hear the clatter of rapid footsteps on wood. "He's moving that way."

They both rushed through a warren of closed booths and food stands on the inland side of the Boardwalk. Just beyond to the north stood fencing high enough to keep the thief trapped within unless he could get beyond them to the rides and over to the beach. Then he'd be free, gone, the whole trip a disaster.

"You take the back row, Tony. I'll follow this down to those trash bins." Dorn ran in the darkness until he tripped over a human form that groaned. He rolled back to grab the man, his stench unthinkable. Some hobo dude perfumed in piss. "Sorry."

Dorn and Tony raced around the two narrow alleys, back and forth.

"Shit, we lost him." Tony gasped for air and leaned back against a booth's plywood wall. "He could be out there, anywhere." He pointed vaguely to the south.

"No, he's still here," Dorn said. "Look low. Might have wedged himself into a hole or a space between stands." They walked slow, kicking at rotted wood flaps and Sheetrock panels as they went. Nothing.

At the east end sat the trash bins, walled in by a wood slat fence just beyond and the high perimeter chain-link fencing to their side. Dorn put a finger to his lips then pointed at the bins. Tony frowned in disbelief.

Holding his pistol, Dorn popped open the first lid. A pungent odor of rotten fish. He tried the next. A mess of damp paper litter, cardboard food boxes, and ice cream cones. When he opened the largest bin, Dorn stared at the mass of banana peels, pizza crusts, discarded stuffed animal prizes. He signaled Tony over. Dorn tore a broken strip of wood trim off the fence and jabbed it down through the trash.

"Ow!" The thief rose up, bespattered in leftover food and liquid filth.

Dorn and Tony grabbed his shoulders, yanked him out and cast him onto the ground. Tony kicked him hard in the stomach. "Where's the bag, shithead?" He kicked him again—in the ribs.

"Ugh, fourth bin." The guy retched up some blood.

Tony tried to dig it out but couldn't. "Bjorn, help me turn this thing over." They lifted the heavy container from the bottom and upended it, then shook it until all the trash spilled out everywhere, over their shoes. No bag. The effort distracted them though. Something in the corner of Dorn's vision.

"He's running." The punk was twenty yards away, hustling along and hauling the damn bag.

"I'll fucking strangle him for making me run so much." Tony took off in pursuit. Dorn followed, realizing it was becoming public. They could all get busted, and if not now, then remembered later by passersby for a police station lineup.

The thief seemed to want to avoid notice too. He weaved through the back areas of rides, jumping over small barricades and jumbles of power cords, pushing past gawky teenagers. Tony appeared to be a good runner and Dorn was fine with that. Let him catch the dipshit then fight it out. Once the real crook had the handoff secured, Dorn could fade fast. So he shadowed both men at a distance.

The brazen jagoff swung the bag and clipped Tony's head, sending him reeling onto a row of barrels. Dorn darted over and helped Tony to his feet.

"Thanks." Tony gestured. "He's heading for the roller coaster."

The thief had scuttled behind the massive Giant Dipper. Its winding tracks rose seventy feet above the Boardwalk, running its constant cycle over and over: the rickety track-clacking sounds of cars in each train slowly creeping up to the summit before the high, girlish screams of riders came during its abrupt plunge downward. Some orgasmic ritual for the kids and teens. Stoners loved the rush it gave them too.

Behind the Giant Dipper, shadowed in darkness were fenced in generators, gears and pulleys, and a seventy-horsepower motor ratcheting away. Beyond them, derelict booths rose on open weed-strewn lots where vagrants stretched out to sleep. They had lost sight of the impostor's fleeing figure, so Dorn and Tony climbed the fencing with the signs stating: *Danger – Keep Out!*

"Where?" Tony shouted over the swoosh and thrum of a Dipper train rocketing by.

Dorn gazed upward. It would've been suicidal to climb the white wood supports that rose seven stories and formed the roller coaster's exoskeleton. He noticed the base of the track, supported by large metal struts, rested almost three feet off the ground. He squinted. Quicksilver motion through the chiaroscuro of dark and spattered fluorescent lighting. "Underneath," Dorn yelled back.

Tony fell flat to crawl beneath, across dirt and mud and grease and oil. Dorn squatted down into a crouch to watch from the sidelines. Tony reached the guy and wrestled with him, pounding the thief with his fists while cursing. After a minute or two, the bogus man broke away and tried to climb the metal ties upward. When he pressed his head through a space in the tracks, his fake mustache tore off, but his shoulders were too broad to snake through the opening. "Help! I'm stuck." He struggled but couldn't lower his head.

Tony ignored him and scampered back holding the money bag.

"Let's go," Dorn said. "The roller coaster runs every five minutes. It'll hit him or they'll brake the train. Either way, the area will be swarming with cops, officials, and carnies."

They both looked around to get their bearings. "You think we can get away over there?" Tony pointed and Dorn turned, seeing only darkness.

Suddenly he felt a wire tighten around his neck, Tony yanking it backward. "Hey," he gasped out.

"It's a goodbye present from Vince," Tony said from behind, hot breath tickling into his ear. "It's not personal, just business. You know too much, have detective friends." He laughed. "Vince has informers, cops on the pad at every precinct."

Only Dorn's thick Nehru collar prevented the garrote from tearing into his flesh. He went limp. Tony loosened pressure for a moment and Dorn hunched down to elbow the thug in the nuts. He grabbed a jagged paving stone at his feet and smacked it into Tony's face. The mobster reeled backwards, blood seeping through one clutched hand, the other fumbling through his pockets.

Before he could find a weapon, four college kids tramped by and noticed the trapped man. Earnest buzz cuts from San Jose or Monterey in chinos and loafers. "Hey, we've got to stop the Dipper." They raced around to the ticket booth in front.

Five years ago in Lawrence, Kansas, Dorn had loathed similar square types. That's why he fled to California, to be with the freaks. But now in 1969, he realized they were the can-do, clear-eyed kids that went into public service, joined the Peace Corps, and got actual shit done. Those Berkeley radicals with Che Guevara posters on their walls were frauds, fighting only for their rights to get buzzed and get laid. And any true believers, who actually wanted to foment bloodbath revolutions in South America, were the truly scary ones: enemies of peace, love, and understanding.

A shrieking squeal of brakes soon followed and the stuck thief screamed bloody murder. Giant floodlights flashed on, illuminating the entire shadowy back area. Tony's left eye had swollen shut after being struck, but the other widened in fear. He bolted with the bag for the chain-link fencing separating the Boardwalk from Beach Street and Santa Cruz's downtown.

Attendants came bustling over with lamps to the train car, barely stopped a few feet from the babbling thug trapped in a halo of light. Curious riders stood in their seats to view the spectacle. The car jerked forward, some residual spark animating it, and pressed over the thief's head. "Get me out of here," he yelled from underneath.

Official-looking men in jumpsuits spoke on walkie-talkies, stern radio voices barking replies. Dorn rubbed his neck and tried to get his breath back. Tony couldn't clamber over the fifteen-foot fence carrying the heavy bag. Instead, he mounted a nearby empty game booth and from the flimsy roof tossed the bag up and over. Gawkers and those waiting in line to ride the Dipper streamed around to see the cause of delay. A rumble of engine noise, then blue and red flashing lights approached; a cop car had actually ramped-up somehow to drive the boardwalk.

The officers rushed over to Dorn, now detached from the crowd, wounded, dirty, and looking guilty as hell.

"What's going on here? Did you cause that accident?" The cop shone his light into Dorn's eyes as if his corneas held deep secrets.

"No." Dorn made a swift decision. "It's a Mob handoff. That guy has the money bag." He gesticulated toward Tony, struggling to get over the barbed wire atop the fencing—his clothes entangled, ripped, hands bleeding.

"You on the fence," the other officer shouted. "Freeze where you are or we'll fire."

Both flashlights were trained on Tony. He tore his pants free as a warning shot rang out. The mobster dropped fifteen feet to the street and didn't get up.

The first cop turned to Dorn. "So you're his partner? And who's the clown under the roller coaster car?"

"I'm working plain clothes for Detective Rodriguez in the SFPD." Dorn handed Victor Rodriguez's card to the stunned officer—whose mouth hung open.

"You're a plain clothes detective?" the other one said. "They must be desperate up there in Frisco."

"We call it San Francisco."

"Yeah?" the first cop said. "And we call it, Fuck You. Where's your badge, your ID?"

"I work one-on-one with Rodriguez. Community outreach. Vince Napoli is a Mob boss delivering a bag of cash down here to an associate." Dorn studied their skeptical faces. "That fool over there intervened, stole the bag from Tony, the Mob associate. He tried to escape and got snarled."

Both cops stood in silence, looking over at the maintenance men prying the jackass from the tracks, then back at Dorn. All three noticed peripheral motion. Tony had risen from the pavement on Beach Street to stagger away from the Boardwalk. Clearly hurt, he moved slow, dragging the bulky bag along the sidewalk.

"You need to stop him," Dorn said. "Get that money."

"Don't go anywhere, you dirty hippie scumbag," the first officer said. "We need to confirm your story. Go sit in our backseat."

Dorn watched the second cop rush past him to their strobing car and grab wire cutters. They were through the fence in a minute and chasing a dazed Tony toward the northeast. Dorn turned and followed them through the cut-out fencing to wait out on Beach Street. He saw blood spattered across the ground, Tony leaving a trail for the cops. Dorn found a small ditch to set his revolver inside before covering it with rocks and dirt. He gazed into the lamp-lit night, seeing the cop uniforms vanish into the maze of small cottages and shacks. The Flats.

Dorn slumped down on the curb, his whole body aching. Fog had rolled in, making it wet and cold, while seagulls circled above and dove for leftover food scraps. He rubbed his sore, swollen neck, feeling zero sympathy for Tony. It wouldn't be long. Dorn heard the cops shout "stop" and "freeze," then a single gunshot followed by a sustained volley of shots. After that, silence.

Yeah, everything would be totally groovy if Dorn just kept driving south, all the way to Patagonia—the tip of fucking South America. As long as he never ever returned to San Francisco, the art gallery, or to see Ali again, his life might continue on in some vague fashion.

DORN GOT RELEASED FROM THE SANTA Cruz Police Station after midnight. It took an hour to reach Detective Rodriguez in San Francisco and he didn't act overjoyed to be awakened. He apparently vouched for Dorn over the phone while the two local cops kept saying, "This is unusual policy" and "How about giving us a head's up next time?" and "If that's what you think is best."

Rodriguez asked to speak to Dorn on the line. "Listen, shitbird," he said. "I told them you were on assignment from me. Totally lied because I want to nab Vince Napoli and his Lieutenant, Antonio Rivaldi. You need to help make that happen. And you ever go off Lone Ranger on me again, I'll let you spend a week in jail meditating on the joys of friendly bunkmates. Understand?"

"I hear you, man."

"Good," Rodriguez said. "Be in my office at noon tomorrow for a full report. Set your watch or whatever you heads use to tell time. Don't make me put out an APB on you."

Dorn handed the phone back.

The lead officer, Harrison, said, "We're releasing you on your own recognizance."

"But I wasn't charged."

"No, not yet," he replied. "We're not pressing charges. Doing this as a departmental favor." He gave Dorn a once-over. "Where are you headed?"

"To the Roadrunner Motel," Dorn said. "Need to sleep now then leave tomorrow." He noted the large autographed wall photos of Richard Nixon and Governor Reagan.

"Fine," Harrison said. "We'll escort you there now. Detective Rodriguez wants that money brought to him." He kicked the retrieved bag at his feet. "Fifty grand was stolen from an armored car delivering to Pacific Coast Credit Union last week. Rodriguez is sure these bills' numbers will match." He frowned. "Are you going to be able to accomplish that, son?"

Dorn nodded.

"Good. Now don't you *ever* come down to Santa Cruz again. Our sleepy beach town don't need some Frisco radical playing cowboy, causing shootouts and carnival accidents. That kind of thing hurts tourism."

"Cleaning up the Flats neighborhood might help you there," Dorn said.

"Did you hear us ask for advice, punk?"

The second cop, Lurbin, said, "You got twelve hours. We see you after that and we're going to get real unofficial with your commie-loving ass." He rubbed his right fist with his left hand. "And get a haircut, son. You're a man, nearly thirty, not some high school girl."

## CHAPTER FOURTEEN
# Change is Now

DORN WOKE AT DAWN. BONE-TIRED, BUT eager to split. Once he'd retrieved his stashed gun near the Boardwalk, he bought a wrapped sandwich and a Styrofoam cup of coffee at a gas station on Ocean Street. Dorn picked up the money bag at the police station then drove north on Highway 1. The slow route, the scenic route, the only route as far as he was concerned.

The road lay near empty on a weekend just after eight; the shuttered cottages, weathered Victorians, and single-story businesses lining the outskirts of downtown giving way to the coastline, to Wilder Ranch, and low headlands fronting the sea. Beyond, he came upon crop field farmland and even migrant shacks of early century design. Rusted and wind-battered outbuildings lay to the west, while on the inland side of the highway, brown and golden hills rose up lazily with sentry lines of redwoods wedged into their clefts and valleys, finally topped off by the jagged peaks of the Santa Cruz Mountains. Dorn watched hawks gliding on thermals as they studied the land, saw dazed cows giving him side-eyed glances, the day just exploding into being. A feeling of renewal after shaking off the brute excesses of darkness, a tang of raw fresh life seeping up from loamy soil dampened overnight by coastal fog.

Instead of racing home, as he could—no traffic cops in sight—Dorn stuck to the speed limit. Because this was the good place, an interstitial zone where time blurred and decades merged. A sense of hope and possibility lived on outside the rush and tumble of city life, of manufactured human reality. The Pacific thundered, in and out of sight, forever crashing against the edge of the continent. Past ranch houses and utility buildings, a few modern geometric residences fanned out on rocky promontories overlooking the sea.

Dorn felt the familiar but impossible desire to live here on the edge, to experience it all, now and forever. Though he knew from visiting Big Sur that you couldn't capture it, keep it, or swallow it deep inside you. The whole fucking thing just too big and wild, rustic and primal, the elements remaining in some seismic dance. Henry Miller understood. Yeah, you could get a peripheral glimpse of it, an after-image burned into your dilated mind, something to feel at a distance, but never to truly stop and touch. The postcard picture framed through your car window, Dorn, was an illusion. In reality, a chaos of creation and destruction, unimaginable powers slamming up against one another. The secret Bohemia, the haven that such places hinted at was temporary at best—unstable matter. Something best kept with faded Kodak photos of lurid sunsets viewed from "Cabinessence" slatted decks perched heart-attack high above the sea.

Dorn had considered such things on previous coastal journeys. The goals always the same: transcend the bullshit, shed your skin, demolish ego games, eliminate your petty agenda.

He decelerated through the tiny town of Davenport, sounding all Cape Cod and paint-faded clapboard cottage whaling town. Pigeon Point Lighthouse lay somewhere ahead through undeveloped land, large private ranches, and parks. Lumber trucks occasionally heaved across the highway to snarl their way up some snaking route toward dense redwood groves.

The summer of '69 and everything in flux. Dorn was a hippie elder. The teenagers on the Boardwalk hadn't patiently grown their hair out as The Beatles became supreme. Nor had they slowly graduated from smoking pot to the psychedelic experience—to reach the next big thing. Crowded up against the end of the decade, Dorn saw the sixties' failures all rising sunlit and blazing into his weary morning eyes.

Peace and dope and free love were a stone groove, but they wouldn't effect any worldwide behavioral or systemic change. The freak population had merely built their own zoo where they could rave and perform for the straights. All the promises of the Human Be-in, of the Monterey Pop Festival, and of the Haight in 1966 had given way to today's foul backwash. A violent undertow of criminal enterprise, hard drugs, and venereal diseases. And that undertow had dragged Dorn down too, gasping for breath, clutching at wet sand. Was he even helping the vibe or just painting it black?

DORN CAME OFF HIGHWAY 1 ONTO 19th Avenue before ten a.m., then turned east on Irving Street and cruised over to his pad on Belvedere. He rented the second floor, which meant enduring the upstairs neighbors stamping about on his ceiling in their hobnail boots. The apartment's front door opened, unlocked. It surprised Dorn, made him suspicious. Break-ins had become routine in the Haight, so he'd installed another door lock and latches on the windows. He removed his shoes, gripped the pistol, and navigated the dim and musty apartment in stealth mode. Just past the entrance in the pantry area, he tripped over a dulcimer and snapped its neck. *Who the hell left it lying on the carpet? That's $10 down the drain.* Melted candle wax and incense embers filled ashtrays. He examined a tiny brown-stained roach. *Damn, too small to light and smoke.*

Faint music played in the living room, a droning Eastern vibe but with menacing undertones. Approaching the stereo, he recognized the Velvet Underground's banana album. He studied the spinning disk. The record player would play the same thing over and over if you didn't stop it.

Dorn lifted the needle and placed the album back in its cover. A vinyl slab of heroin addiction, sadomasochism, and other urban vices, though perhaps it served to remind him that no matter how bad the Haight got, the only other viable option for a freak to live in, New York City, was infinitely worse. Impossible.

The door to his bedroom lay ajar. It smelled of sleep and humanity, sweat and old clothes. He slowly wedged it open. Perhaps worse than rampant thieves, were the homeless runaways who might break into an unoccupied apartment to crash at and shower in. Bracing himself, Dorn approached the bed. *Whoa.* Ali lay sprawled across his pillows, twitching and sometimes murmuring, submerged in a restless sleep.

He crouched down on the mattress edge to softly stroke hair away from her face. She rose up all naked and disheveled and began kissing him, first light pecks and on the cheeks and nose, then on the lips, becoming more impassioned, more saliva-drenched. Though her breath was as fresh as peyote buttons, it still aroused him. Something deep within made Dorn resist.

Ali rustled into consciousness. "Oh, it's you, Frederick." She pulled away to sink her head into one hand.

"Well, yeah, it is my place," he said, feeling tense. "Who were you expecting?"

"I was dreaming, displaced in time, you know, back when we—"

"Lived together?"

She nodded and pulled the covers up to hide her exposed breasts.

"Don't panic, I've seen you before."

"Sure," she frowned, "but I don't want you to now."

"Why aren't you camping?"

"I got scared by noises in the woods. Came home, but what if Scott escaped? He'd go to my apartment." She took Dorn's hand. "Ever since that STP nightmare, I've felt like I'm being followed." She lowered her voice to a hoarse whisper. "I'm paranoid."

"Maybe cut back on the weed."

She swatted him with a pillow. "Fuck you, Dorn, I'm serious."

When he felt her collapse forward to tremble against him, Dorn changed tack. "Yeah, it's cool, I understand, but you left my door unlocked. It's much less safe here for you." He wandered into the living room and put on *Forever Changes* by Love to let her get up and dressed in peace. The first song began with hyper-strummed Mexican guitars and Mariachi horns, but it didn't puncture Dorn's gloom balloon.

After she showered, Ali joined him on the butt-sprung couch covered with a tapestry. "You really think it's dangerous for me to stay awhile?"

"Yes," he said. "I told you how I tried to help get rid of Rat-Man and his fucked up drugs."

"Sure, but that was weeks ago."

"The cops wanted him and so did the Mafia, for separate reasons. Anyway, I got pressed into the middle of that shit sandwich." He inhaled, considering how much he could tell her. "Then the local Mob guy insisted I deliver a bag for them to Santa Cruz. Drug money, money laundering, or something."

"So that's where you've been?" She slid over closer. "I was worried."

"It all went wrong. I got out alive, so that was cool, but the money . . . Police down there shot the handoff guy and I'm in deep shit with the local fuzz for not informing them."

"That's not so bad." She tried to straighten Dorn's hair with her fingers but soon gave up.

"You don't get it." He scooted back away from her. "First off, I botched the handoff, and I found out I was supposed to die after the transaction." He wondered if she understood. "There's a guy named Vince who's about to learn that his money bag was confiscated and I'm still breathing."

"Jesus, Dorn." She teared up, then wiped her eyes and paced the floor. "Talk to Dustin. He's had scuffles with the fuzz and criminals and somehow survived. Can the local cops help?"

"I have an appointment with a detective at noon." He stood up. "I want you to head out of town for a few days. You have that friend, Wendy, out in Sausalito."

Ali stared at him quizzically.

"I'm not asking, babe. You have to go." He gazed around the living room. "I'm not staying here either, but I do plan to leave some booby traps behind. Serious king death shit. So let's have a big breakfast together before you leave, okay?"

Ali chewed her fingernails and nodded.

Dorn met with Detective Rodriguez at Park Station and recounted the events. How Vince had threatened him if he didn't deliver, the whole sordid Boardwalk affair.

Rodriguez said nothing, just moved his mouth around, shaking his head. "Yeah, it's a mess," he finally said. "The officers confirmed what you told me, though they still aren't buying your story, since we both know it's a load of bullcrap that I sent you down there. Tony Giordano is at Dominican Hospital in Santa Cruz in critical condition." He sighed. "The detectives want answers when he comes out of his coma."

"They might need door guards, night and day," Dorn replied. "Not dirty cops."

Rodriguez jumped up, face reddening. "What the hell are you saying about their force?"

"I'd give that thug two days at most." Dorn looked away. "Tony tried to kill me so I don't really care . . ." He lifted the bulging bag to set it atop the desk.

"Ah, the pied piper of peace and love is now Mr. Eye-for-an-Eye?" Rodriguez sat back down to examine the money bag, his expression serious. "And what's your life expectancy, Dorn?"

"Several hours to maybe a week." He wandered around the office. "Someone followed me from my place over here, Detective. I'll help you take down Vince and give you information, but shit man, I need protection tonight at my Belvedere pad."

"You shouldn't be staying there, or at your gallery."

"Sure, sure, I can split tomorrow, find a hidey-hole in another neighborhood, or in Marin, cut my hair, wear square clothes, but tonight—"

"Okay, I'll put your address on the patrol sheet."

"Twenty-four hour watch?"

"What are you, the frigging president? No. Every hour, an officer will cruise by, check your building, listen for noise. That's the best I can do."

"Really?"

"Yes. Do you understand the hoops I'll have to jump through to get a beat cop to give any protection to a local hippie? Your entire support within this precinct is right here in this room." He sank two tablets into a water glass. After they fizzed a while, Rodriguez drank them down. "Okay, we're done."

Dorn slouched toward the door.

"Oh, by the way," Rodriguez added. "There's a ten percent reward for retrieving the stolen credit union money. That's five grand for you. I'll have it in a few days. So cheer up."

Dorn half-smiled then wandered out through the Park Station hallways, as various cops and plainclothes men gave him the stink eye.

CHAPTER FIFTEEN
# Burning of the Midnight Lamp

Dorn left the meeting dejected and confused. The quicksilver essence of life became so much more precious when it seemed to be slipping away. He detoured to Fell Street and strolled to Masonic in search of Van Monk. Ambrosia at the Blue Unicorn said he was recording two blocks away on Page. Dorn made his way downstairs to the funky basement studio known as Sitar Sound.

A performance was in progress, so he joined Magnus, the crazy Swede engineer in the control room. The song sounded weird, extra bright and poppy, unlike most of Van Monk's session work. "Is that you, Dorn?" Magnus said.

"What is this shit?" Dorn asked.

Magnus bobbed his head to the music, pausing to suck on a glassy water pipe. He coughed harshly, his face annoyed at the question. "Be cool. It's a public awareness song funded by San Francisco Health and Services. They paid us all, man. We're capitalists, just like you."

"Yeah, that's groovy."

Magnus squinted at Dorn, his mouth drooping. "Word on the street is that you're a narc."

"You heard wrong."

"Then you're not too pure for this." Magnus outstretched the water pipe.

Dorn waved it away. "Later, not now." Clarity and sobriety seeming wiser choices in the current survival game. He squatted on an area of couch not covered with clothes or damp from cat piss, then placed headphones around his ears. A familiar-looking singer—Dino Valenti?—sang with an earnest expression into the giant Neumann microphone dangling from a Rube Goldberg-like tower contraption of metal, wood, and silver tape.

"Gonorrhea . . . Baby, won't you set me free? Demon lover, please lift your curse off me. Gonorrhea . . . You're the sting right after the flirt. Doctor Leah said bend over, dude, this won't hurt. Peni-cillin, make my dreams come true. Your special medicine, I hope it gets me through. Gonorrhea . . . Leave this town now and be nice. Oh Baby, free love, shouldn't have a price."

After the band finished the take, Van Monk, Dino, and the bandmembers stumbled into the control room with goofy smiles.

Dorn gave them all bro shakes, hugging the guys he knew better. "Dino, your best singing ever," he said. "You wrote the lyrics? They were intense. Van Monk, you *are* the Nicky Hopkins of the Haight." On that, Dorn spoke with utter sincerity. "Rango, no one else attacks their bass the way you do. You don't limit yourself to conventional tuning. And Goat Boy, it's like you never took a drum lesson in your life. Pure energy, no restraint." Dorn sensed he may have carried his bullshit a bit far so he quickly passed the water pipe around as their reward.

He put an arm around Van Monk and whispered, "Are you done? Need to talk."

Van Monk nodded. "Lunch break," he told Magnus. "Back in an hour."

They walked Masonic south, passing the Haight Ashbury Free Clinic and the street theater outside. Pallid junkies with midnight eyes drooped in nearby doorways or squatted on the pavement, knees pressed together, their dope-hungry bodies quivering in pain and desire. Acid heads and speed freaks enacted dramas, yelling about snakes and spiders, banging on the clinic's door then being told by earnest interns to wait outside until called.

Dorn began to turn east on Haight Street but saw a suspicious car idling outside his United Hallucinations Gallery, thin blue-gray exhaust clouds rising from its tail pipe. He noted the CLOSED sign on the front door, glad that Leon wasn't inside, a collateral target for his own malfeasance. He took Van Monk's arm and led him west.

"You okay, brother?" Van Monk said. "You shaved your mustache and I've never seen you wearing a bowler hat or those big, dark shades before."

"I'm sort of in disguise."

"Plus, you're twitchy and really pale." They walked past the Psychedelic Shop and Happening House. Van Monk waved to freaks hanging on the street, some leaning against parked cars, strumming guitars, and playing shrill flutes. Dorn pretended to be a stranger; he didn't interact with anyone.

When they got beyond the bustle and crush of hippie humanity, Dorn said, "Remember what happened to Rat-Man?"

"Yeah, and I'm still not missing him."

"I was involved. Both the cops and gangsters knew about me."

"I heard rumors you were an informer." Van Monk attempted to see into Dorn's sunglasses. "But I figured it was bullshit. I mean you helped nail Rat-Man, then he committed suicide. I can see how local heads might consider that a betrayal, selling out a dealer to the pigs." He took a deep breath. "But I know the truth. You were trying to help me, help the neighborhood. Rat-Man was a disease ruining this community."

"It's bad." Dorn needed to keep it simple. "Mob money got confiscated in transit and I've been blamed. To make it worse, they want me . . ."

"Gone?"

"Like permanently." Dorn led Van Monk into an alcove just past Pall Mall Cocktail Lounge. "I could use your gun, Van Monk."

"Wait, you bought one in June because of break-ins." Van Monk carefully lifted Dorn's sunglasses off his nose, then, as if seeing some painful revelation swimming in his eyes, pressed them back on.

"I need another."

"I can't believe it's come to this: you and me carrying. Where did the brotherly love go?"

"Find us a time machine to 1966." Dorn glared at someone watching them on the street until he moved away.

"Still have my Derringer, my gig gun." Van Monk frowned. "So my keyboards won't get stolen during load-ins, but that's just two bullets, only good at close range."

"Perfect, thanks. I owe you a big favor, for real." Dorn smiled. "Let's go."

They turned north on Clayton then shuffled over to Van Monk's Volkswagen bus. Peace and love and music symbols were painted across its purple-blue exterior. The driver's side was stuck shut with a broken handle, so Van Monk worked the passenger door open using a wire hangar. He scanned the street, then dug the tiny weapon out of the glove compartment, checked the chamber, and handed it over.

"It's a family heirloom, passed down." He gripped Dorn to pull him close, coils of his wild Dylan curls tickling against Dorn's chin and jaw. "Don't lose it, man."

"Impossible. Unthinkable." For a long moment, Dorn wished he was shorter like Van Monk, able to blend in with ease into the neighborhood's sea of long-haired freaks. He'd always stood out, and height didn't provide him with physical strength or allure to women. Just made him noticeable from a distance, the tall, thin joker being buffeted by the wind, struggling against the fucking elements to get a fair shake in this crooked deck of existence.

Dorn flashed a peace sign to Van Monk, then hustled south to find his Volvo. A bunch of errands left to do before nightfall. He'd asked Rodriguez for money in helping the SFPD bust the Mob. The detective gave him fifty in small bills, and when Dorn shot him a "that's it?" look, promised to fix up his car with new tires, filters, and a timing belt at the police garage near Union Square. At least reward money was coming.

Realizing his status at Park Station was of a shady two-bit informer, Dorn didn't expect much police protection on Belvedere overnight. After some shopping at Bay Hardware on Irving, he drove south on the peninsula to an Outdoor Sports World that stocked plenty of hunting and fishing equipment. Dorn felt glad that Ali wasn't in his pad when he returned. Just the Doors playing on his stereo hinted at her recent presence. The dark, creepy vibe of last year's *Strange Days* summed up the current mood. Morrison sang "Unhappy Girl" and Krieger's slide guitar swoops mixed with Manzarek's eerie carnival organ haunted Dorn until he lifted the needle off.

He found records he hid from San Francisco friends, stuff he'd brought from the Midwest. Dorn lay down on his carpet, head propped up on pillows and listened to "What the World Needs Now is Love" from a Burt Bacharach album. The schmaltzy music reminded him of his parents drinking cocktails and watching TV holiday specials in the family living room—everything he'd been desperate to escape. A last vestige of innocence that maybe he never had, but seemed worth reaching for in retrospect.

Later, he made a mixture of the Acetone and bleach he'd bought earlier, before letting it sit in a bowl of ice. For dinner, Dorn ate chicken soup and a hard baguette of bread. When done, he installed a chain lock on the door, then drilled and embedded a one-way peep hole at his eye height. Just outside the apartment, Dorn inserted a blinding 200 watt light bulb on the house's inner stairway. Under the outer stoop of six wooden steps leading to the first floor's landing, he placed two cheap Radio Shack microphones, their wires running back to a powered speaker in his bedroom. With the volume cranked up, he could hear anyone coming inside late at night, and even monitor outdoor conversations. Once completed, he set up a special surprise from Outdoor Sports World. Dorn stayed up to midnight, vigilant. But beyond the upstairs neighbors tromping up to their apartment, no intruders. Just the whoosh of cars whizzing by outside on Belvedere.

Dorn relaxed on his bed. He began to doze off until the phone ringing startled him into alertness. "Yeah?"

"Freddie, are you okay?" Ali asked.

"Sure. Just trying to get a little sleep."

"There's plenty of room here at Wendy's."

"Stop talking." Dorn heard clicking noises. "I'll call you from a pay phone," he added and hung up. Someone was bugging his line. Cops, mobsters, or both?

Dorn was not driving across the Golden Gate Bridge to Sausalito. Candles burned on a side table, but otherwise his room remained dark. He could stare out the nearby window to watch cars rumbling by. Laughter and music came from other houses on the street, the smell of pot smoke and burning food, but no one walked the sidewalks or lurked in the basement alcoves and neighboring stoops. Perhaps Rodriguez hadn't been able to secure police protection.

Dorn put on his fringed suede jacket and made for the apartment door. In the house's foyer he paused, looking through the Art Nouveau-stained glass windows on the outer door. A large Chrysler idled just outside. Too shiny to belong to any local resident. Even successful bands who lived in the Haight didn't strut around in ostentatious new cars. Other vehicles stopped behind it, waiting for it to park or move on, but it didn't budge, so they eventually honked, then drove around it. Bad news. Dorn considered exiting through the back door to the alley, but those latches and rusted locks made a ton of noise and if anyone waited out there in the darkness, he'd be finished.

Finally, another car pulled up right behind the idling one, their super bright lights shining onto the suspicious vehicle. "Please move ahead. You're blocking cross-street traffic."

Dorn had never been happier to see cops. He wished they'd confronted the occupants, but the lingering Chrysler rolled forward, turning east on Frederick Street. The prowl car followed at a discreet distance. He crouched on the carpeted ground and waited. The thugs didn't return. No longer feeling the need to reach Ali, Dorn locked up the apartment then sank face first onto his bed.

A series of dream states: one where he flew above farmlands in the Midwest, another where he swam across a warm red ocean curving over the Earth's surface. Eventually, he noted a feminine scent, Ali nestled against him, her face covering his, lips like silk sheets rubbing against his. Dorn relaxed, smiling, the sense of lucid dreaming and being able to control it. Psychedelics unnecessary; natural tripping. But the erotic nature changed. The perfume held a sweet pungency. Unfamiliar. Ali seemed to be pressing down, a massive weight crushing him. Ali ate lentils, salad, raw vegetables, 120 pounds at her heaviest. Something very wrong.

Dorn coughed then choked. He burst through waking dreams into reality. A pillow was shrouded against his face, the pressure immense, suffocating him. Even in the dark and blinded by the pillowcase, he sensed a sizable intruder just above, grunting and exerting brute strength. His hands couldn't tear the pillow away and Dorn felt his life receding. Drowning on dry land. He reached across the mattress to probe under the other pillows to find a canister. He sprayed the mace in every possible direction. When he heard a snarl and the death gravity lessened, Dorn rolled off the bed, still blind and gasping for breath in the darkness. He grabbed Van Monk's Derringer wedged between the mattresses, just as the huge figure fell over upon him. Dorn misfired a shot right next to the intruder's ear. Another yell as the assailant slid backward away.

The bedroom remained dim, but Dorn perceived the outline of a big woman: a veritable roller derby Amazon. She rubbed at her eyes, face obscured, just a mass of hair visible, while muscled legs extended from a leather skirt. Dorn rushed out of the bedroom. He heard the killer rousing in a fit of gurks and grunts, then saw her stumble forward in pursuit. His parents had taught him to never hit a girl, for any reason.

Well, fuck them. Score another for the generation gap. This lady stood taller than Dorn and seemed twice his weight. When the intruder came through the doorway, Dorn clubbed her head with a two-by-four. The assassin seemed stunned, but remained standing, so Dorn struck her again.

She let out a low-pitched yowl, reminiscent of Yma Sumac or Cher. Jesus, he had wounded and angered a Mama Grizzly. *Get out on the street.* Recalling his preparations, Dorn ran a zig-zag pattern through the living room, then escaped onto the 2nd floor landing. "You'll die for that." The enraged woman lumbered in a straight line toward the front door. A metallic snapping sounded and she howled in contralto pain.

Dorn switched on the living room lights, illuminating a contorted figure on his carpet, the jaws of the bear trap sunken into the meaty flesh above her knee. Then he noticed the wavy, dirty blond wig hanging halfway off the attacker's head, a close-cropped flattop showing beneath. A massive face with a broken nose, scars, and bright red lipstick looked up. Their eyes met.

"Holy fuck," Dorn said. "Hippie Frankenstein in drag."

Flannery tried to pry the bear trap's jaws open. "Let me out," he cried, thrashing about.

Dorn rushed over to his kitchen sink. Underneath he found a rag, soaked it in the refrigerated chloroform solution, and wrapped it around Flannery's mouth and nose.

The evil cop struggled wildly for minutes, then slumped flat back onto the floor. Out. Dorn searched his blouse and short velvet jacket to find a little black book. It contained initials with phone numbers next to them. At the back he found Rodriguez's name spelled out, along with his home number the detective had never trusted Dorn with. Afterward, he only had time to dress before thumping sounded.

The neighbors peered in with alarm when he opened the front door. "I'm Dante and this is Shayla, we live—"

"Upstairs, I know." Using mind expansion deduction powers, he guessed early twenties, recent transplants to the Haight. Still fairly healthy and not heavy dopers—yet.

"You own that junk shop on Haight Street, right?"

Dorn exhaled. "It's an art gallery."

Dante edged inside. "Look, man, we're hip. You want to have wild sex and that's your freak, more power to you. But the yelling and noise. It's nearly two." He rubbed his sleepy face.

"Don't they have basements for bondage parties in the Tenderloin?" Shayla asked. She had a Dutch-German pancake face.

"We're not judging." Dante's features flinched as he studied the grotesque splayed form of Officer Flannery. "Whatever you're into, that's beautiful."

"Enough," Dorn said. "Can I use your phone upstairs?"

"Yeah, but why?"

"Let me give you a few facts of life." Dorn needed to be circumspect. "My phone is bugged. Many are in this neighborhood." He pointed. "Ever hear of Hippie Frankenstein?"

Shayla recoiled and Dante squinted at the recumbent man. "Yeah," Dante said. "The worst of all undercover narcs. But I thought he was like Bigfoot, you know, an urban legend." Dante knelt down. "Did you kill a cop?"

Dorn shook his head and led them out to hustle upstairs. He dialed the number in Flannery's book. After eight rings a hoarse voice replied, "Who the hell is calling at this hour?"

"Rodriguez, it's Dorn."

"How did you get—"

"Shut up. Come to my pad on Belvedere. You know the address from installing wiretaps."

"Wait, what?" Rodriguez coughed as a female voice in the background spoke in Spanish.

"I've got an undercover cop down in my living room. Unconscious. You don't get here in twenty minutes, I'm calling the newspapers, TV, the mayor. I've fucking had it."

"Okay, okay. Coming." He cleared his throat. "This better be good, Dorn."

## CHAPTER SIXTEEN
# Midnight Rambler

Detective Rodriguez got dressed over his wife Maria's objections. "I'll be back in an hour."

"Don't make me a widow, Hector. You know I can't handle your mother alone."

He wanted to laugh, but she was dead serious. "I'm cleaning up a mess. No threat of violence." He went into their kitchen facing onto the corner of 6th Avenue and Cabrillo to swallow two quick cups of Sanka. Absolutely rancid. Rodriguez rang Bud Michaels, the young rookie he was training to be a hip undercover officer in the Haight.

"Hunh?" Michaels answered, clearly roused from deep sleep.

"Meet me at the corner of Waller and Belvedere in twenty, okay?"

"Tonight?"

"Yes, fucking tonight," Rodriguez said. "This is on-the-job training. You've got to be ready, any hour, any day."

"Right, I'm on it." The young cop coughed heavily, spit, then hung up.

Rodriguez parked his unmarked Ford Crown Vic near Dorn's house and waited for Michaels to show up. "Drive me up there, close to the red, orange, and blue Victorian. We need to discreetly transport a body to Park Station."

"Dead?"

"I sure as hell hope not."

Dorn sat out on his stoop looking wired, anxious. "You took your sweet time." He waved them to follow him inside, turning to eyeball the young cop.

"This is Bud Michaels, I'm grooming him for undercover." Rodriguez turned. "Bud, this is Frederick Dorn, my best man on the street."

Dorn flinched and scowled. "What happened to your last partner, McKinley?"

"Couldn't take it. He had a rabbi on the force who got him transferred to Pebble Beach."

"Carmel?"

"Yeah, there's a lot of crime on those golf courses." Rodriguez paused. "Anyway, Bud here will blend in, right?"

"He looks like a recent Stanford graduate circa 1965." Dorn studied the rookie. "Needs to grow his hair out. Lose the sweater and clean blue jean jacket, and burn those corduroys."

Rodriguez felt blood anger coursing through him. "It takes months to grow long hair. I need him now."

"Okay, then he has to sleep in Golden Gate Park for a week. Don't change clothes or shower, stay out of the sun. Unshaven and pale might help." Dorn held his hands up in surrender. "Right now he's as hip as a juvenile delinquent on *Perry Mason*."

"Just a—" Bud started to say.

Rodriguez gripped his shoulder. "Wait, Buddy." He focused on Dorn. "Where's the cop?"

Dorn brought them both into his living room and locked the front door. "Hippie Frankenstein broke in then tried to smother me." He gestured toward the pillow on the bedroom floor. "Was that your idea for the protection I requested?"

Rodriguez circled the splayed, unconscious officer in disbelief. "Flannery?" He pulled the wig completely away and using a rag, wiped the bright lipstick off. "That's him all right. No one else could look that ugly."

"How did he get the Frankenstein scars?"

"In Vietnam," Rodriguez said. "The Green Beret ahead of him stepped on a mine and took the shrapnel, but Flannery's face got scorched by the blast."

"That's tragic, but why was he here tonight?" Dorn crowded up close to Rodriguez.

Bud moved forward. "Listen, sir, would you back away from the detective?"

"Can you tell Junior to wait outside on the stoop until we're done?"

Rodriguez nodded. "We need to talk in private, Bud. Stake out the street and don't let anyone else come in here." The rookie glared at Dorn but obeyed.

Rodriguez bent down to check Flannery. "Breathing. That's good. What did you knock him out with?"

"Chloroform."

"That stuff is dangerous, can be harmful."

"Sure and I'd like to make it to my thirtieth birthday." Dorn shrugged. "He was determined I wouldn't."

"And a bear trap. That's brutal."

"I was expecting armed Mafia goons." He glared at Rodriguez. "Anyway, it took that to bring him down. Jesus, why did you send him?"

He stood to face Dorn. "I requested surveillance, a prowl car to make an hourly check. Nobody wanted the job. No one.

I talked to the Lieutenant and he got a Tenderloin patrol car to make random drive-bys." Rodriguez rubbed his mouth. "Are you saying they didn't show?"

"They did, once. After I went to sleep, Flannery broke in." Dorn showed Rodriguez the rogue cop's black book. "Your number was in here."

"So what? He used to work for me until he got transferred to vice duty in the Castro District. Of course he's got my number."

"But look at these initials." Dorn pointed. "VN and AR right next to each other. I bet if we call them now, we reach Vince Napoli and Antonio Rivaldi."

Rodriguez sighed before squatting down on a moving trunk serving as a coffee table. Dorn was just one piece on a big chessboard. Important, but only in relation to everything else. Rodriguez hated confiding his suspicions to anyone else, especially a mere community assistant like Dorn—helpful as he'd been. But the situation had gone too far out of control now. A dirty badge! The blowback on Rodriguez could be extreme, loss of his detective status, maybe even a transfer to traffic cop duty on the Inner Bay.

"I, uh, suspected Flannery might have been working the other side."

"What?" Dorn paced about. "And you didn't clue me in?"

"I wasn't sure, just a hunch. I mean, in retrospect, how did he find out you were on the Golden Gate Bridge with Rathkin? He was first-on-scene, and when I got there, he had pounded you pretty bad. Vince may have hired him for that."

"Doesn't make sense." Dorn turned his head away as if deep in thought. "I saw Vince two days later and he offered me $500. Congratulated me for surviving police arrest and Hippie Frankenstein."

"Sure, once Flannery got suspended and transferred to another neighborhood, he lost any value to the Mob's Haight operation. By surviving possible death, you gained value to them, though temporary. Vince figured you for a good sucker, a future delivery boy. Totally expendable. And that was Santa Cruz."

"So you didn't warn me Flannery might come for me?"

"He was out of the picture, busting gay guys selling drugs outside of Castro District bars. How would he know you were back, where you lived, unless . . ."

"What?"

"I swear, Dorn, I didn't tap your phone." Rodriguez smiled. "You're just not that important crime-wise for me to go to a judge and get authorization. Major hassle. But Flannery may have done it illegally." He eyed the outstretched giant again. "The three of us are going to lift that piece of shit outside to take downtown for grilling. I hope we can wake him up then because I need to know where Vince is. We've been tailing Antonio, but no one has seen or heard about Vince since last Friday. Have you?"

"Just before I left for Santa Cruz." Dorn scratched his head. "Friday or Thursday."

Rodriguez summoned Bud back inside. The younger cop asked, "Why is Flannery wearing a black leather miniskirt and fishnet stockings?"

"He was working vice detail." Bud's forehead remained furrowed. "Flannery was a complicated man," Rodriguez added. Bud nodded while Dorn laughed.

Rodriguez and Dorn pried open the bear trap then wrapped a towel around Flannery's gouged bloody leg. With help from the upstairs neighbor, they dragged the massive cop down the stoop stairs, and Rodriguez imagined that when

Dorn dropped Flannery a couple times, it was out of spite rather than by accident.

A dazed freak unloaded out of a VW bus to watch the spectacle. "Is this really happening or am I flashing, man?"

"He must weigh three-hundred pounds," Dorn said, as they shoveled him onto the backseat of Bud's car.

"Get Flannery to Park Station and wait for me outside," Rodriguez told Bud. "Need to see the lieutenant first thing in the morning."

Bud munched on a sandwich as a teenage couple approached. Runaways, likely starving.

"Bud," Dorn said, "give them your sandwich."

"Why?"

"Because you can make another when you get home." Dorn took the ham and cheese from Bud's hand then gave it to them. "You know where the Golden Gate Park is?" he asked and the girl nodded. "The Diggers give out free food every afternoon at two." The couple scuttled off.

"We done?" Bud yawned, resembling a graduate student weary from a late-night common room bull session.

"You'll be home in bed by 3:30," Rodriguez said into the driver-side window, then pounded the top of the car with a fist like he did with loaded ambulances. Bud drove off.

"Join me in my ride," Rodriguez told Dorn.

"You're taking me downtown for acting in self-defense?"

"No, you're too valuable as a free man right now." Rodriguez extended his hand toward Waller. "Just a brief chat where we can't be overheard." They strolled to the corner and tucked into the Crown Victoria.

Dorn pressed a finger into Rodriguez's chest. "What did you mean, too valuable?"

Rodriguez pushed his hand away. "Vince has gone underground, but you can draw him out. He can't leave because you're unfinished business. A loose end. After tonight's fuck up, he'll have to get involved himself."

"Great, make me the decoy." Dorn worked the door handle so Rodriguez snapped the auto-lock. "You want me to walk up and down Haight Street wearing a sandwich board with Day-Glo writing: I'm Freddie Dorn? Maybe a target symbol painted on my back too." He slammed a fist against the dashboard. "Let me out. I need sleep, then a hiding place. And don't ask me where."

"Just work at United Hallucinations Gallery for the week, usual hours. You really need to do that anyway for your business. Am I wrong?"

"Unlock the fucking door."

"I'm authorized to give you $100 a day to sit in your office, to sell paintings, if that art in your gallery can be sold." Rodriguez gambled that Lieutenant Malcolm would come through with the payment to take down Vince Napoli.

Dorn slumped back in his seat. "So I just hang out there, a sitting duck, waiting to be offed?"

"We'll be watching the whole time, ready to snag Vince or any of his thugs the second they enter your place."

"Yeah, just like tonight, right?"

Rodriguez coughed. "Totally different. I was working on hunches before. Now we have Flannery with a likely dirty Mob connection. We have a Zero Tolerance policy on police corruption."

Dorn laughed, letting his head loll about. "I want $100 on my desk every day, first thing when I open up. Human sacrifice money."

Rodriguez bristled. "Okay, I'll bring it myself."

"No, that will queer the deal, scare them off." Dorn stared off through the passenger window. "Have Bud bring it. At least he's young, unknown. Could pass as a delivery guy."

They both sat in silence, watching stoned youths and street crazies wandering by outside, some singing. Finally, when Dorn tapped the passenger door with irritation, Rodriguez unlocked it and watched the younger man lope back home.

DORN SLEPT UNTIL NOON, HIS WORTHLESS bugged phone unplugged from the wall. Once showered, he almost felt good. Rested at least. His hair just grazed his collar, but he tied it back tight and wore it under his oversized bowler hat. He found the jacket and pressed pants he only wore for gallery openings. Didn't give a fuck if he looked uncool or a sell-out; survival was the key. The milk in his fridge poured clumpy and smelled foul, so Dorn had Corn Flakes with tap water. God-awful. Finding two slices of bread with no blue mold spots, he toasted, buttered, and devoured them. *You need to do errands, get your shit together.*

After determining the human and vehicular traffic outside as non-threatening, he marched down the stoop standing up straight, just a sober businessman off to work in Freak City, USA. Though disguised, to avoid recognition by lurking goons, he strolled east on Waller and didn't cross over to Haight Street until he reached United Hallucinations. The gallery remained dark and closed, but he noticed a flaw in the window to his office. Close up, he saw it was a bullet hole.

Dorn found a handbill taped to the front door:

> Beware of traitors! Store owners and managers in the Haight are informing on you, brothers and sisters, selling you out to the pigs for money. Giving your names for police lists of suspected potheads and acid heads to bust at their leisure. The enemy is all around you!

Dorn tensed up, feeling the eyes of the world all focused on him. Christ, he wasn't selling names of users. He took down one scumbag dealer and tried to get a girl free from a Marin cult. Dorn scuttled along Haight in full-blown paranoid mode, then noticed the bulletins posted on every shop, cafe, and business—even across the street. He remembered.

Chet Sandberg, the reclusive self-appointed conscience of the neighborhood. He lived atop a crumbling Victorian on Fell Street. Never answered the locked door; he had no telephone. At the wizened age of thirty-six, Chet had been around town ten years. A bohemian from the beatnik days, when it was poetry served with bongo drums and berets, and jazz played at North Beach clubs. Holder of a big mimeograph machine, Chet printed up manifestos and other pronouncements monthly, or sometimes weekly, and posted them in the wee hours before dawn.

Occasionally he was right on the nose, like in 1967 with the infamous local narc: *Beware of Officer Gerrans! He's busted all your brothers, your sisters, and next he'll bust your mothers!* No one was sure if that did it, but Gerrans was soon transferred from Park Station to Central Station, the threat removed. And in 1968: *Runaway teenager chicks are getting free drugs then gangbanged by a motorcycle gang at a garage on*

*Oak Street. Wise up, hippies! Don't become victims of the Haight Street Hustle!*

Dorn keyed the gallery's door then locked it behind, leaving the lights off. Through the large main gallery, down the long corridor leading to a bathroom, art storage rooms, a utility room, and finally his office. Halfway down the dim hall, a figure launched into him. They fell to the wood floor, wrestling. Dorn put his knee and weight against the intruder's chest and pressed the Derringer against the guy's fuzzy head. *Fuzzy?*

"Get the fuck off me, greaser."

"Leon, you idiot, it's me, Dorn."

"Good thing," Leon said. "I was about to cut you with a shiv. Kill your Mafia ass."

"Right, of course." Dorn turned on the lights and helped Leon up.

"Shit." Leon circled around Dorn, examining him. "You dressed as a narc or a Mob guy?"

"Look, you should split, man. They're going to try to kill me. Hippie Frankenstein already tried."

"You mean Non-Soul Brother Number One?" Leon seemed impressed. "And you survived it?"

"For the moment." Dorn wandered into his office to study the window glass.

"Someone drove by over the weekend, early evening, took a potshot then beat it fast."

"You were in here, after I closed the gallery?"

"Because of the man keeping me down, I'm forced to live at my relatives' place in Oakland." Leon put his hands out at the injustice. "So I needed to entertain one of my ladies here, you understand."

"One of?"

"Okay, *the* one." Leon squinched his nose. "But there will be more. By the time I'm as old as you, I'll be living like a pharaoh, sideways Egyptian bitches everywhere." Leon swallowed then turned serious. "You think that was a Mob hit?"

"No, they knew I was out of town in Santa Cruz, and one random shot isn't their style." Dorn sat in his leather recliner by his desk. "Likely a cop, Hippie Frankenstein." Dorn recounted the whole Boardwalk episode, including the recent confrontation in his apartment.

Leon perched atop the desk. "I've never claimed you were smart, boss, but you don't seem stupid enough to just wait for lightning to strike again." He waved toward the street. "Storm clouds out there ain't going nowhere."

"That's exactly what I'm going to do." Dorn took off his jacket. "I've been promised police protection." He frowned. "Please, lay low in Oakland until this is done."

"A promise from the fuzz? Smells like bullshit. You need me here or you'll be one dead sucker."

"If you're determined to stay, I want you invisible, in the utility room. If someone comes for me, you're backup, the surprise." Dorn rubbed his forehead. "You'll need a gun too."

"I can get one." He stared expectantly at Dorn. "For fifty." Leon waited until Dorn nodded. "And you'll be paying me hourly wages to sit waiting to save your sorry ass."

"It's always something." Dorn felt a headache coming on.

"You see that post on our door?" Leon's gaze was piercing. "Almost like you were being singled out."

Dorn sighed. "Neighborhood store owners may be working with the cops. I'm not turning in any users." He stood up, frustrated. "Do you really miss Rat-Man?"

"Not me, personally," Leon combed his afro outward with his fingers. "But some fools are happy to get fucked up on rat poison. They miss him."

FOR THE NEXT THREE DAYS, DORN kept consistent hours, coming to the gallery at ten in the morning and closing at six. Bud Michaels visited at noon each day with a cardboard tray holding white paper bags like a lunch delivery.

"Good disguise," Dorn said on Tuesday.

Bud scowled, a golf pencil wedged above his ear. "Here you go." He set the envelope with a hundred in cash down on the desk, then sat to eat the smelly tuna fish sandwich he'd brought, incorporating his own lunch break into the errand. Afterward, he installed a small tape recorder and a bug inside the bottom drawer of the office desk.

"You can hear that from Park Station?" Dorn asked, and Bud nodded. "It's just temporary, right, until we catch them?"

"So is life," Bud replied. "And for some more so than others." He flashed a big crocodile grin. "Opening the drawer turns the recorder on, and we can hear room conversations clear. The listening device sends a radio signal on the police band. Close the drawer when you want to talk to your girlfriend or boyfriend in private."

Dorn ignored the provocation. "Out of sight, man. See you tomorrow."

Bud left as Leon entered the office and Dorn saw his assistant flinch. Leon had been in some minor scrapes with the law: shoplifting, joyrides in borrowed cars, and dealing in Golden Gate Park. Possible he'd met every cop in the district.

"You know him?" Dorn asked after the rookie detective was history.

"Not in the Biblical sense," Leon replied. "But I smelled pork. Another narc?"

"Part of my protection." Dorn showed him the new equipment in the drawer.

"Yeah, yeah, they're listening, but will they come when there's trouble at the Alamo?"

"You studied history?"

"I've been to high school, middle school, and to low-down school. It's called the street."

No one suspicious or threatening visited that afternoon. Eventually Dorn relaxed enough to call Milo at a printing plant in Burlingame. At first, he'd balked at Leon's idea of stocking posters and T-shirts at an art gallery, but it had become clear that Dorn only made money selling paintings and the original poster art displayed inside at show openings. During the week, sales dropped. Mostly local heads drifted in, said "Far out," then asked for free stuff. Residents and street freaks didn't have the funds to spend on non-essential purchases. They would, however, buy posters by Stanley Mouse, Victor Moscoso, Alton Kelley, and Rick Griffin in the two to ten dollar range. T-shirts emblazoned with album cover and concert poster designs too. Similar items were selling fast at the Psychedelic Shop as well as record stores in the Haight.

"Start with posters of the ten images I gave you," he told Milo. "We'll see what's most popular then do big printings of those. Try a T-shirt from Hendrix, Janis, and the Dead's gig posters. Test marketing. Yeah, yeah, beautiful, man, beautiful."

Paranoia had caused Dorn to buy a second safe that he'd wedged behind the water heater in the utility room. The office safe held only a hundred bucks. If a junkie thief broke in overnight or Mob men demanded a payoff, well, they would get exactly that much. The rest of the money he'd accumulated was locked in the second one. Dorn was saving up for an insurance policy too crazy to tell anyone about. Not even Ali or Rodriguez or Leon—yet.

On Wednesday, after Bud Michaels brought the daily cash, dispensed his usual rude pleasantries, and departed, Dorn heard people enter the gallery. He fumbled for his pistol and tucked it into the sports jacket he wore during business hours. Something about the familiar reedy voice making smart-ass comments amid the laughter of the others put Dorn at ease. THC hilarity. He untied the little pony-tail and shook out his hair. Not long enough for dedicated hippies to respect and yet a scandalous length to anyone over thirty with a day job. He ambled down the hallway with a relaxed gait.

"Freddie Dorn? Is that you, you capitalist, sellout fraud." More laughter.

He recognized the fringed buckskin jacket, a wild mane frizzing out around the visitor's broad forehead. The serene smiling face and twinkling eyes of a wealthy aristocrat stoned on the most primo weed available in California.

"Croz!" Dorn gave the musician a gentle hug, since they weren't close friends, but Crosby drew him in tight for a sustained embrace—like long-separated brothers.

Crosby pulled back, still beaming. "Here to buy a few pieces, Dorn."

"For your houseboat in Sausalito?"

Crosby flashed an "are you crazy?" expression. "No art on my boats, man. These would be for Laurel Canyon."

"You go back and forth?"

"Yeah." Crosby shared the agonizing hassles of owning multiple properties. He took Dorn's arm and led him about the rooms as if he was the gallery manager. "No, not that one. Terrible." The singer lunged about, offering advice and insults, while his entourage of two yes-men and a delicious-looking girl of perhaps twenty followed after. "Yeah, now that's the shit. The Hendrix flaming eyeball one. Rick Griffin, right?"

Dorn nodded, vaguely enjoying this arrogant young prince holding court in United Hallucinations. *Be patient when you smell money.*

"I saw an acetate of the new Dead album."

"*Aoxomoxoa.*"

Crosby frowned. "Sure, whatever, man, but I loved the cover art."

"It's called *Aoxomoxoa.*"

"Fine. I want it. The original art." He turned his head back and forth, then squinted. "Not here."

"It will be."

"I'm buying it in advance—now. We'll sign a contract."

"Okay, but I haven't priced it yet."

Crosby gave him an exasperated look. "Do you *not* want my check? Go to your office and figure it out. We'll be here, just make it quick." He scanned Dorn's features. "Seem tense. You need a Croz special." The musician plucked a joint out of a velvet purse.

"I've been trying to cut back," Dorn tried.

The entourage came to a halt as all four of the visitors stared at him in silent disbelief. Behind them, lurking in the doorway to the storage room, Leon's face showed outrage.

"Well, okay." Dorn took the super-joint. "I can smoke it later."

Crosby's eyes relaxed back to slits and the sleepy grin reasserted itself.

Dorn called a few local numbers from his office until he got Griffin on the line, and they worked out a price for the original *Aoxomoxoa* art. Fairly steep since Rick had wanted to keep it for himself. "I think it may be the best thing I've ever done."

Dorn agreed but didn't say that. "It's a trip, man, but you've got dozens more in you, each one a little better than the last."

"Spoken like a true art dealer." Rick paused, background noise, then, "Okay, let's do it."

Once Crosby had paid cash for two pieces and written a check for the Dead cover inside the office, alone, he gazed into Dorn's eyes. "Man, there are some amazing parties in Laurel Canyon, at Cass Elliott's place and Micky Dolenz's pad. You should come down, Freddie."

Dorn leaned forward to answer yes, but Crosby kept talking rapid-fire.

"It's mostly rock stars, TV celebrities, and go-go dancers from Sunset Strip." He made a curious face. "So maybe come along with Van Monk. Everyone thinks he's cool, even with that time travel rap of his." Crosby laughed. "You know, man, I don't want you judged as a businessman."

"Sure, sure," Dorn replied. Croz could never just be straight with you or consistently nice. Some one-upmanship had to be involved.

The entourage left when a fancy town car pulled up outside. Dorn donated the Croz joint to an ecstatic Leon before shutting his office to field phone calls in private. Near five p.m., Rodriguez called.

"Hey, Dorn, did Bud tell you?"

"Uh, no. Tell me what?"

"Dammit. I'm at Park Station and he's patrolling in an unmarked car. Was supposed to . . ." He paused to clear his throat. "Don't go home tonight."

"Wasn't planning to." Dorn *did* plan to go back and set traps, then sleep at the gallery.

"A fire started in your basement," Rodriguez said. "From reports, it sounds suspicious. Do you store your gallery art or any valuables down there?"

"No, not really. A mattress, old clothes, lamps, mostly junk." Dorn felt blood heat his face. "Who did it, Hippie Frankenstein?"

"Unlikely. Flannery was suspended, pending an investigation into his break-in to your apartment. He's already in trouble for beating up youths in Oakland."

Dorn paced holding the phone, tense. "He patrolled out there?"

"No, he did that on weekends while off duty." Rodriguez coughed harshly. "The fire department put out your basement blaze, but clearly a warning, the instigators hoped the whole place would burn."

"Clearly. Can you give my house real surveillance this time?" Dorn asked. "There's a young couple on the third floor and an old beatnik poet living on the ground floor."

"The lieutenant is determined to wrap this Vince Napoli business up fast, so yes. *The San Francisco Chronicle* ran an editorial hinting that we're in cahoots with the West Coast Mob. We're suing for defamation, but a major bust would quash such idiotic opinions."

Dorn said nothing.

"No support from you on our ethics?"

"Down in Santa Cruz, Tony insisted the Mob had cops on the pad in every precinct."

"Jesus fucking Christ." Rodriguez cursed and slammed drawers. "No visits yet at your gallery?"

"Believe me, you'll be the second to know."

"I'll handpick officers to patrol your neighborhood, Dorn."

"Not Bud Michaels."

"Why? A good narc is hard to find."

Dorn studied the taped-over bullet hole in the window. "I trust you, but not Bud. Not yet."

CHAPTER SEVENTEEN
# Time Has Come Today

DORN AWOKE FRIDAY AT NINE, LYING on the floor of his office. Before midnight, he'd retrieved clothes, blankets and a pillow from his place. The apartment looked the same—godawful—as it had been ever since his tussle with Hippie Frankenstein on Monday. The bed frame in shambles, blood stains on the area rug, shards of glass from when Flannery broke in through the bay window. But worse, it now smelled charred and smoky, the rank odor of burnt carpeting, of cotton and insulation, wiring and other fabrics. To cap it all off was the thirty-day eviction notice taped onto the door from Swedish landlord, Lars Jensen. The man had slipped a note underneath too:

> *I don't know what's been going on here, and realize others are to blame for basement property damage, but you can't smash windows, install bear traps, and have bloody witchcraft rituals in my apartment. —LJ*

Dorn accepted it without anger. He did need to move—soon. Maybe even rent under another name, disguise himself, find a new neighborhood. Though that felt like a retreat, if not an outright surrender. Transforming the Haight for the better had been his noble if unrealistic goal, not to have the district kick his ass and send him packing.

He managed to shave then take a continental bath in the gallery restroom. Fresh clothing and three cups of coffee in the half-kitchen area restored a portion of his will to live. Dorn filled in his desk calendar with plans, made a tentative date for his next art opening party. At noon, Bud Michaels shuffled in. He hadn't shaved, showed dark circles under his eyes, and acted surly.

"Night patrol?"

"Something like that." He glanced around as if searching for something he'd misplaced. "Strange about the fire in your basement."

"Strange?"

"I mean, mobsters would look for you here, but no one has visited. No incidents beyond one gunshot that occurred while you were out of town." His forehead lined. "I wonder if anarchists set that fire. Agitators."

"Why?"

"Because they're un-American commies." Bud slapped the envelope onto the desk. "It could be your last payment. No sightings of Vince Napoli in over a week. The lieutenant may call off surveillance and special treatment by Monday."

"Or is that what they want?" Dorn checked the envelope's contents, still not trusting this cop. "The Mafia can just wait out the police until you get bored, then hit this place hard."

"Life is filled with possibilities." Bud yawned and scratched his ass.

"Looking for your brains?" Dorn said. "Keep it up."

Bud made a fist then let it relax. "I guess if I can look as bad as you, I'll make a good narc." He laughed softly. "You think Rodriguez wants you to just bust a few dealers, some hoodlums?" He shook his head. "The SFPD expects you to be like any other narc on Haight Street, to nail every user—pot, speed, acid, horse."

"Nobody calls it horse anymore, Joe Friday."

"You'll have to turn in all your friends and local addicts until this neighborhood is cleaned up of crime. Then good families can raise their kids on these streets without fear."

"That sounds like a campaign speech, but I'm temporary labor."

"I'll be amazed if you make it through August," Bud muttered as he moved out into the hallway. "Is that other fellow here today?"

"Leon? Out to lunch, why?"

"No reason." Bud marched off toward his car outside.

Mid-afternoon, Dorn opened the window, the late July weather unusually warm, and reclined in his swivel chair. From across the street in the Electric Blue Bookstore's alcove, a Russian folksinger strangled out songs on a beat-up guitar. A curtain of mangy brown hair masked his face and he barely spoke English. That didn't stop him from singing in a bizarre phonetic method. "Hi, Mister Tangerine band, play us all a gong. You're not weepy and there is no space I am rowing to . . ."

Amid the humidity and with the phones silent, Dorn drifted off. A noise startled him awake, Leon approaching his desk, face expectant.

"You okay, boss?"

"Yeah, I was tired. Took a nap."

"If I should live to be as old as thirty, I'll be napping all the time. Sucking soup through a straw, wearing a truss."

"Very funny."

"It's 5:30, man." Leon looked around. "I know we close at six, but nothing's happening. Wondering if—"

"Sure, go home. I'll turn off the gallery lights and lock up."

"Sweet." He slapped Dorn five, then could be heard bustling around in the kitchen before he departed.

Minutes later, the front door to the gallery opened again. Leon must have left something. Dorn heard mumbled voices and hard-soled footsteps approaching. He snapped to attention. Checked the gun in his ankle holster, the knife at his hip, and the Derringer tucked into his inside jacket pocket. *What did he forget to do?* Dorn pulled open the desk's bottom drawer.

An unfamiliar mobster, reeking of cologne and with graying hair slicked back, moved into the office. Two broken-nosed hoods trailed behind.

"Freddie Dorn, I'm Antonio Rivaldi." He gave a shark grin. Slender and average height, though his chest seemed puffed up. "You don't know me, but I know you. Watched you walking back and forth from your apartment, many times."

"I've heard your name," Dorn said. Silence. "What's the deal? I'm not important enough for Vince to take care of himself?"

"Yeah, that's a good one." Antonio pressed the loose sides of his hair back over his ears. "Ain't that funny, boys?" Neither of the sacks of meat in suits laughed.

"I had an arrangement with Vince."

"You got nothing." Antonio turned a wooden chair around and squatted on it, leaning forward. "Vince messed up, paid good money to unreliable cops, brought in amateurs like you. So Vince is swimming out in San Francisco Bay."

The news startled Dorn. "What if his body gets discovered, floating?"

Antonio let out a percussive laugh then stood. "Vince sleeps deep in the bay. You know what a carp is? A bottom feeder."

He walked the room, studying the photos of artists at their gallery shows framed on the walls. "This Santa Cruz disaster. Vince acted on his own, without approval." He perched on the edge of Dorn's desk. "Without him around, *you* are responsible for the missing fifty large, and you have to make good—fast."

"Santa Cruz Police confiscated the money bag from Tony and gave it to the San Francisco Police. They say it came from a local credit union robbery."

"Look at me. That doesn't concern my visit or our situation." Antonio slid on leather gloves.

Dorn rose from his chair, eyeing all three men. They hadn't acted jolly from the get-go, and now resembled gravediggers at the end of a night shift. Eager to finish and go home.

"Ah-ah." Antonio waved a gloved hand. "Stay right where you are. Boys? Search our disreputable friend."

The two goons quickly found the knife and revolver in the ankle holster. They didn't touch his jacket though, slung over the back of the desk's swivel chair. The men held Dorn's shoulders while Antonio punched him twice in the face.

He stepped backwards. "No reason to be scared, Freddie. We're not going to kill you, tonight." Antonio smiled, flashing his eyes at the thugs. "We're just going to hurt you so bad that you understand how serious this matter is, how quick you need to come through."

"I don't have it." Dorn shook his head, vision blurred from the blows.

"So borrow it or steal it. I don't give a fuck. Just get it." Antonio smoothed his jacket and reasserted the shirt cuffs. "You didn't get the message from that accidental fire, so we're going to have to wreck half your gallery as soon as the sun sets. But no reason to sweat. You'll be able to crawl home tonight and leave a trail like a snail behind. That's better than Vince got."

Dorn tried to wriggle free from the thugs' grip but without success.

Antonio pushed past and stared out the window at pedestrian traffic, craning his neck, as if looking for patrol cars. "Someone took a shot at your window." He fluttered a hand by the tape. "Not me. Bullets cost money. I don't waste them on glass." His mouth wedged into a tight grin. "Boys, let him go."

The thugs obeyed, backing away. Before Dorn could wonder *what happens next?*, Antonio crouched down and slugged him hard in the stomach. He let out a groan then collapsed onto his swivel chair. Dorn fished the Derringer from the splayed jacket. No time to think. He fired point blank into Antonio's chest. The gangster recoiled backwards onto the desk, and with an adrenaline surge, Dorn jumped over it to make for the door. He turned, holding the gun high. "Anyone who follows me, dies."

He heard a gargle of choked laughter as Antonio rose up, gripping his ribs. "That hurt, you bastard." The mobster tore open his shirt to reveal the padded vest that had bulked up his chest. "You think I come into enemy territory without protection?"

Dorn tried for the hallway but a thug rushed him. He misfired, the bullet lodging in the wall, but it temporarily stopped the man's advance. Dorn made it beyond the office.

Antonio shouted, "I've got a man waiting just outside. Told him to shoot anyone who comes out before I do."

Dorn got midway down the hall, the three mobsters following patiently behind. His life began flashing by in a corridor. A lousy last thing to see. Why not topless girls dancing with abandon to the Jimi Hendrix Experience in the Panhandle? Something beautiful, ecstatic, mind-expanding.

"Change of plans," Antonio said, closing in. "Going to break every bone in your body and burn this shithole down with you inside it. I'll get the big fifty back some other way. Nobody shoots at Antonio Rivaldi and gets away with it."

They all heard the gallery door slam open and the thunder of bootsteps approaching.

"You called the police? But we had a deal with them." Antonio showed confusion.

"You wish, sucka!" Leon's voice said, though he looked near unrecognizable.

Seven black men in berets, faded green military jackets, and dark shades stomped down the hallway. Leon pointed his pistol, while the others held rifles and carbines, wearing ammo belts like scarves.

"The Black Panthers," Antonio gasped out, his body visibly trembling.

"Drop your motherfucking weapons, or give us a reason to kill you," Leon said. "Please."

"How did you get past my man outside?"

"You mean the sorry honky who was handcuffed and taken by a patrol car ten minutes ago?"

"I-I . . ."

"You hear me, crackers? Drop them. All of them."

Both of the goons tossed pistols, blackjacks, a tire iron, and a switchblade to the floor. Antonio advanced, spread his jacket wide and smiled. "I'm clean."

Dorn remembered an old trick. He wrapped his keychain around his knuckles then swiveled to crack Antonio on the nose. When he brought his fist back it was smeared in blood. The hoods began to move forward but two of the Black Panthers raised their rifles and aimed.

"You broke my damn nose." Antonio held a hand pressed against it, as if it would fall off his face without support.

"Live with it," Leon said. "You been selling shit drugs in Oakland, offering free junk samples, hooking the teenagers, hiring girls to be whores. That stops now. We see any of you greasers out there, that's a death sentence. Immediate. Go back to New York. Better yet, to fucking Sicily." He nodded at the other Panthers. "We're escorting you outside. Never come back again. Dorn donates to the Black Panther Fund, and we do not like to lose contributors. Understood?"

When a thug slipped a hand into his jacket, a Panther hit his head with a carbine butt. Afterward, they slow-marched the Mob trio through the gallery and up the stairs to the street. The Panthers hung back after they exited.

Dorn rubbed his bruised stomach at the doorway to his office. "You just—"

"Saved my job," Leon said. "If I lose my employer, who's gonna pay my salary?"

"I didn't know you were in with the Panthers."

"Well . . ." Leon laughed. "Just with Jesse here." The sternest of the seven men holding the carbine approached and looked over Dorn as if a rare bird species.

When Dorn put out his hand, Jesse ignored it. "You owe me a big one, Leon." Jesse frowned then wandered away.

"But the others?"

The five other men traipsed down the hallway, removing the berets and sunglasses, taking off their military jackets.

"This is my older cousin, Titus," Leon said. "Runs the choir at Fillmore Community Church. Nice enough to bring three choir members along."

"Leon," Titus said. "We went ahead with this foolishness out of respect to your uncle and aunt. But you promised to attend church again on Sundays. And no more cursing either."

They had set their rifles and ammo belts down, so Dorn examined the weapons. "These aren't real. Replica stuff used in plays and movies."

Once out of costume, the men didn't appear threatening at all. One had a horseshoe fringe of hair with big jowly cheeks, another seemed like a librarian in spectacles and close-cropped graying hair. The third was heavyset and had a rumbling bass voice. "You mentioned free food."

Leon clasped his shoulder then led him toward the refrigerator.

Dorn remained stunned. "But what if the Mob guys had tried to shoot back?"

"My pistol was real," Leon said. "And so was Jesse's carbine." He glanced through the window glass. Dorn watched Jesse load bagged equipment into a van just outside the gallery.

"One thing," Leon said, moving close to Dorn. "Watch out for Bud. That narc cop picked up one goombah standing sentry just outside, then drove off. Didn't help in here or call for backup. Shit, that's some fucked-up protection there."

"He knows you, right?" Dorn said. "Past misdemeanors?"

"Um, yeah . . . Something like that."

DORN MET RODRIGUEZ AT KALINSKI'S DELI on Divisadero. A Polish spot, just beyond and downhill from the Haight. A mostly older, ethnic clientele. He wore a floppy mushroom green felt hat Ali loaned him, and giant sunglasses that no one wore—beyond cult leaders and Neil Diamond. They sat in the rear booth where Dorn kept a watchful eye on car traffic and passersby through the picture window.

Rodriguez in plain clothes seemed to be auditioning for the circus. A fez with a dangling tassel sat atop his head, his mustache appeared waxed, and he wore a vaguely Slavic military jacket.

"Are you supposed to be Turkish?" Dorn asked.

"Do I look like a cop?" he whispered.

"Well, no."

"Good." Rodriguez fanned his hands over his face. "Frederick." He never called Dorn that. "Get out of San Francisco." He sighed. "A weekend, a week, a full month—even better."

"What happened?" Dorn propped his elbows on the Formica table separating them. Other diners slurped cabbage soup in neighboring booths.

"We picked up Antonio and his two thugs. Busted them."

Dorn smiled. "Righteous, man."

Rodriguez's mouth sagged. "We'll be lucky to hold them for a week. They've got good lawyers. The conversations we recorded in your gallery would get thrown out of court. All we could charge them on was assault, intimidation, carrying weapons without permits, suspicion of arson." Rodriguez rubbed his red-veined eyes. "The lieutenant is counting on me to find more evidence. We're searching cars and residences for drugs or stolen money, caches of weapons."

"So I'm safe for a few days?"

He forced a grin. "I'm investing. Not in that crazy art, but in the gallery's survival. We're installing locked gates on the entrance door and putting iron bars over every window."

"Sounds like a prison."

Rodriguez paused as a woman hovered above. She could have just disembarked from a trawler or been an extra in *Battleship Potemkin*. "Pierogies for me," Rodriguez said.

"Borscht soup," Dorn added, "on his check."

"Listen," Rodriguez said. "Mob guys have been hiring anarchists, you know, yippies, to burn places, bomb them. We found a cache of dynamite at Hunter's Point last week."

"Why would they do that to United Hallucinations?"

"Well, if they heard you were a narc, working for *the man*." Rodriguez scowled.

"Maybe iron gates are a good idea."

A familiar-looking older couple wandered inside. Rodriguez waved them over, asked them to sit down. "You remember Richard and Martha Duncan, right?"

"Nice to see you again." Dorn took in their troubled expressions. "Is Jasmine, I mean, Meredith okay? She didn't go back to Baba Gagi's commune?"

"No," Martha said. "We call her Jasmine now. She ran off with two young women down to Los Angeles."

"Sorry to hear that, but she is of legal age and—"

"Mister Dorn," Rich interrupted, "those women are radicals. We found three bullets in Jasmine's room. Handwritten plans to kidnap rock musicians and movie stars in Hollywood. There were cut out words from newspapers."

"To make ransom notes? Preposterous," Rodriguez chimed in. "Who would do that?"

"Mister Dorn," Martha said. "We know you can't drag her away this time. But we don't know where Jasmine is staying, or if she's joined their cause."

"Cause?"

"Some People's Liberation thing."

Dorn nodded. Militant organizations were sprouting up everywhere in California. They all foresaw an imminent doomsday and only through violence and bloodshed could they achieve a peaceful utopia. As horrible as Baba Gagi had been, he just wanted sex and control, not to lead a Charge of the Light Brigade into the valley of death.

"I've been thinking of leaving town," Dorn said to Martha. "Los Angeles is a good place for a vacation." He thought a moment. "A hundred a day will cover my gas, food, lodging, and I expect a week's work. Need an itemized receipt?"

"Not necessary," Martha said. "We just want results."

"Do you have any clues?" Rodriguez asked. "A specific area? LA is huge."

"We've already contacted private investigators down there." Martha blushed. "Jasmine was spotted ten days ago at clubs on Sunset Strip, and before that at parties in Benedict Canyon and Laurel Canyon." She stared downward. "That's all they learned."

Dorn considered it. "Great. I'll leave the day after tomorrow." Van Monk had a cabin in Laurel. Make a good base of operations. "So to be clear, I'm finding out if she's alive and healthy, where she's located, and what she's mixed up in?"

"Exactly," Rich said. "If Jasmine becomes a criminal and disgraces us, the scandal to our good family name would be devastating." He wrote out a $700 check. "A solid reputation is easily lost but near impossible to regain."

"I'll worry about your daughter and you worry about your . . . reputation." Dorn glanced at Rodriguez, then left the deli.

Dorn procured his Volvo from the Park Station repair garage. Still rusty and dented, but it ran beautifully now. Inside, cop mechanics were fixing damaged police cars or ripping apart the underside of suspicious vehicles mounted on hydraulic lifts—searching for drugs. He packed a bag full of clothes at his soon-to-be former apartment and drove north to Van Monk's pad on Shrader, near St. Ignatius Church and Fulton Street.

After some energetic doorbell ringing atop the high stoop, Van Monk opened the door, wearing a top hat. "Freddie, I knew you'd be coming."

"Because I called you a couple hours ago and told you."

"Yeah, but I flashed back to the dawn of time and still knew it would happen, man."

"Far out." Dorn glanced around the living room, cluttered with musical instruments, a tangle of cords, and sheet music. "I can crash here on the carpet with a pillow."

"Nonsense." Van Monk doffed his hat to rummage through his curls. "Downstairs is a kitchen and beyond it a back room with a double bed. Don't mind the washer and dryer."

"Perfect, brother. I'll split in two nights. Promise. Need to go down to Laurel Canyon."

Van Monk waved a hand, as if to dispel the jive. "What's mine is yours. I've been to the past recently and the future too."

Dorn laughed. "Be here now."

"Actually, I'm in all three places. It's like a Buddhist club sandwich." Van Monk showed Dorn the guest room before leaving to play a session. "See you for dinner. We'll discuss driving to LA together. Jess is staying there and I'm scoping more studio work too."

Dorn decided against unpacking for a short visit. Instead, he stretched out on the slim cot-like bed, but he wasn't complaining. The warmth of August 1st dazzled him and he slumped into a nap. Smells tickled his nostrils, reminding him of spring in Kansas as he heard the pad of soft footsteps, bare feet. He sensed motion, and wind currents shifting, a lilting voice humming a Beatles melody. He snapped awake to find a young naked woman removing clothes from the corner washer and packing them into the dryer mounted atop. She turned, to startle in surprise, then smiled.

"Hey!" she said. Arms akimbo, hands on hips, completely unselfconscious. Strawberry blond—all over—with a few freckles around her nose, and a tie-dyed headband. "Are you Bjorn from Sweden?"

"I'm Freddie Dorn from a few blocks away." He tried keeping eye contact. "And you're Van Monk's—"

"Yeah," she said. "He told me you were staying over. That's groovy, I like tall guys." She squinted. "You remind me of that singer."

"John Phillips?" Dorn had heard it before.

"Some rock star, but you're less rich or famous-looking." She sat down at the edge of the bed then began stroking one of his knees as if it was a house pet.

"Is Van Monk cool with this, you being with him?"

She sneezed into laughter. "Van Monk's my uncle. I'm visiting for a month."

"What's your name?"

"Sequoia."

Eighteen or nineteen, body still in defiance of gravity. Dorn felt his jeans clenching up as she lay back on the foot of the bed, her splayed legs hanging off. He made a guess. "So you dropped out from Berkeley after two years, Sequoia?"

"No, I'm from Pittsburgh, silly."

Dorn tried, "Uh, Pennsylvania State?"

"Someday." She grinned, crawling up toward Dorn like a feral creature. "After high school."

Dorn recoiled, bunching himself by the pillow and wall. "So you're . . . sixteen?"

"Sweet sixteen."

Dorn moved off the bed to the doorway. He focused on picturing his grandmother, Elmira Scoggins, her features often compared to a mix of writer Ayn Rand and J. Edgar Hoover. "I forgot something upstairs."

"But you're all bunched up." She leaned into him.

Dorn vaulted up the stairs, three at a time. "I'll be back," he gasped out.

Plenty of teenage runaways infested the Haight, and certainly older hippies shacked up with underage girls, usually consensual. Dorn knew he was in deep shit with the Mob and had undercover cops watching him. Supposedly for his protection, but in the case of Bud Michaels, for a private agenda. Had this enticing tableau been set up by Michaels to discredit him at Park Station? Sex with a minor? An easy way to get Dorn busted, shutter his gallery, lose the funds he needed for a crucial future insurance project. Not to mention piss off local friends and get himself pummeled into ground hamburger meat by other prisoners when in jail.

He gazed through Van Monk's front door peephole. A man with bushy reddish facial hair stood across Shrader Street staring back at the house. Was it Porkchops, a local vagrant, or a narc disguised as him? Dorn scampered to the rear window and saw two shirtless black men kissing each other out in the garden of the adjacent house. Were they hip gay dudes or actually undercover men? *Jesus, I've got the fear, heart tremors, and I'm still stiff.*

Sequoia traipsed upstairs in a long T-shirt and showed a puzzled expression. "Is everything okay? Am I ugly to you?"

"No, baby, totally beautiful." He remembered reading Hemingway in high school. "See I suffered a war injury, stepped on a mine. Ever since, I've lived like a monk in a monastery."

"You were in Vietnam?"

"No, South Bronx. Wait, just a minute." Dorn made it to the downstairs kitchen in three leaps, opened the fridge, and wedged the ice tray from the freezer into his pants. After that, he locked the guest room and listened to Aretha Franklin's *Songs of Faith* until Van Monk returned.

CHAPTER EIGHTEEN
# Wasn't Born to Follow

VAN MONK WENT ALONG, BUT FELT annoyed initially. Dorn insisted on leaving to Los Angeles before noon the next day for a seven-hour drive down Highway 101. With one stop, in San Luis Obispo, they could make Laurel Canyon and Van Monk's cabin by sunset.

"The plan was to go tomorrow," he reminded Dorn. "I was recording keyboards till three last night. Can never crash right after a session. It's a high, man, nailing the perfect part." Van Monk huddled half asleep in the Volvo's passenger side. "I don't know what your problem was with my niece." He opened one eye, trying to see inside Dorn's brain.

"She kept coming into my room to do laundry."

"So?"

"For someone who's always washing her clothes, she never wears any."

"Oh, man, she's beautiful and free." Van Monk studied the tire repair garages and car dealers sprouting alongside their route toward San Jose. "You used to be open-minded."

"I'm aging fast this summer," Dorn said. "You don't feel anything when she's naked?"

"No way, she's family." Van Monk lifted the Cossack hat he wore and frowned. "Not all nudity is erotic, sexual. Do you get excited seeing a nude in a museum painting?"

"No, except Modigliani's girlfriend was out of sight, long nose and all." Dorn glanced over sideways then back at the shifting traffic ahead. "Anyway, everything's cool with Sequoia. She helped dye my hair and cut it this morning."

Van Monk craned his neck. "Not much shorter, but lighter colored, and bangs in the front." He giggled. "Are you trying to join the Byrds . . . four years ago?"

"My hair was too dark to turn blond, but we got it sandy at least." Dorn sighed. "I need any disguising I can get."

Van Monk wiggled his fingers in the air. "Because you're a world-famous art dealer. No autographs, please."

Dorn elbowed him. "I told you what went down at United Hallucinations."

"Those mobsters are in jail. They're not going to follow us to LA."

"But I need to trace where Jasmine ended up. Her parents said local investigators down south never located her. I need some anonymity to work my thing."

"Whatever that thing may be."

"Exactly." Dorn laughed. "If we can ever figure it out, then it's sure to disappear."

Van Monk flashed to the future then bounced back. When he felt stable in the present, he put *Cheap Thrills* on the car's 8-track and they listened to Janis belting it out, raw and painful.

LAUREL CANYON LAY SHADOWED IN DARKNESS when they arrived. The sky retained its baby blue, some reds and purples bleeding into the cottony clouds suspended out to the west. Still a mellow place, all birds and trees and lawns, a nearby escape from Hollywood business jive. Tons of musicians living nearby in cottages or cabins.

Van Monk told Dorn, "Jessica split San Francisco in June. Stays here now." They crossed the driveway to his two-bedroom house on Lookout Mountain Road. $175 a month. That's why all the musicians lived in Laurel. The cheapest canyon. He noticed a handwritten note taped to his door.

*Van Monk, I had to split. Vibes are bad. I got the fear. Staying at my parents' place in Palos Verdes. Love always – Jessica Sky Bird.*

Bad vibes? He only saw serenity and nature out the window. Van Monk went through the mail while Dorn wandered the rooms. "Find a nook to call your own, man." He tossed the envelopes into a corner to ponder later, but found an invitation to a reception at Capitol Records.

Dorn, being annoying and taller, ambled back to read over his shoulder. "Hey, can we go to that thing? I can show Jasmine's picture and see if anyone remembers her."

"Okay, maybe." Van Monk moved away. Since he hadn't done any Capitol sessions for near two years, it might be good PR to show his face, say that he was available for recording. "Be back soon. Find a bed, relax."

He darted across the road to check on his neighbors Burt and Ellen, maybe they'd want to share dinner. Odd. A big cyclone fence encircled their property. When Van Monk pressed a buzzer at the gate, a dog started growling. *Their place had never been locked up before.* Retreating to his pad, he scrounged together refrigerator leftovers Jessica left behind while Dorn showered.

The next afternoon, they parked Dorn's Volvo on Vine next to Barney Kessel's Music World and entered the famous

Capitol Building—shaped like a stack of giant 45 records. Van Monk flashed his invite to security, the lobby decked with gold albums and photos of jazz greats. During the elevator ride to the roof, he said, "Listen, Freddie. Lots of heavies upstairs."

Dorn snorted. "I've been around famous people before."

"Be mellow. I know you want to find Jasmine, just don't be too demanding. For my sake." Van Monk brushed lint off the brown crushed velvet jacket he'd loaned Dorn. "They think I'm nuts, after my Rat-Man bad trip on OM."

"Yeah?"

"I said a lot of crazy stuff. Made sense to me, still does, but no one else grokked it." He rubbed his nose. "It's much more business-oriented down here. About acting professional."

"I'll keep all my clothes on. Definitely won't howl at the sky."

Outside on the roof, the gathering was in full swing. Van Monk peered beyond the suits and radio people. Local scenester Rodney Bingenheimer stood close by his hero Davy Jones.

"Davy, this is my good friend, Freddie Dorn."

"Hey, Van Monk, you're back." Davy slapped him on the shoulder. "Nice to meet you, Eddie." Davy turned. "So Lenny, are you feeling better?"

"Much better." Van Monk grabbed a drink from a waiter passing with a tray. "I'm hoping to record again with you and the Monkees." Davy Jones' face pinched into sadness. Immediately, Rodney's features drooped in solidarity.

"You know," Davy whispered, "our days as a band are numbered." His eyebrows raised and he became cheery again. "I'm planning a solo album once it's official, after the press release. Song and dance tunes mostly."

"I'd love to be involved." Van Monk immediately felt he'd come on too strong.

Davy's business mask reasserted itself. "My people will be in touch with your people." He hurried off.

Van Monk watched Dorn questioning Rodney Bingenheimer while he scrutinized photos. "Looks familiar," Rodney said. "I've seen her at the Whisky, maybe the Troubadour too."

"Thanks," Dorn said.

Van Monk eyed the various congregations of music biz people spread across the roof. *What was the gathering actually for? Damage control?* All that insiders talked about were rumors of the Beatles breaking up soon. Capitol executives remained stoic. What hope did any group have, if the best group in the universe couldn't keep it together? No wonder the Monkees were in chaos. A TV band formed to capitalize on the success of the Fab Four. From session work, Van Monk remained a conduit of all the industry gossip. Capitol's other major pop act, the Beach Boys, had their catalog deleted so the company wouldn't have to pay out royalties.

Despite that, Dennis Wilson stood near the edge of the roof patio, face downcast. Van Monk introduced Dorn to the rugged, bearded drummer. "You look familiar."

"I know, like John," Dorn said, nodding sheepishly.

"No, that actor cat, Harry Dean Stanton."

"Wow, isn't he over forty?" Dorn frowned.

"Age is a concept, time doesn't exist." They all laughed. "Things are different lately," Wilson told Van Monk. "It's not cool to look like us right now." Wilson gulped down his drink. "Not sure why I came today. Just wanted the bigwigs to know I don't hate them."

"Over the lawsuit, ditching the Beach Boys catalog?" Van Monk asked. "But why come?"

"Death. I fear it." Wilson paled, his handsomeness leaching away. "We made a deal with the devil so I want to set things right, just in case."

"That sounds dire. Things can't be that bad."

Van Dyke Parks, who knew everyone in the Southern California music community, sidled up to them. The man-child spoke in a theatrical manner. "Salutations, fellow travelers, astral and otherwise," he said. "The manifestations of past imperfect characters have transformed the aesthetic here to one of less expansive inclinations, wouldn't you agree?"

"How's Brian doing?" Van Monk asked. Nobody had seen Brian Wilson in months.

"Alas, he is still unwell. In then out of a hospital, hunkered down in his home." Parks' hands fluttered about his face. "I hope someday Capitol releases *Smile*. Brian's been depressed ever since Mike Love rejected the album as too experimental. Capitol butchered the original. I fear he won't write new material for the boys of the beach until this base injustice is righted by the powers that be." Parks formed a wistful smile. "Last time I saw Brian, he said he was scared."

Dorn extended the photos. "You're connected, know everyone. Have you by chance seen Jasmine. She's been missing for weeks."

"I've met several Jasmines. So many lost girls in our local canyons." Parks rubbed a finger between his lips. "Anything else to go on?"

"She may be traveling with two women in their twenties. No makeup, bad hygiene. Militant radical types."

Van Dyke Parks flinched. "An incursion of undesirable elements into our serene world. Some come from the Bay Area."

He gazed into the distance. "I sense very bad outcomes. Greek tragedy and other phantasms. Farewell, gentlemen." He saluted before moving toward Barbara Hershey. She stood by the rooftop outdoor bar, almost mirage-like, the West Coast hippie dream of 1969.

"That was weird," Dorn said. "As if he knew more but wouldn't say."

"Maybe. But finding anyone down here takes time." Van Monk watched women sway past with ironed straight hair, or wearing hair lacquer that suspended their teased creations, women in miniskirts—their Coppertoned breasts heaving up out of low-cut blouses into the dazzle of Hollywood sunlight—desperately trying to shed caterpillar pasts and begin their butterfly futures at once. He took in the view of Hollywood, the ocean tucked somewhere off in the distance, fused with the smog and haze.

An A&R man approached to shake Van Monk's hand vigorously. "Stan Filberg. You're in town for a bit? Beautiful. Mark Volman and Howard Kaylan asked if you were available." Stan laughed nervously. "Stories keep floating around about your condition, so I need to ask, what year is this?"

"It's 1969." Van Monk made eye contact. "The Turtles are planning another record?"

"They're working on a new album with Ray Davies, and they need you to flesh out their recordings." Stan laughed in a bogus, industry manner. "Mark and Howard love ya, baby."

Dorn intruded to show the Jasmine photos. The record company hack became irritable. "Who are you exactly? Why ask me? I don't date San Francisco freak girls, or abduct them."

"Course not, just wondering if you'd seen her," Dorn tried, while Van Monk nudged him.

"I wear blinders." Stan put a hand on each side of his face. "Have no idea what goes on at those canyon parties. Don't want to get involved. I read about it later in the morning papers, like everyone else in the business who wants to stay in the business." He moved briskly away.

"People are freaked out about something," Dorn said.

"I asked you to be mellow." Van Monk studied the industry types nearby, but they looked square, remnants from the Dean Martin era. The bartender in a monkey suit kept giving them both the evil eye, as if they'd crashed the shindig. On the way out, Van Monk bent down to hug Paul Williams. "Good to see you, man. Keep in touch." They both shared a moment watching minders try to keep a staggering Harry Nilsson from tumbling over the side of the building.

Dorn waited by the elevator, taking in the whole plastic event with a cynical scowl.

THE NEXT MORNING CAME ON BRIGHT and sunny. Up early, Van Monk decided to hitchhike down to the Laurel Canyon Country Store. Strangely, car after car descending the twisting route refused to stop.

"Hey!" Van Monk waved when he recognized Ken Forssi driving by fast, the old bassist for Love. Van Monk hiked past a former log cabin roadhouse that had been Frank Zappa's sprawling home with grounds and a treehouse. Bluebirds dove through the branches while jays squawked. Again, a brand-new locked fence encircled the property. Weird.

The roads snaked around in the Canyon, and everything man-made stood vertical: pointy little wooden houses jutting up on small parcels of land cantilevered over the roadway or fenced at their boundary line before the earth plunged off precipitously. The ghosts of Errol Flynn, Harry Houdini, Tom Mix lingered in the dust particles carried by warm afternoon wind gusts. Van Monk wondered what would happen if the Big One hit and the epicenter was Sunset Boulevard? Would all those wooden shacks on stilts propped high on Lookout Mountain come tumbling down? A wake-up call that the Garden of Eden had weeds, that bliss is temporal, and the microcosm of a scene you inhabit with impunity is only alive for a moment—then dying—before shifting to someplace else.

Outside Van Monk's cottage, near the bamboo wind chimes hanging on his porch, Dorn swayed in a rocking chair, sipping tea. Later in the afternoon, Van Monk tried calling Jess, but her parents said she'd gone out. He watched *Dark Shadows* and later a bit of *Laugh-In* with Dorn before heading down to the Sunset Strip.

First, they checked out the Troubadour where a mellow vibe emanated. Some earnest songwriter chick—patterned after the reigning Queen of the Canyon, Joni Mitchell—performed, Monday being audition night. The bar throbbed with life, glasses clinking, drinks mixing, female laughter, and male boasts all spilling out toward the stage area.

Dorn went to question the staff while Van Monk scanned the dim room. Recording engineer Kip Stanley from A&M Studios spoke to a familiar rocker.

"Dave, I didn't recognize you," Van Monk interrupted them. "You helping your brother Ray produce or on your own trip?"

"Trip?" Dave Davies said. "I stopped doing hallucinogens ever since I took some untested acid and met The Captain.

He's this heavy dude who lives on a whole other level. A different plane."

"Dave, did you take Orange Marmalade?" he asked. Most who had taken Rat-Man's OM were in psych wards. Perhaps Van Monk had found a brother to help him get through his own ongoing confusion. "It made me jump around in time, flash to the future."

"Uh, no." The Kinks guitarist stared at Van Monk. They reached a Zen unison moment where each one doubted the other's sanity, then both laughed.

Kip stubbed out a butt and stroked his goatee. "Everyone's on the Elvis trip now."

The "Elvis trip" meant pharmaceuticals: painkillers, sleeping pills, diet pills. Mother's little helper. That's how far the counterculture had come around in a circle, reduced to blotting out daily anxiety and pain, just like their parents' generation. "I'm in town, if you need me." Van Monk gave out his card.

Kip lifted his fist in the Black Power salute. "Right on."

Van Monk never knew whether to give the peace sign, the soul shake, make the weird elbow grab, pump a fist in the air, share a tight bear hug, or just utilize his father's firm handshake. Being hip in 1969 required a sign language dictionary and a secret code book. Afterward, he found Dorn slouched in a red-lit corridor leading to the restrooms.

"The bartender, Kevin, definitely remembered Jasmine," Dorn said. "He insisted he had to eighty-six her two female friends earlier tonight."

Van Monk felt confused. "They never bounce women. Men, all the time."

"Kevin claimed they were saying crazy shit to customers, and he caught them holding eye droppers near the drinks."

"Jesus, that's so San Francisco, 1967."

"Anyway, Jasmine followed them outside." He half-smiled. "So they're still traveling together, and she's with them voluntarily."

"What did the servers say?"

"Thought the three women were headed to the Whisky, but the staff are all freaked out. Cops have been looking for a guy named Bobby. For a killing in Topanga Canyon last week."

"Right. Think it's related to Jasmine?"

"I hope not." Dorn rubbed his face with a fist. "I'd hate to take seven hundred dollars from the Duncans just to tell them their daughter was mixed up in murder."

Outside, they drove the Volvo and parked by a gas station on Horn, then strolled over to the Whisky. An off night. The action centered at the bar or out on the street. Women in floppy hats and bell bottoms, suede vests and miniskirts, crocheted caps, batik scarves and sandals. Men who looked like tanned movie actors cast as hippies smoked regular cigarettes so the heat patrolling up and down Sunset Strip wouldn't bust their asses. The bartender had seen Jasmine in the back room, but warned, "If you're carrying anything, ditch it. Cops have been hassling customers, searching them too."

Fortunately they weren't, so Van Monk and Dorn pushed through the swell of people—*"Hey, what the hell?"*—to the back room, lights low, male and female bodies pressed close. No sign of three women hanging together so Van Monk asked a security guy.

"Those strange girls? One smelled rank. When I asked her to wait outside, they all went to the parking lot. Maybe twenty minutes ago."

Dorn bolted for the exit door and Van Monk followed out into the parking lot where various dramas went down. Usually freaks sharing a joint, a friend walking another drunk friend around to get air. Not tonight. Van Monk overheard weird hippie pickup lines like, "Come see my sitar collection" or "Baby, let's throw the I Ching at midnight."

Fifty yards away they saw a VW bus grunting and churning into life, then it buzzed away from the curb.

"That must be them," Dorn said. They both raced over to the Strip and headed for the Volvo. Almost made it. Blazing lights focused on them from an unmarked car, then two obvious plainclothes cops rushed over.

"Where are you two going in such a hurry?" one narc asked. "Who are you?"

"Lenny Van Monk and Frederick Dorn from San Francisco."

"Up against the wall." They were jostled over then frisked. The younger cop went through their wallets to check drivers' licenses. On a notepad, he scribbled the details down with a golf pencil, and examined the Volvo's plates.

The middle-aged cop, who wore a flat cap and a worn tweed coat, resembled an Irish cab driver. "Where were you anarchists on the night of July 27th?"

"In San Francisco, where we live," Van Monk replied. "We drove down on August 3rd. I have a place on Lookout Mountain Road—"

"Up in Laurel Canyon with all the freaky musicians and radicals." The older man checked his notes. "Do you know anyone named Bobby? We're looking for him."

"You should be over in Vietnam," the younger cop said to Van Monk, "fighting for our country against the Communists."

"What's this all about?" Dorn asked him.

He turned. "Did you just sneer at me?" The Aryan-looking blond took a leather blackjack and struck Dorn's shoulder with force. "Don't sass me." When the cop grazed his skull, Dorn folded over.

The older man interceded. "That's enough, Clint." He gripped the young cop's wrist until he relaxed. "We have their information and an address to reach them." He glanced at Van Monk. "Time to drive home. You won't see us," he said. "But we'll be behind, to make sure you do."

## CHAPTER NINETEEN
# Baby You're a Rich Man

DORN KNEW JASMINE WAS INDEED SOMEWHERE around the greater Los Angeles Basin, but where exactly? Much could be learned at tonight's party. Dorn prepared beforehand by washing his hair, then parting it on the side, so his new bangs angled into the longer hair. He went through Van Monk's sizable hat collection until he found a green wool cap. He felt self-conscious about the bump on the back of his head from the cop's blackjack. *Could anyone see it?* He wasn't sure, but didn't need some monstrous swelling panicking the image-obsessed Hollywood types.

"I don't know if you should wear that hat," Van Monk said as they drove.

"I've got a lump on my skull." Dorn lifted the cap.

"I can't see it." Van Monk squinted. "Why didn't you tell that asshole pig you were working for Detective Rodriguez?"

"Because that story barely flies in San Francisco." Dorn steered with one hand while massaging his head with the other. "Anyway, this Jasmine search is a private job for her family, so I gave those fuzz fuckers nothing."

Dorn parked his Volvo behind a line of fancy cars snaking along Horseshoe Canyon Road toward Micky Dolenz's home. A single-story ranch-style house set on an acre of land. They walked amid the cooler night air breezing in from on high while the heat of the day lingered atop the sunbaked ground, warming pockets of the canyon. As they approached, Dorn noticed Van Monk wobble on his feet, disoriented.

"Are you okay?" he asked. "No acid, right?" Dorn had stayed straight—beyond the odd joint and cocktail.

"No tripping since Rat-Man." Van Monk still seemed confused. One day normal; next day orbiting the stratosphere.

Through the open front door, they walked into the swell of hip beautiful people: canyon cowboys, luscious nightclub dancers seeking a stepping stone, producers with high foreheads and long fuzzy sideburns, TV character actors from *Mission Impossible* and *Mannix*, eager songwriters trying to connect with talent, musicians laughing too long and too loud at jokes by sports-jacketed record executives. Colored lights shifted in patterns and competing music came from several directions. Black blues, Dylan folk, psychedelic rock, free jazz saxophone.

"What's the date today?" Van Monk asked as local legend Nurit Wilde listened nearby.

She squinched her eyes into creases. "Van Monk, are you time traveling again?"

*Had everyone heard about his condition?* Dorn wondered. Worse, it had become a kind of in-joke. Nurit's eyes widened when he glanced at her DayGlo minidress and white go-go boots.

"I'm serious," Van Monk said.

"It's August 6th, 1969," she said. "We're on the cusp of Cancer and Leo, the cusp of oscillation. It's groovy but weird. Be careful."

"I feel like I'm oscillating," Van Monk replied.

"Trippy." She wiggled her fingers in front of his face, then moved off.

From the distance, someone chanted their mantra as *The Soft Parade* by the Doors played on the living room stereo. Van Monk carefully stepped over Gonzo, drummer for the Sky Seeds, who lay on the carpet staring upward. A vest made of yak fur appeared to sprout from his chest.

"We're all living in a cube," Gonzo said, as odd spasms inhabited his body. "You dig what I'm saying?"

Dorn crouched down. "Yeah, I dig."

Micky Dolenz stood cloistered with friends and his British wife Samantha drinking wine in the pantry by the kitchen. He'd watched them both enter from the corner of his eye, even frowning at Dorn.

"I'm getting bad vibes from Micky," Dorn whispered. "What did I do?"

Samantha rushed out to hug Van Monk. "Lenny! You came. Do you fancy some poached eggs?"

"Not right now, Sam. I'm trying to figure who I am and why I'm here?"

"Ah, the big questions." Samantha's mouth tightened, her grown-out bangs falling in her cherub face. She moved close to Van Monk. "I don't think you're bonkers. I believe in psychics and mediums." She squeezed his arm. "How long will all this last? You know, the parties, Micky's fame, everything being so perfect like this?"

Van Monk went quiet. A tense silence. But something in his expression must have conveyed a message. Her face drooped, eyes watering. "Nothing this beautiful could last for long." Samantha sighed. "Otherwise we wouldn't know how special, how magic it was."

A crash of breaking glass through the swinging doors to the kitchen. "Nilsson." Samantha shook her head. "Harry's on a three-day bender." She seemed happier suddenly, the super-hostess racing back into the fray.

The stunning Catherine James waved at Van Monk before disappearing down a hallway.

From behind, David Crosby clutched Dorn's shoulder. "Come outside, right now." He wore his fringed jacket and bolero hat. The smaller man didn't wait for a reply, he nudged Dorn toward the sliding glass door. Soon they were moving herky-jerky across the patio, beyond the eerie blue-white glow of the heated swimming pool and onto a manicured lawn that stretched fifty feet to dead end at low fencing on the edge of the canyon. Beyond there, a long precipitous drop-off through scrub brush, rock, and dirt.

"Fucking Freddie Dorn. What the hell, man?" Crosby pointed at him as he stomped around, his face red and pinched.

"You got a problem? Spill it."

Crosby glared at him. "You come to a party at Micky Dolenz's house with your hair like that, wearing that hat?"

"What?"

"You're dressed like Mike Nesmith," Crosby said. "Same green cap, same hairstyle."

"I-I don't really follow those guys, or their fashions."

"Don't you know the Monkees are on the verge of breaking up? Peter split already and Mike is planning to. That leaves just Micky and Davy Jones. Jesus, how unhip could you be?"

"Well, it's pretty unhip for you to tell me how unhip I am."

Crosby leaped up to snatch the cap off Dorn's head, then tossed it far off down into the canyon. Dorn couldn't even see it, only the lights of Hollywood glimmering in the distance.

"That was Van Monk's hat."

"Sorry, but I'm protective of Micky. He's beautiful but also a child. Sensitive." Crosby wandered back toward the throb of music and overlapping chatter of voices at the house.

When Dorn made it to the patio just outside, a diminutive man with a British Invasion haircut approached.

"Rodney," Dorn said. "Good to see you again. I was at the Capitol Records shindig."

Rodney Bingenheimer poked a finger toward Dorn's chest, but due to his size landed it closer to his stomach. "Get this straight, whoever you are. *I'm* the fifth Monkee. Me, not you." He contorted his baby face into disgust. "Everybody in LA knows that."

Dorn ducked into a tiny bathroom by the kitchen and wet his hair down before parting it in the middle. For the moment it looked darker and he sort of resembled his old self. He strolled away from the living room down a corridor to a room with its door ajar. A couple were standing, making out in the dim lava lamp light. The woman startled backward out of their embrace when she noticed Dorn. "Wait, you're not John." Michelle Phillips of the Mamas and the Papas, while the sheepish cowboy was Gene Clark of the Byrds.

"I'm not and have never been," Dorn said. "I'm looking for a young woman."

"Who isn't?" Michelle said.

"Get lost, *friend*." Gene Clark's voice came pitched between wanting to share a joint and preparing to kick some serious ass.

Dorn darted outside. No sign of the hosts, so he poured himself a drink: whiskey on the rocks. From somewhere came the husky, unmistakable sound of Mama Cass singing then laughing. Hallways everywhere. He paused by another door, but heard groaning, a mattress squeaking, so he kept on. Spying an open bedroom at the far end of the corridor, Dorn hesitated. A trembling voice sang over an acoustic guitar.

Inside, a man crouched on a bed, dirty black hair obscuring his face. Two pale women, who looked like Berkeley students, sat cross-legged on the floor, eyes shut and heads swaying to his music. Beneath their torn T-shirts, the outline of braless breasts visible. Dorn peered in from just beyond the doorway and listened.

"That is so heavy," one of the girls said. "It's beyond heavy."

The man attempted to tune his guitar without success. "My music is beyond conventional tonality." The girls nodded. He started plucking the strings before strumming in jagged bursts of sounds—occasionally thumping the guitar's body with a fist.

"Last night I dreamed I was inside you, baby, but then you turned into my mother and I was all the way inside you, trapped up with your fluids. I'm drowning. Placenta, let me out of here! I burst from your womb like a flesh volcano, and you died and left me alone, baby. I guess it wasn't true love after all . . ."

The singer locked eyes with Dorn. "That's a good song I wrote. That's really good, right?"

"It's unconventional, unique."

"Don't tell him that shit," one girl said. She pulled back her matted ginger hair to reveal a freckled complexion. "You're hiding your truth, we can tell."

Dorn had seen the dude before, possibly in Golden Gate Park years ago. Another would-be songwriter trying to get a break by nuzzling up to the famous, forcing demo cassettes on anyone connected to the business.

"You're vibing me, man." The singer smiled like a leer. "Hear the ocean? The tides have shifted. I'm out of here." He grabbed his guitar and scuttled down the hall.

Dorn entered the room to see, beyond the weird girls, two other women who resembled twins. They chattered to each other with British accents. "And *who* are you, darling?"

"Freddie Dorn."

"I'm Segolene," said the most attractive of the pair, her hair bobbed and layered, with thatches descending into her eyes in preordained chaos. "And this is my younger sibling, by minutes, Forsythia."

The sister giggled. They both wore paisley blouses and wire-rim glasses with candy-colored lenses.

Dorn approached them but overheard the other two weirdos in rapt discussion. "We have to free Bobby. They found him on Cuesta Grade, up north."

"I'm down here looking for my former old lady," Dorn said to the twins. "Her name is Jasmine Duncan. Came down to find out if she's all right." He set his drink on an end table.

"Sorry love, we're visitors. Can't help you there." Segolene took Forsythia's hand to lead her out into the corridor.

The two weird women restrained Dorn and sat him down on the bed between them. They smelled awful. "Looking for *who*?"

"Jasmine. She's nineteen or twenty, from San Francisco. I'm concerned."

"Everyone's free," the redhead said. "I mean, you don't own her, can't own anyone." Scratches or a rash showed across her bare arms. "Maybe she found her truth."

"I dig," Dorn replied. He noticed the brunette stroking his leg, moving her hand upward. Distracted him momentarily. "I lost all touch with her. I'm just worried she might be hurt, gotten robbed or beaten up, man." He sighed and made a forlorn face. "I don't want to call the local fuzz to find her, because that would be such a drag."

The two girls stared at each other, their features twitching, some silent communication.

"No, you don't want to bring in the pigs, man," the brunette said, her hand gently working Dorn's crotch. "We might know where to find her. There's this old man with property outside of town—"

The redhead backhanded the brunette. "Enough, sister. We need to talk outside—now!" She tugged the other woman into the hall and when Dorn tried to follow, she slammed the bedroom door on him, somehow locking it from outside. After taking a big swig of whiskey, he wedged the window open enough to slither out, landing on the paving stone pathway that circled the house.

Dorn entered the living room through the sliding glass to locate the suspicious women. Darker inside than before, just blue and green lights now, mostly shadows and smoke. Ten minutes passed; no sign of them. Van Monk staggered out from a bathroom to embrace Dorn. The whole house a fuzzy pointillist parade of people, each room teeming with life and joy, music and conversation. Twenty minutes passed. The back of Stephen Stills head talking to Peter Tork: *"We have to go beyond the sixties, man, and deal with heavier stuff." "You mean, like, the seventies?"* A smell of sweet incense mixed with weed and spilled booze, the musky odor of sex lurking behind that. In the corner, a pile of scarves and threadbare jeans cackling. Janis? No, a Joplin look-alike. The brief immortality of youth, just a flicker. Grab it fast.

A half hour without finding anything.

"I'm onto something," Dorn told Van Monk. His friend laughed then chased after a female figure. Guests blurred into shapes, and when they moved, motion traces formed in the air. Dorn remembered playing in a sandbox as a child, imagining the five-year-old girl he held hands with, but she became scaled, reptilian, and slithered off into tropical foliage.

Dorn shook his head. *Fuck, oldest trick in the book.* The psycho chicks spiked his whiskey. While one stroked him, the other played the mad scientist. At least he hadn't downed the whole glass. Dorn felt tiny needles stabbing inside his head. This shit wasn't acid. More like morning glory seeds and strychnine. Every head in the Haight had encountered that buzz once—the newcomers' welcome.

"You okay, Dorn?" Crosby pressed close, beaming. "I love you, man. The past is past. We're good now, right?"

"Sure," Dorn said, trying to focus. "Two messed up chicks are here. I asked them about a missing girl from San Francisco but they spiked my drink and ran off. Pale, no makeup, smelly."

"Bummer," Crosby said. "Let's find them. Surprise dosing someone isn't cool anymore."

He took Dorn's arm as if he was blind and led him room to room, past melting faces, some famous, others anonymous, all smiling to greet them, then receding like spent waves. It seemed an hour or maybe just five minutes.

"They must have split," Crosby finally said. "Don't stress, man. You'll feel normal in twelve hours."

Dorn closed his eyes, rainbow lava eruptions, the eyelid film festival of synaptic stutter-stop glory—a nickelodeon for the soul. Cecil B. DeMille meets Owsley Stanley in lurid Technicolor. When he opened them, Van Monk was studying him. "Some crazy woman dosed me." Dorn spidered a hand around his forehead. "It's not good stuff."

"You need some Niacin, dude."

The reversal was stunning; Van Monk looking out for *him*. "That will bring me down?"

"Sort of. It flushes your system, turns you beet red, sweats the toxins out."

"Really?"

"I don't know for a fact." Van Monk put an arm around Dorn's shoulder. "But it helped me once." He handed two capsules over.

Taking mystery pills from Van Monk seemed on par with hiring Rasputin as your personal dietitian, but Dorn needed relief. He swallowed them. "Those two girls know where Jasmine is. Let's search outside."

They reached the lip of the patio. Van Monk restrained Dorn from falling into the pool, where skinny-dipping guests were playing Marco Polo. Dorn noticed an orange glow in the distance. He saw a phoenix, the giant bird rippling its wings, coal black smoke draped around the outline. It was fucking glorious.

"Outrageous." Dorn knelt down on the wet grass, ignoring the sprinklers that had turned on. "You see it, brother?" Van Monk stood close but seemed a million miles away.

Sounds grew, a growing chorus of alarmed voices, and the vibes becoming decidedly un-mellow. Dorn got caught up in a group lurching forward toward the flickering spit of colors. Words unclear but clearly tense, the whole far off view coming closer, heat rising, a collective anger palpable. Dorn wanted to be part of it, the communal commotion, but he remained wrapped in gauze, running in place, the planet spinning out of control. "It's like July 4th," he said. "Someone's shooting off—"

"Fire! The greenhouse is on fire," a man nearby yelled.

And the massed guests rushed toward the paroxysm, some entranced, others alarmed. Then Micky Dolenz emerged from the bunch, no longer a Monkee, but a concerned homeowner responding to this unwanted chaos. They took shovels and rakes to shatter the glass windows, Samantha spraying the flames with a garden hose, both ridiculous and brave. Naked swimmers rose from the pool, rendered into non-erotic pale amphibians, to splash buckets of chlorine water on the fire.

Dorn saw Crosby close to tears. Two youthful groupies supported his unsteady stance. "They'll never survive," he said. "We lost them."

"Are there people in there?" Dorn asked. No reply. "Are cats or dogs trapped inside?"

Crosby removed his hat then slumped to the lawn. "Worse, man. We were growing killer Croz weed in there. It's all gone." He lay down then compacted into a fetal position.

Micky Dolenz grabbed Dorn's shirt to yank him close. "This whole party has gone wrong since you crashed it." His contorted famous face and permed afro blotted out everything else in Dorn's perception. "Who did this? Answer me!"

"Probably the women who drugged my drink," Dorn replied. "No makeup, greasy hair. Smell really bad."

"Those girls from the ranch?" Micky asked. "Dennis Wilson told me they were cool."

"They're out here somewhere," Dorn said. "Let's find them before they get away."

He felt disoriented, head throbbing, visions of Spiro Agnew in drag dancing through his frontal lobes. He'd never been a Monkees fan, but now, in the fiery heat of the moment, he felt proud to sprint with Dolenz around his darkened outdoor property, to be the Robin to his Batman, the Tonto to his Lone Ranger. Secret heroes. They dodged barking dogs, hurtled over spritzing sprinklers, and pushed nude revelers aside. Dorn spotted two shadowy figures, small and crouched, darting off.

"Over there," he yelled to Micky, and they ran after them as if the world was on fire, because it was. Because your private little reality is the only one that matters in the present moment.

Dorn tackled the lanky brunette and held her down, while Micky restrained the redhead. "Did you start that?" he asked. "You did, I feel it. Why would you do that?"

She scratched Micky then broke away. "Because you're sell-outs, plastic TV phonies, pigs." The brunette squirmed out of Dorn's grip. Both ran toward the far edge of the property—the end of everything.

"Hey, wait!" Micky shouted.

He and Dorn tried to catch up. The women reached the low fencing at the property line and hesitated for an instant before diving forward. By the time Dorn got there, they were tumbling, in a free-fall down the steep hillside through brush and jutting rocks, descending hundreds of harsh canyon feet to the neighbor's spread far below. He and Micky heard their screams but remained frozen. *What could they do?* Dorn saw all the lit houses on Horse Shoe Canyon Road as well as on nearby ridges, and visualized the cults, the criminals, the psychos, the bizarre musicians, sex freaks, Satanists, former movie stars turned dark and kinky. The whole Utopian "California Dreaming" vibe turned rancid and polluted, stacked up vertical before his dilated eyes.

"You okay, man?" Micky asked as he retreated, his concentration back on the embers of the greenhouse.

Dorn's head spun, so he collapsed onto his ass and let the planets revolve around him. Dizzy, nauseous, disassociated, wanting to find some jewel of truth in this madness, yet unable to break through the sludge. A volcano within, heat rising, magma churning.

British voices chattered. "We'll help you, darling," Segolene said, and Forsythia echoed her words. Van Monk stood somehow wedged between them, Siamese triplets looming above.

"You look so healthy, flush with color, Freddie," she said. "Just need to release your pent-up energy."

"Those women," Dorn stuttered. "I needed to find where they have Jasmine. Blew it."

Segolene stroked his forehead as he shrank into an infantile form merging with her crouched motherly self. "They invited Forsythia and I to their compound. We know where."

"Compound?" Dorn tried to nod—so goddamn happy to hear it—but a spasm of pain contorted his body and everything went black.

CHAPTER TWENTY
# Tomorrow's Just a Nightmare Away

DARKNESS, A SUSTAINED VOID. ABSOLUTELY NO perception or sensations, until an ocean wave crashed over Dorn and he sputtered back into consciousness. Reborn. "What the hell?" He craned his wet body forward on a mattress tangled in sheets, with Segolene grumbling into awareness beside him. She covered her breasts with a pillow and raked at her explosion of hair. He rubbed his eyes in disbelief. A never-ending bad trip.

Ali hovered above them, holding the bucket she had just drenched him with. "You idiots," she said. "I thought you were in danger. Van Monk called yesterday, said you needed me down here." She banged the bucket against the cabin's wood floor. "Seems like you got a helping hand or two." Behind her, Van Monk staggered from his room, wrapped together with Forsythia in a draped sheet.

"Crazy women drugged me last night," Dorn tried. "Can't remember anything after the party."

"These two?" Ali looked back and forth, eyes like slits.

"No, different ones."

"Sounds like you've been quite *busy*." Ali faced Van Monk. "And you. I thought you came to visit Jessica."

Van Monk looked sheepish, knuckling sleep from his eyes. "She split from San Francisco, and now wants to stay at her parents. I love her." He paused. "And I love you too, always."

Dorn remembered that Van Monk had been with Ali in 1967 while he was living with Ramona. They hadn't lasted long, Van Monk always at recording sessions, always traveling. Now Ramona was dead and Van Monk was functionally insane, and Dorn didn't feel that far behind either of them. He waved to get Ali's attention.

Segolene moved to the side of the bed, elbowing Dorn in the process. "My god," she said to him. "Last night you looked flushed, almost seemed like an American Indian. You were filled with a primal force." She smiled. "But now you're as pale as any British bloke on Carnaby Street." Her face held a greenish tint. "I must go to the loo." She hopped off the bed holding the pillow to grab her sister, and they stumbled giggling toward the bathroom.

"I'm really glad you're here," Dorn stared at Ali's tense face.

"That makes one of us."

"This is just a distraction. Totally unplanned," he said. "I'm going to find that missing girl, Jasmine Duncan." He couldn't seem to get through to Ali. "I got so close last night."

"Is that the current fantasy?"

Dorn felt as if a dump truck was unloading inside his skull.

Ali's expression remained scornful. "You're determined to save the day, be the hero. Aren't you caught up in some big ego, savior jive?"

"Two months ago, you called me a businessman, a long-haired capitalist, in it just for myself. Now I'm trying to help people in the Haight—"

"For a price."

"Help people in the Haight."

She snorted. "The cops, mobsters, millionaire parents?"

"And you too," he said quietly. "Maybe I couldn't protect you from your ex Scott, but I tried. I fucking tried." Dorn felt bad playing that card, but it was a firing squad at dawn situation.

Ali stopped arguing to stare at the ground, her head trembling. "I'm going to make a big breakfast," she finally said. "Get showered and dressed, both of you. The house is a mess and it smells like a North Beach strip club."

She stamped toward the kitchen.

Van Monk stood grinning, like a just-released outpatient wondering what to do with his life.

"How did you let this happen?" Dorn pointed at the bathroom. "And you invited Ali down without telling me?"

"We all love each other man, and I was trying to do you a favor."

"My gratitude has its boundaries." Dorn forced his way into the bathroom and, over the protest of both sisters primping by the sink, commandeered the shower for the only glorious twenty minutes of his recent life.

After breakfast, Dorn got the basic location, if not exact address where to find Jasmine before the twins left. Van Monk drove Segolene and Forsythia back to their hotel, leaving Dorn alone with Ali. Her mood improved, but she said nothing, busying herself cleaning up dishes and making a brave attempt at sorting out clothes, musical instruments, and paraphernalia.

"I'm not touching the bed sheets," she announced while bouncing through the rooms. "My advice: burn them."

Dorn knew not to argue, plead, or offer up any candy-coated bullshit. Instead, he slumped into an easy chair and recounted in exhaustive detail everything he'd learned over the last days at Capitol Record, the Sunset Strip clubs, and what he recalled from the party—leaving out any salacious details. Ali didn't seem to be actively listening, but he didn't care. It was a Kafkaesque confession, delivered by the accused without any knowledge of the charges. He eventually finished with, "So I need to go to that property at sunset tonight, get photos, or some evidence that Jasmine's alive, and bring it back to her parents." He paused. "If I could do that, then this whole odyssey will have a purpose."

"Odd is right, Dorn." Ali swept the floor with a distressed whisk broom. "And I'm coming with you when you go."

Dorn flinched forward. "Too dangerous. I didn't bring a gun or anything."

"Who's going to sneak in? Not you. If those crazy girls recognize you, you'll be captured or worse, with Jasmine jeopardized. Take photographs? I'm the only one of you mental giants who actually owns a camera." She ran her hands up and down her slim figure. "These compounds always want more women, not more hairy horndogs looking for leftovers." Ali went to the corner and played Van Monk's dulcimer while singing quietly.

Dorn didn't want it, didn't like it, but knew it would have to be that way.

CHAPTER TWENTY-ONE
# Wishful, Sinful

ALI PREPARED HERSELF IN THE BATHROOM, needing to look derelict but desirable. Washing her hair would seem too pampered, too clean, so she wet it down and went with a center part, leaving it flat and dull-looking as it crested on her shoulders. She had brought an open blouse with a flowery collar that she usually wore over a thin shirt. She ditched the shirt then tied a scarf as a bra, showing a lot of skin, including her belly button. Thinking they might attend a local bash, Ali had packed special jeans. As she struggled to pull the slim pants up her legs, she intuited Dorn and Van Monk would never be invited to another Hollywood party. The hip-huggers sat tight, exposing much of her lower stomach between navel and what Dorn called the "secret garden." At the bottom, the jeans flared over sneakers. Using nail scissors, she cut holes in the denim around her knees. Slinging a suede carry bag over her shoulder, she took one last mirror glance, "A stone-cold fox," psyching herself up while laughing, then swayed outside.

Dorn's jaw dropped. He pretended to concentrate on reading *Kaddish* by Ginsberg.

Van Monk never hid a thing. "Wow, you look amazing, Ali. Where we going again?"

"Are you sure you want to be that exposed?" Dorn finally said.

"If I get caught, I need to seem like a drifter, a hitchhiker who's endured some bad rides." She stared at them. "Let's go before I change my mind and drive back to San Francisco."

Ali curled up in the backseat of the Volvo while Dorn drove them to Highway 101, then north on Topanga Canyon Boulevard, away from the familiar ocean side and Neil Young and all the outcasts who lived up there. It was a slow twenty miles, the low sun bleeding through the windows and aggravating their eyes, even when wearing shades.

"How much longer?" She tried not to sound nervous.

"Not far," Dorn said. "If those twins gave me the right directions."

In the background, the Stones *Let It Bleed* played on the car's 8-track player, yet no one sang along or tried to turn it louder. A tense quiet hung in the air as they climbed to higher terrain. Signs announced Chatsworth directly ahead, but Dorn turned west on Santa Susana Pass Road and followed the twisting, narrow route through brown hills crowned with giant rock outcroppings. Traffic had dissipated, allowing Dorn to cruise along at a fairly slow speed.

"I think that's it." Dorn pointed at a dirt road with a wood frame around its entrance and split rail fencing on either side. Like a ranch without a name sign. He passed by it, but only scraggly trees and barren rises lay beyond, so he turned around to go back, pulling off the road onto hardscrabble flat land fifty yards from the entrance. "You stay here, Van Monk. If I shout your name, drive in and get us fast." He ejected the 8-track tape. "No music. Focus."

Ali walked in the open gate then moved along the tread. The sun had set, though she could still see. No one around, just animal noise in the scrub bushes, bird calls. Eerie. Dorn followed out of sight somewhere behind. Said he'd only show himself if trouble occurred. The rising moon looked to be near full and she had a small flashlight to guide her. Ali wanted to hum or whistle, knowing she couldn't. Something to distract from the creepy vibe. The twisted branches and trunks of scraggly oak trees formed disturbing silhouettes on either side of the road.

After a hundred yards, Ali came into a wide opening. She froze until she ascertained she was alone. No voices, lights, or movement. The clearing held the ramshackle remains of a western town: a saloon, cafe, undertaker's parlor, a sheriff's office and a jail. Something out of a TV show or cowboy film. Ali scampered along near the wood buildings in the shadows. Across from the line of storefronts sat a frontier wagon with big white wheels, an old-fashioned water trough, and ten vehicles. Rusty old trucks, a dented Volkswagen Beetle set on cement blocks, and several new-looking cars—Buicks and Chryslers. A few had license plates removed. She didn't understand what any of it meant, but photographed each one with her Pentax 35 mm. Quiet music came from the distance, somewhere beyond another scrim of oak trees. Ali glanced behind; no sign of Dorn.

The air had turned colder, making her shiver in her scant clothing. Ali wanted to retreat but the desire was outweighed by her intent to prove to Dorn that she could do anything he could, and was no shrinking flower child. She walked ahead, past the last outbuilding and around an empty stables and . . . "Fuck!"

She collided with a small but powerful man, who grabbed her arms, held her tight. "What the hell are you doing?"

"I'm-I'm," she sputtered.

"Shhh!" he said, gazing around. "They'll hear you." He released her and squinted. "You're not one of the regulars. It's dangerous to wander here at night."

"Who are you?" she whispered.

"Shorty," he replied. "I work for George, the owner of this land." He had a lined, leathery face and dark, greasy hair. "I'm a ranch hand. Now who are you?"

"I'm looking for Jasmine, my, uh, younger sister." Ali fished inside her suede carry bag then showed Shorty the photos Dorn loaned her. She illuminated them with the pocket flashlight.

"Turn that off," Shorty said. "I can see fine at night. Part of my job." He led her to the edge of the oak trees. "Down that path is a bunkhouse. Twelve women camp inside. The five or six men roam around, stay in other derelict shacks or out in tents." He gazed at her. "I think that girl in the picture is down there, a newcomer." He sighed like an asthmatic gasp. "You should turn around and get out of here."

"I need to get a photo of Jasmine." She realized his suggestion sounded way better. "Will you help me?"

"Lady, I'll stay right here to make sure no one sneaks up on you from behind. What's going on is wrong, but I'm just a watchman working for the owner." He paused. "Look for a big structure, more modern and ugly that the rest. Stick to the trail. The grass has dead branches, sticks that will crackle. Don't dawdle. Some of 'em drove off on a mission. The others will be waking up soon."

*Were they vampires?*

Ali advanced to the end of the big clearing where a slim trail wound gradually downward. Darker now, woods surrounding, but she dared not use the flashlight. A loud zipper noise came. She flattened onto the dirt road and strained her eyes. Then she saw. A long-haired man had unzipped a tent flap thirty feet away in the woods. He moved behind the tent until she heard a trickle spattering foliage. A minute or two later, he shambled back, disappearing into the tent. Once she felt confident he wouldn't pop out again, she strode down the pathway. The outline of buildings loomed ahead.

Ali crept toward the largest one. A wide, single-floor structure with two paneled glass windows, each holding sixteen panes. Dim candle light emanated from within. She rested on her haunches at the side of a window preparing the camera and small zoom lens. Ali peered in to glimpse the interior. No furniture, a dump. Several bare mattresses were scattered across the big room and various women lay on them either alone or bunched together. Some were topless, others semi-dressed. She saw dirty clothes, ashtrays, a record player, small file cabinets used as tables. The females appeared semiconscious or drugged, and a man's voice repeated simple phrases over and over from a cassette player. Ali got ready to take photos when a naked dude approached the panel of windows, pressing himself against it. She recoiled and shrunk down, freezing in place. He stared at the moon while scratching his ass, then moved away.

Ali adjusted her Pentax's light filter and zoomed in as much as she could to snap shots of each young woman. Some were propped up on an elbow or in a lotus position listening to the tape, so she could capture their faces, while others lay staring at the ceiling. She lost track of time. Something moved on the edge of the roof and startled her. An animal, maybe a raccoon. Then whatever it was, fell, crashing down into the bushes nearby. A pale freaky creature emerged with pink eyes. A twitchy possum.

Indoors, lights switched on. A murmur of voices, then a few women rose from their mattresses alarmed. The naked guy started dressing. Ali took off, rushing through the darkness, a clawing canopy of tree branches blotting out the moonlight. *Just keep going.* Ali picked a thick dead tree branch off the ground for protection. She saw the same tent flap opening near the trail. Wired on adrenaline, Ali clubbed the emerging man's head, then the tent, breaking the supporting cords until the whole thing collapsed around the guy. Tangled, he struggled to extricate himself. From behind her came the sound of screen doors springing open and slapping shut.

She soon reached the ramshackle western movie set, saw the outline of a figure. No, not Shorty. Too tall, yet not skinny enough to be Dorn. Racing across to the opposite side, she ducked behind the frontier wagon. Whoever the man was, he didn't realize what had happened at the bunkhouse. Yet.

"Hey, is that you, Susan?" he said. "You just wake up?"

She crouched down behind one car, then darted to the next and the next. By the time the guy arrived at the water trough, she was fifty feet away and nearing the far edge of the clearing. At that point, she flat out sprinted for the exit road leading back to the highway. *Where was Dorn?* Too many behind her, she needed his support. But was that love or just for protection? Hustling through the overwhelming darkness, she ran directly into him. They both tumbled onto the stone-pocked dirt ground.

"They're after me." She hugged him. "We're way outnumbered."

Dorn brandished the only weapon they had on this reconnaissance mission, her canister of mace. Watching him squint into the deep night, turning one direction then another while pointing the slim dispenser made her crack up momentarily.

"Let's go," he said. "I hear people coming." Dorn opened the side of her bag.

"I've got my camera and photos."

"Good, I want your flashlight. Doesn't matter if anyone sees it anymore." They heard a rifle fire from somewhere behind.

Using the flashlight's thin beam, Dorn took Ali's arm and scurried along the tread until the post fence came into view. Someone revved a whining engine back in the clearing, trying to turn it over.

"Van Monk!" Dorn shouted. "Get your ass over here, now."

The Volvo met them just outside the gateway. Ali got into the back while Dorn slid into the driver's seat and accelerated east toward Route 27.

"Did you see her?"

"I think so," Ali told Dorn. "I took pictures of every woman in their bunkhouse. The older guy I met, Shorty, recognized Jasmine from your photos. Said she was a recent addition to the compound."

"Compound? Was she a prisoner?"

"They were all there willingly from what I could see. No locked doors or any restraints."

"Bummer." Dorn exhaled. "Well, we found her exact location. Too dangerous to try to rescue her. That was no commune, more like a death cult. It's up to the Duncans on how to act. Some of those cars by the western set looked hot, stolen. Newly painted and missing license plates. That's an angle cops can use to investigate."

Dorn drove them south on Topanga Canyon Boulevard and Ali began to relax as they neared Highway 101. No one following.

"The Duncans paid you, right?" Ali asked.

"Uh, yes," Dorn said, voice halting. "A hundred a day."

"So don't you think I earned my hundred tonight?"

Dorn inhaled then exhaled as if on life support in a hospital bed. "Yeah, I guess you did."

Ali knew he would pay her, but had to go through a routine of pained and indignant expressions, groans and muttering. After that, Dorn drove straight back to Laurel Canyon, none of them saying a word until they reached the familiar calm of Lookout Mountain Road.

DORN MET RICHARD AND MARTHA DUNCAN inside Detective Rodriguez's office two days later at six p.m. As he wandered the hall of Park Station between cubicles and desks, cops and plain clothes detectives glanced at him. Some showed amazement that he was still alive, a few wore masks of disdain—they worked in Hippie Town and he was the enemy—while others nodded and gave him a thumbs-up. Minor progress.

Martha rushed over to hug Dorn when he entered the office, her veined eyes close to tears.

"Martha," Rich said. "Remember, he's still a radical, a stranger to a bar of soap."

Dorn glared at him. "I bathe once a week, whether I need it or not."

"He smells fine," Martha told her husband. "What did you learn?"

Dorn sat, scooting the wooden chair closer to Rodriguez's desk. "I found Jasmine and she's alive." He paused. "But part of a bad scene, an evil crowd." He lay Ali's just-developed photos out across the desk top, two that showed Jasmine's face.

"That's her," Martha said.

"Are you sure?" Rich asked. "Most of those girls have long, ratty hair."

"A man who works as a night watchman on the property identified Jasmine from your pictures." He returned the color prints. "Said she was part of their gang."

"Gang? But what do they do?" Martha raked at her black dyed hair.

"Not certain, possibly a cult." Dorn frowned. "Definitely a car ring. Stealing them, maybe breaking them down to sell parts." He showed Rodriguez the vehicle photographs.

"Our daughter, a car thief?" Rich's face showed purple veins throbbing on his forehead. "We bought her expensive clothes, unlimited tennis lessons."

"Where is Jasmine?" Martha demanded.

Dorn rose to perch on the edge of the desk. "On private property north of Los Angeles, in the hills near Chatsworth. There's a derelict western movie set and some outbuildings where those people are living." He rubbed his mouth. "It's called Spahn Ranch."

DETECTIVE RODRIGUEZ SURPRISED DORN THE FOL-LOWING day at United Hallucinations. Only a couple of pedestrians had braved the new accordion gates and barred windows to view the gallery art. The whole place seemed solemn, no crazy rock music playing as in the past. He shuffled along the hallway from the large gallery toward the office.

When he entered, Dorn held his revolver at the ready, expecting an attack. His assistant Leon clutched a fire axe.

"It's okay, boys, I surrender." He held his hands up. Neither laughed.

"Could you wait outside for a minute, son?" Rodriguez asked Leon. "We need to speak confidentially."

"Don't call me son." Leon placed the axe back into its restraints on the wall then left.

Rodriguez shut the door behind. "Have you seen the papers?"

"Not really my thing." Dorn appeared fed up, eyes weary.

Rodriguez showed the August 9th *San Francisco Chronicle* to Dorn: *Five People Murdered in Benedict Canyon of Los Angeles, including pregnant actress Sharon Tate.*

"Holy fuck." Dorn took the paper to read the article.

Then Rodriguez showed him the current August 10th edition: *Leno and Rosemary LaBianca Brutally Murdered in Los Angeles Hills. Police found writing in blood across the walls: "Death to pigs" and "Helter Skelter."*

"God damn," Dorn said.

"A music teacher was killed two weeks ago in Topanga Canyon. Tortured beforehand. Police arrested a Robert Beausoleil last week."

"I heard about a 'Bobby' while I was in Laurel Canyon." Dorn put the first newspaper down then picked up the second. "Everyone in the hills and canyons was scared, really tense. No one wanted to talk about it directly. Like hoping it would go away." He read more.

"Things are still hot for you here, Dorn." Rodriguez wondered what he could share that might help. "Still, I bet you're glad to be out of that snake pit, back to swinging San Francisco."

"Sure, sure." Dorn turned in his swivel chair, seeming to study the freak parade outside through the slats in the barred window. "Welcome home to the city of brotherly love."

## CHAPTER TWENTY-TWO
## The Wicked Messenger

Dorn waited until nightfall the next day, when darkness shrouded Haight Street. Still plenty of longhairs loitering on the sidewalks, vagrants panhandling, and narcs hassling locals. While the straights were out having a look-see at the brightly colored hippie world they'd read about in *Time Magazine*. Evening was safer for Dorn to blend in under a felt hat, hair tied back, body cloaked in a long green raincoat. Decided it best to avoid the gallery by day. Raspy voiced threats over the phone, cops he didn't know dropping by, rocks hurled at the window bars, and a locked entrance with a doorbell to announce visitors and potential buyers. Barely open.

Dorn slipped into an alleyway by Voodoo Guru Records and made for the rarely used back door to United Hallucinations. Three locks to key, and even after opening them, the metal door had rusted in place to the frame. He finally shouldered it open and wandered the dim interior hallway, using outstretched hands to feel along the walls. Dorn tapped on the utility closet door then turned the knob. Leon waited within, his apprehensive face illuminated by five candles.

"This is like wartime," he said. "Hiding in bunkers from attacks."

"Yeah, maybe so." Dorn smiled. "You *did* study history."

He made a quick check of the premises. The front door leading out to Haight Street remained locked with the metal fencing set in place. Inside the gallery and office, some panes of glass cracked but not shattered. Overall, the fortress safe for the moment.

"Are we open anymore or closed?" Leon asked when he returned.

"I wanted you to meet me here to discuss—"

"Yeah, you're expecting trouble," Leon said. "That shit-bird Antonio is either out of custody today or will be tomorrow."

"I don't want you caught in the crossfire." Dorn knew things were serious because Leon had stopped joking. "So, can you hang out at your relatives' house for a while, until . . ."

"No way, this is my job. I'm not running. I'll do what I can, within reason."

Dorn slid slowly down the wall to sit on the floor. Leon reclined sideways on a futon mattress he crashed on some nights, his head propped up by an elbowed arm.

"I need an insurance policy." Dorn stared into Leon's eyes.

"What do I know about that shit? We don't get insurance in the ghetto."

"Stop with the foolishness. You told me there was a guy."

"Don't ask."

"I'm asking."

"You don't know what you're asking."

Dorn untied his hair, shook it loose. "About a guy that could be hired who would—"

"Wait, wait." Leon shifted poses to sit up. "I was speaking in the abstract, speculating." He scratched at his scalp. "First off, you'd need ten grand."

"I've saved eight large from the National Bank reward and Santa Cruz bag retrieval reward for a down payment."

Leon looked agitated, forehead perspiration gleaming in the candlelight. "The dude I spoke of is as serious as a heart attack."

"Where is he? I need to meet with him."

"Impossible."

"Right away. Both of us will go."

"No way, can't help you."

Dorn stared at the small utility window. "Okay, then I have to close up shop, move out of town, hide out way up north."

"Northern California?" Leon seemed startled. "No brothers live up there. You know why? Rains all the time, windy as fuck, and no soul food or soul music. Even the pussy is cold."

"I'll send postcards to your aunt and uncle's place." Dorn stood. "Going to crash in my office for a few hours. Don't surprise me, I sleep with a gun now." He shuffled into the hallway.

DORN SAT SLUMPED DOWN IN THE Volvo in a neighborhood of Oakland he'd never been to before, and hoped he'd never have to visit again. Far from Berkeley, the student dorms or the professors' hillside homes. Beyond where the hardworking black families lived as best they could. This area was made up of condemned houses, burned down buildings, and small corner markets emblazoned with graffiti. Up the hill in the distance, a large brick project loomed, all late sixties modern—cubist grotesque. Where they had parked, behind a brown Lincoln missing its tires, was adjacent to a vacant lot. Rubble and weeds and clothes and junk strewn across it.

Dorn felt nervous so he tried levity. "This guy's name is Moses? What does he do, part the Red Sea?"

Leon had crumpled himself into a cannonball position on the passenger's side. His shoulders shuddered. "No," he said. "Moses parts your skull, then the red sea flows—directly."

Two rickety structures like watchman shacks sat at the far side of the lot next to the remnants of a small building. Just the first floor evident, the upper stories demolished by a wrecking ball. *Keep Out* signs were posted on the lot's perimeter, but children occasionally scuttled through the ruins, while ragtag mutts and feral cats acted quite at home. It resembled a construction site that had accomplished the destruction part and then abandoned the renovation.

The sun drooped low behind them, sinking into the Golden Gate Bridge and the massed bank of fog creeping in to the west. Dorn squinted. "So we wait over by those shacks? Does he live there?"

"You're going to wait," Leon whispered. "I'm staying out of sight right here. Somebody has to identify the corpse after he hands you your ass." Leon made grumbling sounds. "He don't live there. Has a few places of business in Oakland. Keeps on the move. If you're lucky, he won't show up tonight. This is the only spot I've heard about."

Dorn checked his mirrors, hoping a cop car would sidle up and tell him to move along. No traffic. Just the sound of a few teenagers slapping balls against the ground by a basketball court more than a block away.

"If he is there, please don't say I told you." Leon's face had contorted with a fear that Dorn never witnessed before. "Turk isn't prejudiced at all. He'll off a whitey, a brother, or a Mexican without batting an eye."

"Turk?"

"Moses Turk."

Dorn's only other option was to sit in his gallery and patiently wait for Mob death to come. He got out, feeling unsteady immediately, his skeletal frame wobbly, guts churning in protest. "I'll shout if I need you—"

"—to call an ambulance," Leon finished, from inside the Volvo.

Dorn entered the lot, navigating the abandoned sinks and junked fridges, the broken glass and jagged chunks of building rubble. The land rose up on humps of dirt sprouting sickly grass, then fell away to pits and puddles of brownish water with gas slick surface reflections. Leon had begged him to leave weapons behind, but now Dorn felt vulnerable.

He nearly reached the shacks in twilight when he spied a small dog rustling in the grass below. He bent down then recoiled. *Christ, a fucking giant mutant rat!* Dorn pushed his way into the first shack, the door squeaking open. Empty. Nothing inside but a mess of papers and a scarred wooden desk. Maybe the foreman's temporary office during whatever job they had abandoned. A loose window shutter banged in the wind, but Dorn felt safer than being outside. Exposed.

From the doorway, he peered out into the new dark and across at the stone building's foundation, its cave-like opening resembling a maw into some unknown hell. He thought he saw a blur of movement, likely human. No one came. The last blue in the sky died and darkness became absolute. The slapping shutter distracted Dorn so he reached out through the glassless window frame to secure it. *Shit!* Someone gripped his arm and pulled him tight. A fist shoved Dorn backwards to topple over the desk.

When he rose, a tall figure in the doorway shined a flashlight on him. "Who the fuck are you, and what you doing in my office?" He slid leather gloves onto his hands.

The shadowy man wore a hooded sweatshirt, but Dorn could see that one of his eyes was wide and angry-looking, the other barely showing, its pupil opaque, and a scar ran above and below it. Dorn had never believed the phrase "shitting yourself in fear," but at the moment, anything seemed possible.

"I've come looking for you, to meet with you."

The man grabbed Dorn and tossed him hard against the wall. "I don't take meetings," he said. "The only thing you come looking for here, is to die."

He gripped Dorn's collar then slugged him in the stomach. "Someone hired you to kill me, right?" He threw him onto the floor. "Must be a trick. You ain't built to kill Moses. No one is, but definitely not you. Hundred and forty pounds of scrawny hippie out here in no-man's-land? That shit ain't right."

"A hundred and sixty." Dorn picked himself up.

The man backhanded him down again. "They sent you as a decoy to find me, right? Other guys are coming with guns." He frisked Dorn. "Tell me the truth or I'll have to cut you."

"I came to buy your services," Dorn said, his jaw twitching. "There's someone I need protection from."

"You want me to do a hit?" Moses picked him up by his shirt then dropped him. "I'm not a contract killer. Never was." He glanced outside. "I don't see no one, which is good because I'd have to off you immediately, but it's also really stupid. You out here alone. Jesus."

"I need insurance," Dorn sputtered out. "From someone who wants to kill me."

"Yeah, you do." Moses laughed before mumbling to himself, then he tensed up. "Who told you where to find me? I'll kill that motherfucker."

"I can't betray my friend."

Moses took the remains of a chair and hurled it at Dorn. "Yes, you can." He kicked Dorn in the chest.

"He's a kid from Oakland." Dorn coughed up blood. "More scared of you than I am."

Moses seemed to relax enough to stop attacking. "A brother from the neighborhood?"

"Yeah, he works for me. He didn't want to tell me and wasn't even sure you'd be here. It's my fault, I forced him." Dorn braced himself.

"Hmm, this merits—what you call—some investigation." Moses switched on a small lamp with a dim bulb under the desk. "Name and business?"

"Frederick Dorn, United Hallucinations Gallery on Haight Street."

"Don't be moving," Moses said. "I need to confer with my associates."

Dorn wasn't sure he *could* move from his position, sprawled out in pain on the ground.

Moses went outside the shack's door. He soon began talking in a low voice to another man by the ruins of the nearby building.

Time passed, twenty minutes, Dorn swimming in and out of consciousness.

"You still with us?" Moses asked. He had squatted down by Dorn to offer him water in what looked like a plastic dog bowl.

Dorn accepted it without comment.

Moses sponged away blood on Dorn's head that had trickled into one eye and fuzzed his vision.

"I had my guy verify your story," he said. "Checks out. Tall hippie art dealer with a local brother working in his gallery."

Moses sighed. "Word on the street is you're in trouble with the law and the mob." He helped lift Dorn into a folding chair he'd brought along. "You got to know that anyone who comes looking for me on my turf is a problem, a threat." Moses lit a cigarette then handed it over to Dorn. "And I better tell you straight, I won't off a cop. They may be pigs but 'cop killer' would bring down too much heat on me. We good? Okay, spill it, man."

"I took a bag of cash down to Santa Cruz for a Mob guy, Vince Napoli."

"I know that scumbag." Moses pinned a rat to the wall with his massive boot. He picked up the squealing beast and flung it out the gaping window frame.

"The handoff went wrong. The police retrieved the money."

"I don't give a shit."

"Then Vince got drowned in the Bay as punishment."

"Hallelujah," Moses said. "Fucker ran the skag deals killing people out here."

"Antonio Rivaldi took over Vince's position," Dorn said, the nicotine smoke somehow making him feel healthier than just before. "Blamed me for the money loss. He's getting out of jail and is determined to deal with me, permanently."

Moses walked around the enclosure, head bowed and thoughtful. "Did your coworker tell you the program, how I work?"

Dorn could see him clearer in the lamp light, the hood now thrown back. Bald and clearly a once handsome man, Moses had paler scars etched on his dark facial skin, and showed a damaged eye and odd ridges rising on his skull, but also feminine, sensuous lips. A mythical, grotesque beauty who could somehow charm and mesmerize before destroying everything and everyone. He looked somewhere between thirty-five and a hundred. Without asking, Dorn knew he'd been in 'Nam, had seen the worst of what it had to offer. His face was the war, in each wound and brutal line, the distortions and pock mark craters. His one clear eye showed a sense of betrayal, a deep heartache turned to anger in its gaze. A gaze that was impossible to meet for long.

"Yes, he did," Dorn finally replied. "I pay you the fee and if anything dire happens to me, you deal with the person, with Antonio Rivaldi."

"In that case, you'll never know that I got him. Never have the satisfaction of justified revenge."

"I was told just the threat of Moses Turk having your name makes people think twice about pursuing their target."

"Unless they're a dumb-ass." Moses sniffed. "I can't fix stupid." He tightened his lips. "You got ten in cash for me?"

"I have eight," Dorn said, "and can get two more soon."

"Not on you."

"Nearby. I didn't know who I'd run into out here."

"Smart." Moses perched on the edge of his desk. "Of the last seven policies I got paid for, I only had to act on one." He laughed, strange and high, almost girlish. "That's good news. You're paying me for life to continue as it is. Some clients don't understand that special value and come back asking for refunds."

"I understand and won't be back." Dorn thought a moment. "What if they destroy my business but don't kill me?"

"Then Antonio's home gets blown up. And the warehouse where they stash their supplies has a sudden fire sale." Moses pointed at his damaged orb. "An eye for an eye. Except I double the payback so it don't never happen again."

Moses put both of his massive hands over his face as if exhausted, as if he hadn't slept since the dawn of time. "I would love to snuff this cat Rivaldi. His people, Vince's people, give out smack samples in Oakland, to teenagers. I hope for your sake Antonio doesn't take you out, but I would sincerely enjoy making a full payment on your policy."

"You against drugs?"

"Done them all. Most I took voluntarily, over there, in the jungle." He jerked his head toward the east. "Others were tested on me in Menlo Park when I was in training." He moved closer to Dorn. "If you a grown-ass man, go ahead, fuck up your life. But if you're a poor neighborhood kid and some big, ugly honky dressed as a hippie hands you a free powder lunch, then I got something to say about that. And not in words."

*Hippie Frankenstein?* Dorn wondered.

Moses spoke Spanish to his associate outside then returned. "You go get the cash. My man will follow and watch, so it don't get lost in-between. Dangerous neighborhood out there."

He twitched before smiling, and helped Dorn stand up. Moses dusted off Dorn's shirt then smoothed his collar. "Nothing personal, just business. Think about how I greeted you times ten, and that's what Antonio and his family members gonna deal with if they fuck with you, Mr. Frederick Dorn."

"Dorn or Freddie is fine. And can I call you—"

"Don't call me. Ever."

## CHAPTER TWENTY-THREE
# It's All Too Much

DETECTIVE RODRIGUEZ SUMMONED DORN TO HIS office. Even he didn't want to risk visiting the gallery. "Jesus, Dorn, what happened? Every time I see you, you're bruised and beaten."

"A new self-defense class I signed up for," he replied. "I'm not learning fast enough."

"Right." Rodriguez shook his head. "Rivaldi's lawyer, Jerry Stimson, asked to meet, speak to you as soon as possible. What's that about?"

Dorn formed a puzzled expression.

"Look, the Captain wants to bust Antonio bad. We picked up a street dealer yesterday who squealed on Rivaldi. We can keep him locked up for a couple more days on suspected drug dealing charges, that won't hold up in court. So if you know anything, or if his goons just decorated your face, please share it with me." Rodriguez waved his hands while pleading, and momentarily seemed Italian.

"What happened to Hippie Frankenstein?" Dorn recalled what Moses had said.

Rodriguez's expression soured. He shuffled papers on his desk as if delaying speech. "We suspect Flannery was involved in trying to kill you in your apartment."

"Only suspect?"

"He's been suspended indefinitely." The detective rubbed his face, then his eyes. "Internal Affairs wanted to interview him, but he bolted. Skipped. There's a warrant out on him."

"That's not all of it, right?" Dorn waited. "He hated me, but not enough to kill me."

"We also believe he may have gone rogue, was taking bribes, and eventually working directly for Vince Napoli and then his successor, Rivaldi."

"Maybe you should search Oakland for Flannery. I got a tip he's dealing out there."

Rodriguez seemed unconvinced. "Manpower is limited. We need a sighting, witnesses, a definite neighborhood."

"Great, another guy who could murder me is on the loose." Dorn approached the desk. "I'll meet with Stimson. Can you arrange a neutral public location?"

Rodriguez scratched his forehead in thought. "We could plan for a busy restaurant on a crowded street. Assign a car to watch." He exhaled. "This lawyer is semi-legit so he won't hurt you, but likely *will* threaten you. Do you want to wear a wire?"

Dorn knew they would be trading threats. "No, not necessary. We meet and talk. If I don't come out in fifteen minutes, have your guys come and cuff me, then take me to their car."

"Really?"

"Yeah. I don't need thugs or street people thinking I'm working with the cops. You know, the enemy of your enemy is your friend's enemy's friend."

"Just shut up and leave." Rodriguez stood then sat. "I'll call you when I know the location. Your phone's clean now."

Dorn angled his head.

"The bug's been removed."

"MY CLIENT IS DISAPPOINTED IN YOU," the lawyer Stimson said, as they sipped tea and coffee outside the Andalusian Dogs Cafe on Scott Street. "You owe him a debt, a financial one, and have not been forthcoming."

Dorn gazed at pedestrians, then at parked cars, wondering which one held the detectives in it. Did they have any kind of boom mic to pick up distant conversations? "I owe Antonio nothing." Dorn cupped a hand over his mouth. "His connection in Santa Cruz lost the money bag, not me."

"Be that as it may." Stimson yanked a dark hair protruding from his nostril. "You've lived a long, lucky life, especially recently, when unfortunate accidents occurred at your former apartment and business. Why press your luck? A man in your condition could live until the ripe old age of forty, if he played the game by the rules."

"I have a message for your client that I wish you to deliver personally." Dorn slapped a custom-made tarot card down onto the table. It showed a gargoyle with one giant eye and the other squeezed shut. Instead of The Hermit or The Fool, it simply read: *The Turk.*

"Moses Turk?" Stimson spoke between a whisper and a gasp. He straightened up. "Everyone knows he's an urban legend. The boogeyman of Oakland." He forced a laugh, then coughed. "Sure, I'll bring this to Antonio, but it won't change anything. He doesn't believe in ghosts."

Two men in jackets approached their table. "Frederick Dorn?" one asked. "Can you come with us? You're wanted for questioning." He glanced at Stimson. "Mr. Attorney, is this one of your crooked clients?"

"No." Stimson frowned. "He can't afford me."

The pair of detectives led Dorn across Scott Street when a break in traffic came. "We drop you three blocks away then you find your own transportation."

"Swell."

Before 8 p.m. that night, Dorn hustled over to the payphone on the corner of Haight and Central Avenue in a hat and coat, collar up. He gave a Buena Vista Park drifter a buck to beat it from inhabiting the booth. Waited. One minute after the hour, it rang.

"Is that you, art dealer?"

"Dorn here," he replied. "I gave your card to that certain person's lawyer."

"And?"

"Said he didn't believe in you, like you were Sasquatch or Bigfoot."

Turk allowed a low rumbling laugh. "Bigfoot exists. Give me twenty-four hours to send a message, to prove I'm for real." He hung up.

The following morning, Dorn woke at ten, his back sore from sleeping on his office floor, but he remained recumbent. The gallery was locked up tight. No rush to achieve anything; the outer gallery phone rang but he ignored it. Eventually, a reel-to-reel machine picked up. He'd review the messages later.

Around eleven, tapping sounded at the door, then knocking. Dorn played dead. He felt like that anyway. "Hey, wake up." Leon forced his way in. "Come out and rap. It's important, but hell, put on some damn clothes."

It looked safe outside. Dorn cracked open the window, the smell of greasy breakfast food wafting in from nearby. "Hang out while I wash up." Dorn shaved, except for his mustache, rinsed his hair in the sink, and cleaned himself as much as possible without a working shower. He'd never expected to be forced to live, to hide out in his workplace.

In the lounge by the big gallery space, Leon had the *San Francisco Chronicle* out and attempted to straighten its folds. "You probably haven't read the news yet."

"I rarely do," Dorn said, his wet hair slicked back. "Since when do you buy the papers?"

"Since never. Saw the headlines when I got donuts this morning." He rustled the edition over to Dorn. "Curiosity."

A grainy photo showed a near naked man dangling from a bridge. *"Late-thirties male found hanging from the Bay Bridge wearing only his underwear. Though severely beaten and unconscious, the as yet unidentified man remains alive. Plastic packets of street heroin were found lodged within his anal cavity. A long hair wig had been duct-taped to his foot."*

"Jesus," Dorn said, "that's—"

"Your buddy, Hippie Frankenstein." Leon glanced at the photo and back at Dorn. "I thought you were crazy to make me take you to Oakland, but this is beautiful, man."

Dorn rubbed a towel through his hair. "You think Moses did this?"

Leon shot him a look of disbelief. "Who else has the stones to take on that psycho cop? Dude was tall, muscled, and armed, but Turk has no fear. He's told people he died a few times in combat hospitals then came back to life."

"Wow, if the cop worked for Rivaldi, that will send a clear message." Dorn chuckled.

"If?"

The main gallery phone rang and continued ringing. Dorn shook his head. "Ignore it, the tape machine will pick up."

"I turned that off," Leon said. "I mean serious shit is going to go down due to this news, so best for you to know how deep you'll be swimming in it."

"Thanks for your concern." Dorn cracked his neck and shambled into the gallery.

"Dorn, have you heard?" the detective asked when he answered.

"The Bay Bridge thing? Who was that guy?"

Rodriguez sighed long and slow. "Flannery. We've delayed identification to the press." He cleared his throat. "What do you know about it?"

"You think I have the strength or courage to have done that? I wish."

"I asked if you *knew* anything."

"I told you, word was Flannery had been dealing junk to teenagers outside high schools in Oakland." Dorn squinted at the photo. "He's in his jockeys." He laughed. "Look, the dude was hated, despised by the black community. Are you asking me to cry about a maniac who severely beat then tried to kill me because he used to be your partner?"

"Don't remind me." Rodriguez sipped at something. "You mentioned him the other day. Afterward, you meet with Antonio's lawyer and this happens. Any connection?"

"Good question." Dorn relaxed on the throw cushions. "Lawyer Stimson takes his marching orders from Rivaldi. Maybe Antonio told him that Hippie Frankenstein had become a liability. Too notorious. Flannery's main asset was his being in the SFPD, the Mob's inside man, as it were. His current value as a white dope dealer in Oakland was probably negligible."

"That's just really tidy." Rodriguez said, the sound of his metal desk chair scraping. "The Mob takes care of him—"

"Well, your guys either didn't or couldn't even find Flannery. So if it took Rivaldi to do it, I'm totally cool with that."

"Hip, hip, hooray. But I think you know more, Dorn. Who tipped you that Flannery was dealing?"

"Unnamed sources." Dorn heard heavy breathing from Rodriguez. "You want to hassle me because a psycho rogue cop got his ass kicked by his employers?"

"I do not," Rodriguez said robotically, "but I do need you to settle up your business at United Hallucinations and leave town. I asked before, now I'm telling you."

"I've been planning to visit my family in Kansas, head out on vacation." Dorn considered it. "Give me a little time to hire someone, a manager." He paused. "Leon can't handle it alone."

DORN WENT TO SAINT FRANCIS MEMORIAL Hospital the next day as requested. The stark whiteness of the walls and staff uniforms under fluorescent lights snow-blinded him. Intercom announcements for doctors and interns broke the reverent hush, the antiseptic solvent smell burning into his nostrils. He tried to find his own way, not speak to desk nurses giving the stink eye. They hated hippies. Too many freaks taking up their valuable bed space after bad trips. Worst place to recover in. The straight doctors would shoot you up with Thorazine then discharge you while the side effects of dizziness, constipation, blurred vision, and drowsiness were still hitting hard.

"Uh, ma'am, I mean, mister?" said the stern woman showing a lined forehead under a sanitary napkin hat. "You need to sign in for visiting hours." She beckoned with a meaty hand.

Dorn spied Rodriguez at the far end of a hallway leading to patients' rooms. He waved back to the nurse and dashed across the slippery, shiny vinyl flooring.

"Just wanted you to see him, Dorn. Maybe jog your memory." Rodriguez gestured for the cop guarding the door in a folding chair to let them by.

Inside, Flannery lay breathing through a tube, his head bandaged like a mummy, and both legs and one arm set in casts, raised and suspended. Alive, but either heavily sedated by painkillers or in some limbo beyond consciousness.

Rodriguez removed the top sheet and opened the hospital gown to show the bruising across Flannery's sides, stomach, and chest. "It's been determined that whoever did this wore gloves. Took his time, maybe a half hour. Bare knuckles would have scraped, even bled a little. We would have gotten something, but no skin or hair or nails or blood." Rodriguez clammed up, waiting on Dorn.

Dorn recalled Moses Turk's leather gloves when he was getting pummeled at the Oakland shack. "I'm not a police detective, like you," Dorn said. "But it looks pro. Maybe the two thugs with Antonio who roughed me up in my gallery did that."

"Maybe." Rodriguez held a bitter expression. "We have warrants out for them, but tough to prove with no hard evidence or witnesses." He stared at Dorn.

"I swear and can take a polygraph that I was asleep in my office, not on the Bay Bridge whenever Flannery's beating happened."

"You were on the Golden Gate Bridge back in July—"

"Once. Never again." Dorn studied the pathetic bandaged form, looking more like the Frankenstein Monster on a laboratory slab than ever before. Dorn felt zero sympathy. *Karma, man.* "Is that it?"

"No, the lawyer Stimson is down in the cafeteria waiting. Begged me to speak to you for five minutes, then we're taking him to Park Station for a major grilling." Rodriguez smiled. "After that, you can plan your imminent vacation."

"And why are you ordering me out of San Francisco?"

"Either you know more about this"— he pointed at Flannery —"than you're telling me, or just your presence in town is triggering violence and destruction. People want to kill you, but instead, others keep getting hurt. So for your own safety and for the Haight district, I'm banishing you. Two months minimum. Got an issue? Take it up with the mayor."

Dorn exited into the hallway then rode the elevator to the cafeteria.

Moving through the crowd of interns in scrubs and visiting family members, he traversed the long line of metal food trays holding tuna fish sandwiches, macaroni and cheese, enough potato salad to feed an army, and a thick log of mystery meat drenched in dark brown gravy.

He saw Stimson sitting docile with that shithead Bud Michaels. The slimy young detective was not necessarily linked to the Mob, but maybe with Internal Affairs. Likely watching both Detective Rodriguez and Dorn too.

He joined them. "Bud, I need to speak to our attorney friend alone. Why don't you go get a fistful of sauerkraut to suck on?"

Bud's eyes thinned. "We're escorting Mr. Stimson downtown. I was assigned—"

"Your senior partner just gave me permission." He craned his neck. Rodriguez waited outside the glass-walled cafeteria with folded arms.

Bud grunted his way over toward the food display.

"I don't need or want any more threats," Dorn said in a low voice.

"Threats, from me?" Stimson asked. His shirt collar looked damp, oily, his suit's cheap polyester blend revealed under the harsh lighting. "My client received your tarot card, and the subsequent message in the newspapers . . ." His voice trailed off. "Antonio insists there's been a misunderstanding in accounting." Stimson smiled, salad matter wedged between two teeth. "Our apologies. You owe him nothing. Antonio would also like to buy a piece of art to support your fine gallery." He handed over a signed statement detailing what he'd just said from Rivaldi Exports LTD.

"Great." Dorn felt happy he could pay Moses Turk the rest of his fee. "I don't want to see your client or his associates anymore, not on Haight Street nor hassling my coworkers or friends. Any subsequent property damage to my business will be responded to in an overwhelming fashion."

Dorn slid a piece of paper over with Rivaldi's home address, his mistress's apartment, a storage warehouse in Oakland, and Stimson's home address in Daly City. "Are these correct, in case the boogeyman needs to deliver a Christmas card?"

Stimson swallowed and looked slightly green. "Yes, that's all in order."

Dorn watched Rodriguez enter the cafeteria and Bud returning from the food line.

"Always a pleasure, Stimson." Dorn stood. "And I hope this is truly goodbye."

## CHAPTER TWENTY-FOUR
# Back to the Garden

DORN HAD BEEN SUMMONED TO JOIN this event, the current fantasy, a hello-goodbye to all his dear friends—before the next thing. Whatever exactly that was. They had already scattered since the colorful July nights at the Bard Theater. Moon Girl went away for treatment at a famous hospital in Salem, Oregon, while those who remained in the Haight, like Dustin Blazer, sought to escape to new cities, different states of mind. As always, Dorn had reservations about his part in the proceedings. Was he one of them anymore, or had his foolish Quixotic quest left him compromised and alone? Now they were pulled back together.

He waved to Dustin when they found each other—kismet—after parking along the endless line of empty cars. They hiked into the grounds, part of a long march of freaks determined to celebrate this zenith of everything that had been building up since 1966.

"You just get back?" Dustin punched him in the arm. "Is the Kansas sabbatical over, so soon?" Moon Girl trailed behind the taller journalist, quiet and wide-eyed at the unending parade of humanity.

"It depends on a lot of things." Dorn trucked along, a knapsack hanging from one shoulder. "Depends on my funds, basically. Been meaning to call. How are things at the gallery?"

"Not making bread, but not losing." He grinned. "You worked at your father's hardware store and paid our rent. That's how you wanted it, right? Then sweep back in and be the savior."

"No." Dorn shook his head. "I had to split, for my health and the collective vibe. You being the manager and getting my artists involved in a co-op was the only way United Hallucinations could stay open."

"That's the problem." Dustin scratched a few frazzled dark strands of hair then set his poker visor back on. "Those artists all think that they're in charge. No one listens to me. I will not be bossed around by Mouse or Griffith or fucking Dorfman." He let out a sniff-laugh, did a little spastic dance, then embraced Dorn. "Good to see you again. I get it. You tried to make things better in the Haight. But fixing one problem causes two more to occur. It's like the Myth of Sisyphus, but with scumbags instead of rocks."

They hiked upward on the dirt road with deep tire tread marks and muddy trenches. "Sorry about what I said in July about you being a narc. Rat-Man went down, and Antonio Rivaldi is behind bars now. Who cares? They never did a fucking thing for me." Dustin turned around. "Keep up with us, Moon."

ALI TRAVELED FAR FOR THAT FAMOUS concert, that festival. They all did. Some hundreds of miles, others thousands. Her friends Van Monk and Jessica came far from his Laurel Canyon cabin, a hideout to escape the bad juju that infested Hollywood after the Manson killings. Dustin picked up Moon

Girl in Oregon and journeyed from there. Dorn hadn't told Ali he was joining them too, but it was cool because it would be uncool for her to manifest it not to be. Yes, she'd been annoyed that everyone seemed to know about him coming but her. But beyond that, Ali was glad her friends all loved each other and had been part of a special time—longer than a season, shorter than an era. Something had changed though, so she felt wistful.

A group trip.

In the sunlight of a beautiful afternoon, Ali estimated the crowd inside the concert grounds. A legend of the future being written today by footsteps imprinted in dirt and mud. Three hundred thousand? A half million? Enlightened youth tracking in from all points on the compass. The state highways clogged with barely moving traffic, even before reaching miles of cars abandoned on the road approaching the event. Swarms of people milled toward the entrances. The hills and fields already pocked with blankets, and the encampments of those in for the long haul. The Pied Pipers of the Acid Generation had led followers from everywhere in America to this perfect convergence.

Ali took off the top hat she liked to wear to special events and shook out her wavy, dirty blond hair. No one asked about her ex-husband in Vietnam anymore, not after his insane visit to the Haight in July. Now he was MIA, assumed dead. *Keep the vibe positive*, Ali thought. Even with the scope of the event, history in the making, she refused to get high today—on anything. Well, maybe a hit of a joint.

"So you guys are cool?" Ali said to Jessica.

"Yeah." She laughed. "Lenny has been stable recently." Jess spoke as she leaned into Van Monk. "It's only when he loses his sense of time and place that I get scared and go crash at my folks' place." She squeezed his thigh.

"This is amazing." Van Monk pointed at the gathering. He felt his mass of brown curly hair mushrooming out beneath a flat cap. "A giant peaceful tribe."

Van Monk's left arm draped across his girlfriend's shoulders. *I'm living in the present. It's 1969,* he kept telling himself. *Be here now.* Jessica had American Indian markings etched on her face and a headband embellished with flowers and peace signs.

"I'm so glad we made the long journey," Van Monk said. "We'll tell our kids about it someday." He imagined two sons and a daughter. When he time tripped to the future, he met them, knew their faces, but as soon as he zapped back to the present, those future memories disappeared.

Jessica frowned at his last words. "Kids? But *we're* the forever children."

When they discovered an uninhabited space of brownish dead grass atop a hill a good distance from the stage area, they spread out a large blanket. Dustin Blazer, followed by Moon Girl and Freddie Dorn, soon found them. Dustin really liked Moon Girl, but being from Texas, wanted to get all the free love possible out of the sixties before the store closed up for good.

"I can write a decent story out of today. Definitely." Dustin stared out over the hills and flats to muddy farmlands beyond. A riven and rucked world that he could claim for his own. Though he was over thirty, the oldest of them, and a sometimes rock journalist, he felt cocksure and powerful. Someone who could realize their own plans. In control. Today he wore a paisley vest and a visor and never took off his shades. Inside his brain, he could feel his scalp tingle, where his short dark hair was thinning. *Need to make my mark soon*, he thought. *I'm going to be famous if I don't fucking explode first.*

"So many great bands," Moon Girl said. "I hope I can stay awake until dawn."

Around their blanket on the slopes and flats, Ali saw sleeping bags, ramshackle tents, knapsacks, and wine bottles, she heard guitars playing folk songs, the throb and thump of bongo drums, watched dogs rolling in mud and tiny children stumbling through a bizarre universe they were too young to form memories of. Made Ali relieved not to have any. Kids were part of the eventual plan, but not in the here and now.

The few cops present looked glum. Most stood in pairs by the entrance gates and the road leading in. Solo officers on vague patrols acted lost or shook their heads, frowning. They could never have faith, believe in something vast and amazing like this.

"Don't eat the brown acid" had become a familiar joke to repeat with a grin.

Who needed to? Scads of blue sunshine circulated through the audience, given out freely by a mystery provider rumored to be Owsley. Dustin and Moon Girl partook in the offerings while Van Monk sliced up mushroom stems into a putrid-smelling wine mix.

Jessica seemed unenthused, her forehead scrunching. "Are you sure, Van Monk?"

"Not for me," he said. "A gift for the rest of you." No one looked especially grateful.

Time passed until they all smiled and grooved when Crosby, Stills, Nash & Young performed. Their twinkly, sparkly acoustic guitars strings resonating in hollow wood then miked up and sent reverberating out through the fields and hills, as the singers' amazing ghost harmonies rode atop the *plink-plink-strum-strum* to summon echoes of the Byrds and the Beatles. The audience embraced in a warm blanket of an aural hug from legends barely born into the Aquarian Age, here to bid farewell to the end of whatever this was and usher in the beginning of whatever would be. *Soon, soon, be patient.*

"We are the anointed ones." Dustin nodded at his own statement, pulled a joint from his vest pocket, lit it, and passed it around. "The radio says maybe four hundred thousand." Even with the live bands playing, Dustin held a transistor radio pressed against his ear to hear news, sports, and whatever else his information-starved brain needed to thrive. That was his scene. "Dig it, the upstate highways are jammed for fifty miles." He felt so pleased. Any event that upset the natural order had to be beautiful. Life was a gas.

Occasionally, messed up people stumbled and tramped across their blanket, as the whole event had become free. A test.

When they did encroach, Dustin inhaled weed and said, "Relax, man, relax," to himself.

Getting into a scuffle at a rock festival could only bring him bad karma. Though set far back from the stage, they held an excellent vantage point for the event. Somewhere, maybe two miles down the road, sat the cars they planned to sleep inside later on. If sleep was even on the agenda.

Jefferson Airplane's music provoked Moon Girl and Jessica to dance together. So happy over hearing one of "their" bands far from home. Ali could see no end to the people, the massing crowd. Most concerts stabilized at a certain point, but this one just grew. When the Airplane played

"Volunteers," Ali jumped up to join her girlfriends shaking and swaying.

"Start a revolution!" she sang along with Marty Balin. The band stopped their set a couple of times, though Ali was used to delays from outdoor shows in Golden Gate Park. People argued over the PA system, the words muddled, indecipherable at their distance.

"Are the Dead going on next?" Jessica asked.

"Not sure," Van Monk said. "Maybe they played before we got here, or they go on later."

"I need to pee." Moon Girl glanced at Dustin to accompany her, or for a reaction. Nothing. She set out for the rare portable toilets down on the flats to the south.

Dustin heard on his radio that there were only two hundred of them. "That means one toilet for every two thousand asses," he told the others. "That's insane."

*Is this our future?* Ali wondered. Bunching together in vast open spaces to listen to the distant clamor of bands that mirrored a generation's own feelings? The youth of America rejecting everything from their parents' generation: indoor plumbing, refrigerators, privacy, cleanliness, and the basic structure of law? Was the whole tribal, back-to-nature trip a step forward, or a stumbling return to some primitive caveman past?

A group on the faraway stage started playing country-sounding music, pedal steel guitar swooping, all twang and drawl. It momentarily calmed the restive audience, who came to be fed a never-ending buffet spread of amplified bands, not silence.

"Nice." Dustin waved his fingertips before his eyes. He stood but got a dizzy head rush and squatted back down. "Is that Country Joe and the Fish?"

"No," Van Monk said. "Canned Heat maybe, or the Flying Burrito Brothers."

"Why didn't you go along with your lady?" Ali asked Dustin. "Help her find the toilets."

"She's a grown-up, a big Moon Girl." Dustin laughed. "Self-reliance is key." He turned to massage a woman's shoulders on a neighboring blanket.

Dorn tried to talk to Ali but the scene was too public, his thoughts too private. "Sorry, I didn't tell you. Me coming here was kind of a last minute thing."

"It's cool," she said. "I love you." Ali quickly turned. "I love all of you—so much."

"Me too," Jessica replied, crossing the wide blanket on her knees to hug Ali.

The music drew listeners down the hillsides, magnetizing them toward the stage area already crowded with fans and whatever security there was. Ali and her friends had been to lots of outdoor concerts. They knew to stay away from the front of the stage, the stomping ground.

Moon Girl returned distraught. "Too many people down there. More keep coming in. They're not giving anything, they just want, want, want." She turned to Dustin who sat in his own blissful acid bubble, despite the herky-jerky advance and retreat motion of those around them. Ever since she got back from the treatment center, she couldn't seem to communicate with him.

"I think we should leave while it's still light," she said. "We can come back later when the vibe turns mellower, more positive."

"You want perfect vibes?" Dustin's smile twisted into a sneer. "Come on. You know if we go, we'll never get back in."

"What do you guys think?" Moon Girl asked, her hands fluttery, agitated. She had hoped Dustin would back her up today. He was always flying on his own solo ego trip.

Jessica had swallowed the mushroom and wine blend, her complexion greenish. When no one else had volunteered to try it, Van Monk decided to sip some. "Just a little, I can handle it. What's the worst that can happen?"

Afterward, Dustin stole the bottle away from him and handed it to a wandering man with dirty rags for clothes. At present, Van Monk struggled to act content. "I can't move right now because my stomach is churning."

"You can puke that stuff out," Dustin said.

Ali waved her hands defensively. "Not on the blanket, please."

"Let's split as soon as he feels better," Jessica said, "before it gets pitch black." Late afternoon cirrus clouds blotted out the low sun, but they had forty minutes before sunset. She wrapped herself in a shawl as the temperature dropped. "Please."

"I agree," Ali added.

"Okay," Dorn said. He really wanted to stay though, for the music, and this was part of his stupid assignment from Rodriguez. Finding a needle in a hippie haystack. Last favor ever for the SFPD because shamus retirement lay directly ahead.

Van Monk nodded. "Cool."

Dustin pounded his fist on the blanket. "I came all this fucking way to see these bands and I'm not leaving early. You going to tell your kids in the future that you split from the rock festival of the century because the vibe wasn't right?" Dustin shrugged. "Okay, go ahead, lightweights. I'll meet you back at the cars by midnight. I have a flashlight." He rolled over, facing away from them.

Suddenly, a big man lurched into their midst, collapsing on his knees at the center of the blanket. His clothes looked etched with dirt and mud, his face bruised. An almost palpable body odor surrounded him like a force field. He wore thick-framed glasses and sported a grown out crew cut.

"Hey, man." Dustin jumped up. "We're full up here. Keep on truckin'."

Then Ali recognized him. "Scott, is that you? Oh, shit, what happened? I thought you were lost in Cambodia."

Scott turned. "No, I got discharged, Ali. Been bumming around Napa and Vallejo, but I heard the call for this, in the wind." When he spit onto the ground, his saliva showed blood.

"Who hit you?" Ali asked. Scott's eyes looked vacant—a breathing ghost.

"Down there." Scott pointed at the stage. "It's just like Vietnam, where the enemy of your enemy is *not* your friend. Just you against the world."

"No, that can't be." Jessica's lips trembled. "We're the Woodstock Nation, peaceful and united in music and love."

"But this isn't Woodstock," Scott said, and handed a pair of compact binoculars to Ali. "Astrological forecasts all predicted this."

Ali focused on the stage area, already lit up by scaffold lights in the muted gray-blue of dusk. She saw Hells Angels with pool cues pummel audience members heads. A plump naked woman was pushed toward the stage then repelled, and a black man who stood close by watching got punched in the face. When a motorcycle toppled, Hells Angels lunged out to punish anyone in the vicinity. They clubbed spectators using sticks and bats. The stage rose only four feet off the ground with no fencing around it. The press of the crowd spit out random fans, casting them first up onto the lip of the stage—until they were beaten—then tossed back like broken furniture into a landfill. Unable to watch, Ali lowered the lenses to see a roiling mass of people propelled down the hillside by the gravity of their desire. The music a siren call to the stage.

Tears streamed down Jessica's face. "Joni said we all have to return to the garden."

"That was about Woodstock," Scott said. "Not this."

"No, we're in the Garden of Earthly Delights," Ali whispered. "Hieronymus Bosch."

The roar of a procession of motorcycles approaching the stage drowned out all music. Moon Girl embraced Ali in a trembling hug then passed the binoculars to Dustin.

"Oh, shit," Dustin said over and over before surrendering the binoculars back to Scott—the only one among them smiling. By then, the Rolling Stones played an out-of-tune version of "Sympathy For the Devil" that kept halting and restarting. Jagged and time delayed, the song echoed through the vast raceway. Dustin noticed movement around him as the hillside masses surged forward. *Charge of the light brigade . . . Into the valley of death!*

When Ali saw Dorn photographing Scott, she gripped his arm and whispered, "What the hell are you doing? When did you buy a camera?"

"Just trying to capture the event." His comforting smile must have looked bogus. Dorn snapped a picture of her.

"Stop that. I don't want to remember this scene, it's horrible." She shoved him away.

"They're all here today," Scott announced, his eyes bulging. "Manson, the Angels, me."

"I thought Manson got arrested in October."

"In spirit he is," Scott told Dustin. He pointed at the tiny figure singing onstage in a red cape. "And there's fucking Lucifer himself." Scott grabbed an empty wine bottle off the blanket. "I just came up for a breather, so I could see the battle clear, like Napoleon would."

"You're crazy," Ali said. They all stood while Dustin and Van Monk folded the dirty blanket. The surrounding hills and landscape lay shadowed in darkness, a faint powder blue making a last stand high up in the sky. Reason fading fast. "Who are you fighting, Scott?"

As if from some cosmic telepathy, Mick Jagger's voice came from faraway loudspeakers. "People . . . Why are we fighting?"

No one could or would ever answer that question logically.

"Vietnam kept growing, spread all the way to California," Scott said. "So I'll keep fighting until the war is over." He made a mad dash downhill, swinging the wine bottle to clear a path. No surrender, no retreat, no salvation.

Around Ali, audience members argued, some descending, others fleeing. Most didn't care about the disjointed music anymore. The environment, the elements became the thing, not attending a free concert to see favorite bands. That myth had already receded, become a relic of the past, a religion without believers.

Ali and her friends edged backwards, away from the suction of the flood-lit maelstrom. A cold tule fog ghosted in from the Central Valley, adding to their shivering disorientation. It took forever, a stumbling retreat over trash and abandoned gear, and sometimes across sprawled figures, wrapped like mummies in blankets. They pushed shivering through layers of people frozen in anguish, then beyond others too intoxicated to care, while the sound of the Stones playing "Carol" diminished behind them.

Finally, Dustin led them by his flashlight toward the boundary fencing around the racetrack. It took an hour to locate their cars amid the mass of parked vehicles. Both had been broken into, though at least not stolen. Ali saw the guys put on brave faces, but in the glow of fleeing headlights, they looked aged by the experience.

DORN STUDIED THE UNENDING TRAIL OF red taillights ahead of them, the traffic barely moving. Feeling no real rush to join that crawl, he noticed Dustin leaning on his own car. They locked eyes. Both of them alike, control freaks who thought they could solve problems, had the grit and determination to get shit done, and yet here amid this vast spectacle, this mass scale bummer, they were powerless. Dark primal forces no one understood had been unleashed. Neither one spoke a word, yet their sustained knowing glance was the most coherent communication they'd ever shared: a collective gut punch. The hangover that hits before you even drift off to sleep.

Dustin cracked a wistful smile before sinking into his Galaxie 500 next to Moon Girl and Ali. Behind Dorn, Van Monk was hunched over, vomiting by the wooden fenced side of the muddy exit road. Jessica held his head. The retreating raggle-taggle army of haunted concertgoers barely noticed, their imaginations stretched and warped to some other place.

Dorn lay across the hood of his Volvo, opening himself up to every lost soul at the event, and what led them to this muddy racetrack.

They were strangled by society with its phony jobs and its whole sitting on a porch watching the corn grow in some American Gothic, Norman Rockwell, bland, insurance company, town factory of a factory town, among the suspendered Middle America of slicked back hair and sock garters, girdles and beauty salon curlers, brick patio barbecue, fallout shelter fear, where the ignorant locals say, *"Kill the commies, punch the fags, lynch the coloreds and the longhairs,"* and go fight a war no one understands because to question it means you hate the USA, hate your ever-loving mother. Get married to start a nuclear family, join your pop's firm, work hard, and someday become the manager of the local hardware store with Elk's Club bowling teams and weekly poker nights. Haunted by midnight train whistles, by the fervid belief that something beautiful is happening out there, something electric and alive, dancing on the periphery, a rainbow explosion of possibilities and the pied piper leading off to a world that must be better because how could it be worse, and you can't ever miss home if you never had the guts to go and leave everything and everyone behind.

And somehow, you do escape to where it's new and outrageous, horizon unlimited, childlike wonder from morning to night. But after a while there's no job, no purpose, the band breaks up, the paint dries, the visionary trip ends, and your lover leaves you shattered and alone in the harsh burnout of dawn. To admit that it went wrong, that it didn't all add up, and it's not a utopia, but just a different way to live . . . No, that's way too intense to deal with, man.

AFTERMATH

## CHAPTER TWENTY-FIVE
# All Tomorrow's Parties

TWO DAYS LATER, DORN MET RODRIGUEZ inside the church by Van Monk's place. They spoke in the outer hallway, where candles were lit to honor the recent dead and holy ghosts of ancient saints, beyond the mass in progress and organ swells piping outward. "What's this atrium area called?"

"It's a narthex, and over there is the baptismal font," Rodriguez said. In plain clothes, he looked like a middle-aged Catholic come to worship. "You made it back all right?"

"Guess so," Dorn replied. "I can't believe you sent me to that disaster."

"You would have attended a free rock festival anyway."

Dorn shrugged. "Yeah, probably." He opened a manila envelope and pulled the glossy prints out.

"Saw the news, read the papers. Meredith Hunter and three others dead. Altamont sounded hellish. That's all?" Rodriguez went through the photos. "Not many here. Fuzzy too."

"Everyone looked guilty at the concert, or felt guilty afterward. I just photographed five people who vaguely fit the description you gave me." Dorn felt uncomfortable.

Rodriguez studied each one, either frowning or allowing slight grunts of doubt.

Dorn scanned the churchgoers walking in and out, his brain in permanent paranoia mode.

"The good news is, that it's relatively safe for you to live in town again." Rodriguez smiled, but it vanished fast. "Antonio Rivaldi got charged in connection with the murder of Vince Napoli."

"They fished his body out of the bay?"

"Yup. Only identifiable through his dental records." Rodriguez winced. "We pressured Antonio's two thugs, the guys who roughed you up. They eventually broke in exchange for leniency. Implicated Antonio in that murder and for drug operations in both the Haight district and out in Oakland." Rodriguez put his hands in a prayer pose. "He should be locked up for ten years, at least. The others for three to five."

"Great," Dorn said, without feeling much relief. "I still plan to leave town in early January."

"But why?"

Dorn didn't mention the recent letter from Selective Service; the draft had finally caught up with him. "I've told you over and over, I'm done." He sighed. "This whole detective fantasy, it ruined my business. I left California to make money in Kansas and keep the doors open, but I'm back and broke. Can't pay rent past December."

"I thought United Hallucinations became a co-op gallery?"

"Yeah, that kept it afloat for a few months." Dorn listened to the haunting dirge tones of the pipe organ. "The gallery only stays alive if I'm present managing it. Leon is good at what he does, and someday I'll figure out what that is. Dustin Blazer helped this fall, but he's on his own trip, not a selling art kind of guy."

"That's a shame." Rodriguez scratched at his mustache. "Your place was legit. No drug dealing in back rooms or any other illegalities that other Haight Street businesses pursued."

"Some artists won't show in my gallery anymore. Think I'm a narc. Who knows, maybe they're right. I had good intentions at first." Dorn laughed, short and sharp. "I'm having an event next weekend. Shhh, it's a closing party. Drop by, just pretend you don't know me."

Rodriguez dug two drawings from his coat's inside pocket.

"Who is he?"

"Police sketches of the Zodiac Killer." Rodriguez eyed him. "Your photos are blurry. See anyone similar at Altamont?"

"My friends thought it was jive, me taking pictures, so I stopped." Dorn sighed. "You expected me to find someone I don't know at a huge concert?"

"The SFPD hired ten people to photograph anyone with a buzz cut and sunglasses."

"You'd need ten dozen."

What disturbed Dorn is that the police sketches resembled Scott Coburn. Not exactly, but similarities existed. Dorn considered his minute chances of ever getting back together with Ali, and how that would be affected if she knew he fingered her ex-husband. Scott was unstable, insane, and desperately in need of treatment, but had he been back from Vietnam long enough to embark in an ongoing and deliberate murder spree?

"Again, did anyone look like him?" Rodriguez extended the sketches.

"No, not really." Dorn took them. "I'll ask the others I went with, then get back to you."

Dorn shuffled out of the church into the harsh light of a winter San Francisco day.

IN THE RUN-UP, IT SEEMED MAGNIFICENT, everything falling into place. Dorn's Christmas party art opening on December 19th was really a closing, but very few knew that. Though rumors had been floated in Herb Caen's *Chronicle* column about "a certain local gallery holding its last hurrah."

Detective Rodriguez helped out, speaking to various non-hippie businesses about the contributions United Hallucinations made against crime in the neighborhood. Because the gallery was having hard times, he urged restaurants and delis to chip in and support this end-of-the-sixties event. They did. Two servers loaned out for the evening. Cases of wine, beer, and appetizers began arriving the morning of the party, the kitchen's refrigerator soon packed with cheeses, ham, celery and carrot sticks, baguettes of French bread, small egg salad, and tuna fish sandwiches with their crusts sliced off. Leon had a stomach ache by noon sampling everything.

"I'm the taster. Making sure you don't get poisoned," he insisted. "Heavy work. Need a nap now."

"Stay in the utility room, let the rest of us get ready."

Ali arrived, casually stunning in faded jeans and sandals, with a thin, floral batik shirt and a bandana scarf as a choker around her neck. Dorn noted she wore a bra, which in California in 1969 was a conscious choice, and strangely, he approved of it. Some throwback to his Midwestern repressed background, or maybe that like onions, people needed to be peeled in layers, then slowly revealed.

"You've been avoiding me, Dorn." She set down a grocery bag of supplies and hugged him.

"Do you mean while I worked at my dad's hardware store in Kansas during fall?" He removed plastic cups and napkins from her bag. "Eighteen hundred miles tends to separate friends."

"I meant since Altamont." She perched on the counter in the kitchen. "I'm still processing the event. We, the collective culture, didn't need an epic bummer."

"True," Dorn said. "I've wanted to talk to you, but have been trying to get my head together and plan this thing."

She placed a finger under her lower lip. "This feels final, like a big blowout." When he started to speak, she interrupted, "Don't bullshit me, Frederick. Acid made us both transparent to each other."

Dorn feared the number that lay within the unopened Selective Service envelope locked in his desk. Cursed with bad luck, it was likely between one and one hundred.

Instead, he said, "I need a break. Can't manage this place or make the monthly rent and live here." He took both of her hands in his. "None of my artists grooved on working in the gallery, so the co-op plan didn't fly."

"I see," she said. "Then back to Lawrence, Kansas, with your parents?"

"Hell, no," he said. "A few months was the limit. Had to cut off two inches of my hair."

She laughed, throwing her long, wavy mane back. "Granny Dorn?"

He scowled. "Eighty-eight years old and can still kick my ass." He sighed.

"I sort of . . . "

"Missed me?" Dorn asked.

"Well, I missed all of us being together at the Bard Theater."

"I heard the owner booted Blazer out of there." Dorn stared off. "Think I'm going to open a small gallery up north and get lost—"

"On the Lost Coast?"

"Yes."

"And you didn't tell me, or ask me if I wanted to go along?"

"I figured . . ."

"You figured nothing, Dorn." She slid off the counter. "Okay, let's get this party ready." She faked a smile. "We can talk about the rest afterward, right?"

"Deal."

Guests arrived in a molasses of slow motion until they were massed inside the main gallery. Some spilled out onto the streets or wandered the hallway. Mayor Alioto showed early with two bodyguards and wormed through the assembled glad-handing friends and strangers. *Look* magazine had accused him of Mafia ties in September so he was suing them for libel. Now, he seemed to be railing against organized crime on television every day. Alioto cornered Dorn.

"I've heard you've been helping eradicate criminals in my town, and let me show my sincere thanks"—he extended two fingers—"by giving you a hearty hand clasp." Alioto soon vanished amid a cloud of fake bonhomie and forced laughter into his limousine waiting outside.

Ali helped the servers navigate their appetizer trays through the crowd. Yes, no, okay, he told curious strangers who pretended interest in buying pieces that Dorn knew they had no interest in. He spotted Rodriguez wearing a Cossack hat and bushy mustache disguise. Made him paranoid for an instant, but sniffing the air, no one was smoking weed. David Crosby's entourage seemed a welcome change from the swells in jackets and ties who'd dropped in on their way to dinner parties because the shindig had been featured in Herb Caen's column. Art *was* being bought. He had three deals circling in his brain. If only things could have always been this way before, then, but no.

"Hey, Dorn," Crosby said. "I've decided to forgive you."

"The hell are you talking about, Croz?"

"My weed stash at Micky Dolenz's greenhouse. It got burned up, remember? Your fault."

"No. Those crazy women turned out to be Manson girls. Squeaky something."

"Maybe the Manson chicks actually started the fire, but you were the catalyst." Crosby formed his I-know-everything smug expression. "If you hadn't crashed the party that would not have happened."

"Be that as it may."

"I held onto my anger for a couple months." Crosby's eyes became thin slits and a sly smile curled up. "Then I meditated on it in a hot tub at Esalen, with four beautiful naked women. At a certain point, it just didn't seem important anymore."

Dorn slapped him softly on the back. "Glad you made it. Have some wine."

"I want to buy that Alton Kelley piece with the flowers." Crosby jerked his neck and his young hippie associate opened a leather clutch bag. He began to pull out wadded bills.

"In my office, if you please."

Afterward, Dorn began to feel the second—or was it the third?—glass of red wine. Alone in the utility room searching for a corkscrew, he felt an arm wrap around his neck to choke him.

"Did you think I'd forgotten you," said a clipped voice.

"Tarick? What the hell?"

"You brought us trouble. Our commune has fallen apart."

A smacking noise sounded; Tarick's grip loosened. Rodriguez handcuffed the dazed man.

"Aggravated assault. Want to add resisting arrest?" He smiled. A new clean-cut, junior partner came in and escorted Tarick outside to a squad car. Rodriguez approached Dorn. "I didn't think I'd need to protect you tonight, but that bozo didn't get the memo."

"The memo?" Dorn rubbed his neck.

He tapped Dorn's chest. "Flannery wasn't dangled from a bridge as a warning to the police department, but to the Mob."

Dorn feigned deep thought. "You're the detective. I've shut my private third eye. Just an art dealer."

Rodriguez shook his head. "I don't know how you pulled it off, but no Mafia goon is going to touch you." He smirk-scowled.

"What happened to your partner, Bud Michaels?"

"Scum. Worked for Internal Affairs and the Mob. Can you believe it? Rumor is he's hiding in Omaha somewhere under an assumed name."

"You've had a lot of unique partners."

"Yeah, ever since you volunteered." Rodriguez made for the hallway. "Happy whatever."

The crowd looked hipper now, younger, gallery artists vying for his attention, wondering about the future, making Dorn respond with grins, slapping them five then continuing on, a shark in constant motion, fearing death—as anything alive does—along with disgrace, insolvency, and other modern age maladies.

The Duncans approached, their daughter in strangely formal clothing, freed from two cults and now brainwashed into whatever rich people called normalcy. She met Dorn's eyes for a moment then stared away, as if they'd shared some deep horror in the past which he had triggered flashbacks to.

"Thanks for everything you've done for our family and San Francisco," Richard Duncan said. *Sure, pin a medal on me, build a statue, give a speech at the ceremony, chip in for a sweet headstone.*

"Hey man, you've come a long way," said Peter Coyote of the Diggers.

"Yeah, from helping the community in your troupe to becoming a bread-head, a capitalist sellout, right?"

Coyote gently removed the third—or was it now the fourth?—plastic wine glass from Dorn's grip. "I wouldn't phrase it like that." They stared at each other. "I heard you tried to make things better last summer. I may disagree with your methods, but your heart was in the right place."

"Pete, you've got the fucking best gravelly voice. Have you ever considered radio work?"

Coyote chuckled raspy. "I'd like to act, but Hollywood is so plastic." He became serious. "I'm here on business. There's going to be quality leftovers when this party ends. Will you donate the food to the Diggers to distribute in Golden Gate Park?"

"Definitely." Dorn felt shark death consuming him, so he flexed his fins and swam on.

"I knew this would be a great scene." Van Monk hugged Dorn and they stayed frozen in a mutual support sculpture. "Because I've attended it a few times before."

"You flashed here?" Dorn became curious. "How does it end?"

"With the sixties. One big bang."

"Van Monk, I thought you went back south afterward." No one wanted to mention Altamont, how it had closed out 1969 with an exclamation point of disgrace. And now 1970 loomed outside, peeking in the windows, gauging the damaged property it would soon inherit.

"No, not yet. Some sessions with Paul Kantner's thing." He pushed his dangling curls upward to reveal his rumored but rarely viewed pale forehead. Jessica appeared behind Van Monk, drooping onto his shoulder. She waved at Dorn, low and secretive, without speaking.

Through the press of the crowd, Dorn spied Peter Fonda holding court, making it hard to break through the handsome man's ring of admirers. Instead, Dorn found Dustin Blazer and Moon Girl making out in the utility room. Leon sat on a nearby couch with a young black woman, glaring at the couple who had invaded what he considered his sanctum. Dorn finished his cup of wine, did a little dance step routine, and exited amid their laughter.

Bill Graham appeared, grinning and swarthy. "Congratulations, Dorn," he said. "You and me, we're alike. Music, art, and rent aren't free. No crime in providing a service that makes a profit." He became distracted by a frizzy-haired babe in a low-cut shirt. "Hey, did you get the fresh tangerines I sent over?"

Dorn nodded, having no clue what he meant. Graham went back into motion and became a figment of the past. Three women in conventional business dresses hugged Dorn while thanking him. Immersed in his wine buzz, he felt puzzled. As their faces came into focus, he recalled them as clerks during the July bank robbery.

"Glad you made it, ladies, stay as long as you like," he greeted them as he departed.

Someone had gotten into his locked office. Dorn forced the door—blocked by a leaning chair—open. Dustin Blazer held court with friends. "The Beatles are singing about you, Dorn."

"What?"

"You're one of the beautiful people," Blazer replied. "Not physically or mentally, but socially, yes! You've got politicians, civic leaders, professors, and rock stars out there. You can ride this moment to Seacliff parties, to Palo Alto pussy."

"Not interested." Dorn saw white powder atop the desk, Blazer showing his *what's wrong?* expression. Two seedy longhairs stared enraptured at the drugs, and no Moon Girl.

"Jesus, Blazer. Uncool. Cops were outside just before."

"I know, that's why I broke in here then secured the door. For your sake, man."

"Can you move your little private party elsewhere?" Dorn knew rich musicians did coke, but it hadn't really hit the street. Too expensive.

"Stuff is good for you," Blazer insisted. "Women in South America chew coca leaves every day to get them through their work. I can't believe *you* would be anti-labor." Blazer shrugged. "Try it, then tell me I'm wrong."

Dorn sniffed a line and stars pulsed on the periphery of his vision. "Finish it," he said. "Then everybody out."

"A 'thank you' would have sufficed." Blazer feigned an indignant look.

Dorn ushered them into the corridor before locking his office. Blazer exited the party, Moon Girl discarded somewhere. Ali embraced Dorn, whispering, "You'll make it through."

"Will you drive up north with me?"

"No," she said, eyes flitting about.

"Will you come visit me when I've settled in?"

"Well . . ." Her face went mysterious, clouded. "Just when you're sure I'm not coming, that's when I might." Ali's mouth twitched before she rushed back to referee the chaos.

## CHAPTER TWENTY-SIX
# All You Need is Haight

AS DAYLIGHT DRAINED FROM THE SKY, Dorn surveyed his land, his temporary real estate. Candles burned in the lounge where people acted reverent, slumped on low chairs and pillows, in some wordless demigod trance. Moby Grape played delicate and beautiful from the stereo. Dorn traversed the hallway for the thousandth time into the main gallery. Guests had spilled out onto the street, somehow remaining in orbit, like rings of Saturn attached to an immortal party whose true value can only be gauged by departing it. A celestial glow, the fleeting everything, all transitory, the decade's ending summoned up in a shouted farewell to a shining forever friend. "I love you, man!" Fading already, shadowed into the just night.

And Ali left, kissed your cheek and promised to return to help close up, causing some primal sadness to swirl acidic in your stomach, Dorn, though she rarely lied and why tonight of all times? Deals to be completed, so stay alert. The coke brought you up to the surface, out of the wine submergence for a time. Yes, that original poster is eight hundred, two thousand for the big canvas, and one thousand for its little sister. Robert Crumb asked, Why is there only one piece of my art on these walls? Because I dig your Janis album cover, Robert, but you're mostly underground comix, *Zap* and such. Come show me paintings in January—*when I'm gone.* Crumb isn't pleased, attired as an old hobo banjo player, contrasting with a baby face obscured under his vintage mustache and odd spectacles. A man out of time. A blur of gray hair tumbling over a white shift that resembled a nightgown: Baba Gagi, pointing a scolding finger and bowing as he retreated up the few steps to Haight Street to his waiting Mercedes-Benz. How did you miss him? Do you miss him? Hell, no. You hallucinated Ramona gesturing at the end of the hallway where a dying lightbulb flickered. It's only a strobe ghost, Dorn, turn away. You shared a perfect moment. Most people never even get that much. Don't forget, but don't look back.

The stereo blasted "All You Need is Love," and maybe a year or two ago it felt true, but goddammit, not in December '69. You also needed shelter, and bread, and a car, and maybe even a fucking weapon. *Breathe, Dorn.* Negative space showed through the remaining people, and stories and laughter came from departing guests strolling Haight toward Masonic or Clayton, the vibe spreading, a moment of goodness and hope in a year burned down to its nub. Just a scant roach left to puff on. A familiar-looking giant strode around with a pointed pharaoh's beard extending conical from his chin. *Where have I seen him?*

"Stanley? Stanley Hayden?" Dorn stared up agog at the six foot five actor as if a statue in the Louvre. Dorn stood to full height, but not high enough. He was a giant, broad-shouldered, with tree trunk legs.

"Ha ha, that is quite funny," Hayden replied. "It's Sterling, though I was in two Stanley Kubrick films."

"*Dr. Strangelove,*" Dorn said. "Welcome to United Hallucinations, for the first and last time." He made a Three Musketeer flourish with his hand.

"May we speak on a matter of importance?"

"Sure, Doctor." Dorn gently moved the last inhabitants of the lounge into the gallery, and hopefully on their way home, then sealed the door. "My dad loved you. *Johnny Guitar*, right?"

The actor nodded. "A profound experience occurred to me." He crouched down on the sofa to converse eye to eye with Dorn. "I had success in Hollywood, in westerns, crime films, Viking epics. Married a fine wife, owned homes, cars, and sailboats. The American dream, right? Happiness, yes?" He sucked in a deep breath. "No, I was an empty shell. Nothing I achieved enriched my soul, you know?" The actor ended most statements with a question, an extra piercing gaze. "Then last year I turned fifty-two and smoked marijuana for the first time." His whole face relaxed and went young. "It saved my life."

Dorn laughed. "That's pretty funny."

"I'm dead serious." Hayden stiffened. "I visited your gallery before, in October." He extended his long legs over the couch and armrest. "A rude fellow typing up front. No mental connection, if you catch my drift."

"Yeah, Dustin Blazer." Dorn smiled sadly. "I was indisposed."

"Getting high has been excellent in cutting through my tendency to bullshit." Hayden's eyes widened. "May I get to the heart of the matter?"

"Please."

"The rumor is, your gallery will close at the end of the year." His expression turned stern. "Unacceptable."

Dorn chuckled, checking if he missed a joke. "Hey, if you want to take over the lease—"

"That's exactly what I propose!" Hayden stood suddenly, his head striking the Japanese paper lantern lampshade descending from the low lounge ceiling. He slumped onto an adjacent chair. "I'll take over the lease for six months." Hayden smiled. "The work in here is astounding, profound, childish. I can tell these artists have been thrown out of the very best art schools. And one feels joy to look at it, no?"

Dorn tried to shake his woozy head, jostle his brain. "You want to manage my gallery?"

"Sure. You're going on a journey, according to a young female partygoer, on a walkabout, like Wandering Aengus."

"Far out, you've read Yeats?"

Hayden waved a finger. "Marijuana saved my life. I want to be part of this freak parade." He scanned the room, searching. "Must get back home to Sausalito now. We'll sign a deal tomorrow, then I'll speak to your landlord." A deep rumble of laughter. "I can be quite persuasive."

"I believe it."

"You'll have the option to return on July 1st," Hayden said, eyes gleaming. "By then I'll have new plans. I'd like to navigate a barge through canals in France, write my journal, you dig?"

"I completely dig." Dorn felt dizzy as they shook hands. The actor was like a Neal Cassady. An aged bohemian landed from a previous world, rushing to catch up on all he missed before the flash faded. And from the looks of it, poised to beat the hippie freaks at their own game of both enlightenment and intoxication.

# Everything is Everything

Dorn rises out of a nap, finds himself bidding goodbye to the final stragglers, puts on a brave face to Leon, who knows the deal, and finds a ride for Moon Girl—so lost and lonely. The servers are leaving too, one singing in Italian, as they melt into the evening street crowd. He wants to lean and does, into softness, into Ali. "I'm back." She patrols the gallery rooms, sends a bearded, bald man clad in a paisley bathrobe on his way, then blends back into Dorn's trip.

"You here to tidy up with me?" He tries to be stable, ignore the wine, weed, and coke, but keeps fumbling, keeps swaying.

"We can clean up this mess tomorrow," she whispers close to his ear though they are alone. "I came back to collect you, Dorn. You can't sleep here." She is right, of course, pointing at empty bottles, at plates on the floor, spilled ashtrays, and discarded junk. "You're staying with me tonight."

Dorn is blurred, hardly noticing himself lock the front door, slide the metal gate shut and step up to Haight Street. "I am? Why?" he says, as she assists his veering stride.

"My goodbye," Ali tells him.

Dorn is in a fug, both muzzy and muddled, but not brain dead. Doesn't share that he won't leave San Francisco for two weeks. Haight Street expands, becomes an electric-lit shadow canyon where a psychedelic black Santa Claus rings a bell, and says, "God bless you, Freddie." Smiling, Dorn falls into Ali's trip, surrenders all, confident that what can't be accomplished tonight, will be in the morning.

AFTER THAT? HE TEARS UP THE envelope from Selective Service without seeing the draft number. Tossed away. *Change your name to Teddy Bjorn and just forget it.* Inhale a day; exhale a night.

One week passes, then another. A slew of minor hassles before it's just him sitting in the trusted rusted Volvo, windows rolled down, barreling up Highway 1 in search of some displaced Cape Cod of the mind. All gray wooden cottages and forgotten whaling dreams of ancestors bubbling into the collective consciousness. The road twists and turns, rises and plummets, his ears pop, a burst of pure sunlight blinds, then fog sweeps in wet and cool. Seagulls flap above, lonely promontory lighthouses and monolithic offshore rocks come rushing toward him, while his future waits patient with a mysterious smile—reflected in his rear-view mirror—just three hours drive ahead. You're going to make it, Dorn. You already have.

# Acknowledgments

EARLIER VERSIONS OF THE "On the Bridge" and "Boardwalk Shuffle" chapters were first published in *The Dark City* crime magazine. Special thanks to Genna Rivieccio for her editorial advice, and thanks to my writers group, FOWG, for their input on several chapters.

## About the Author

MAX TALLEY WAS BORN IN NEW York City and holds a B.A. in literature. He has been a professional musician, playing at CBGB and Bleecker Street clubs in Manhattan in the late 80s and 90s. Talley's stories and essays have been published in sixty journals, including *Vol.1 Brooklyn, Atticus Review, About Place Journal, Whiskey Tit,* and *The Saturday Evening Post.* His short story, "Celestial Vagabonds," won best Fiction Contest from Jerry Jazz Musician. Previous books include the novels *Yesterday We Forget Tomorrow* (Damnation Books) and *Santa Fe Psychosis* (Dark Edge Press), the literary short story collections *My Secret Place* (Main Street Rag Books) and *Destroy Me Gently, Please* (Serving House Books), and the genre collection, *When The Night Breathes Electric* (Borda Books). In California since the mid-90s, Talley currently lives in Santa Barbara.

# RECENT AND FORTHCOMING BOOKS FROM THREE ROOMS PRESS

## FICTION

Lucy Jane Bledsoe
*No Stopping Us Now*

Rishab Borah
*The Door to Inferna*

Meagan Brothers
*Weird Girl and What's His Name*

Christopher Chambers
*Scavenger*
*Standalone*
*StreetWhys*

Ebele Chizea
*Aquarian Dawn*

Heather Colley
*The Gilded Butterfly Effect*

Ron Dakron
*Hello Devilfish!*

Ron Dakron
*Hello Devilfish!*

Robert Duncan
*Loudmouth*

Amanda Eisenberg
*People Are Talking*

Michael T. Fournier
*Hidden Wheel*
*Swing State*

Kate Gale
*Under a Neon Sun*

Aaron Hamburger
*Nirvana Is Here*

William Least Heat-Moon
*Celestial Mechanics*

Aimee Herman
*Everything Grows*

Kelly Ann Jacobson
*Tink and Wendy*
*Robin and Her Misfits*
*Lies of the Toymaker*

Jethro K. Lieberman
*Everything Is Jake*

Eamon Loingsigh
*Light of the Diddicoy*
*Exile on Bridge Street*

John Marshall
*The Greenfather*

Alvin Orloff
*Vulgarian Rhapsody*

Micki Janae
*Of Blood and Lightning*

Aram Saroyan
*Still Night in L.A.*

Robert Silverberg
*The Face of the Waters*

Stephen Spotte
*Animal Wrongs*

Max Talley
*Peace, Love and Haight*

Richard Vetere
*The Writers Afterlife*
*Champagne and Cocaine*

Jessamyn Violet
*Secret Rules to Being a Rockstar*

Julia Watts
*Quiver*
*Needlework*
*Lovesick Blossoms*

Gina Yates
*Narcissus Nobody*

## MEMOIR & BIOGRAPHY

Nassrine Azimi and Michel Wasserman
*Last Boat to Yokohama: The Life and Legacy of Beate Sirota Gordon*

William S. Burroughs & Allen Ginsberg
*Don't Hide the Madness*
edited by Steven Taylor

James Carr
*BAD: The Autobiography of James Carr*

Judy Gumbo
*Yippie Girl: Exploits in Protest and Defeating the FBI*

Nancy Kurshan
*Levitating the Penttagon and Other Uplifting Stories*

Hédi A. Jaouad
*The Immortal Journeys of Isabelle Eberhardt*

Judith Malina
*Full Moon Stages: Personal Notes from 50 Years of The Living Theatre*

Phil Marcade
*Punk Avenue: Inside the New York City Underground, 1972–1982*

Jillian Marshall
*Japanthem: Counter-Cultural Experiences; Cross-Cultural Remixes*

Alvin Orloff
*Disasterama! Adventures in the Queer Underground 1977–1997*

Nicca Ray
*Ray by Ray: A Daughter's Take on the Legend of Nicholas Ray*

Aram Saroyan
*Before I Forget: A Memoir*

Stephen Spotte
*My Watery Self: Memoirs of a Marine Scientist*

Christina Vo & Nghia M. Vo
*My Vietnam, Your Vietnam*
Vietnamese translation: *Việt Nam Của Con, Việt Nam Của Cha*

## PHOTOGRAPHY-MEMOIR

Mike Watt
*On & Off Bass*

## DADA

*Maintenant: A Journal of Contemporary Dada Writing & Art*
(annual, since 2008)

## MIXED MEDIA

John S. Paul
*Sign Language: A Painter's Notebook*
(photography, poetry and prose)

## HUMOR

Peter Carlaftes
*A Year on Facebook*

## FILM & PLAYS

Israel Horovitz
*My Old Lady: Complete Stage Play and Screenplay with an Essay on Adaptation*

Peter Carlaftes
*Triumph For Rent (3 Plays)*
*Teatrophy (3 More Plays)*

Kat Georges
*Three Somebodies: Plays*

## TRANSLATIONS

Thomas Bernhard
*On Earth and in Hell*
(poems; German and English)

Patrizia Gattaceca
*Isula d'Anima* (Corsican & English)

César Vallejo | Gerard Malanga
*Malanga Chasing Vallejo*

George Wallace
*EOS: Abductor of Men* (Greek & English)

## ESSAYS

Richard Katrovas
*Raising Girls in Bohemia*

Vanessa Baden Kelly
*Far Away From Close to Home*

Erin Wildermuth
*Womentality*

## SHORT STORY ANTHOLOGIES

### SINGLE AUTHOR

*Alien Archives: Stories*
by Robert Silverberg

*First-Person Singularities: Stories*
by Robert Silverberg

*Tales from the Eternal Café: Stories*
by Janet Hamill, intro by Patti Smith

*Time and Time Again: Sixteen Trips in Time*
by Robert Silverberg

*The Unvarnished Gary Phillips: A Mondo Pulp Collection*
by Gary Phillips

*Voyagers: Twelve Journeys in Space and Time*
by Robert Silverberg

### MULTI-AUTHOR

*The Colors of April*
edited by Quan Manh Ha & Cab Tran

*Crime + Music: Nineteen Stories of Music-Themed Noir*
edited by Jim Fusilli

*Dark City Lights: New York Stories*
edited by Lawrence Block

*The Faking of the President: Twenty Stories of White House Noir*
edited by Peter Carlaftes

*Florida Happens:*
edited by Greg Herren

*Have a NYC I, II & III: New York Stories;*
edited by Peter Carlaftes & Kat Georges

*Songs of My Selfie*
edited by Constance Renfrow

*The Obama Inheritance: 15 Stories of Conspiracy Noir*
edited by Gary Phillips

*This Way to the End Times: Classic & New Stories of the Apocalypse*
edited by Robert Silverberg

## POETRY COLLECTIONS

Hala Alyan
*Atrium*

Peter Carlaftes
*DrunkYard Dog*
*I Fold with the Hand I Was Dealt*
*Life in the Past Lane*

Thomas Fucaloro
*It Starts from the Belly and Blooms*

Kat Georges
*Our Lady of the Hunger*
*Awe and Other Words Like Wow*

Robert Gibbons
*Close to the Tree*

Israel Horovitz
*Heaven and Other Poems*

David Lawton
*Sharp Blue Stream*

Jane LeCroy
*Signature Play*

Philip Meersman
*This Is Belgian Chocolate*

Jane Ormerod
*Recreational Vehicles on Fire*
*Welcome to the Museum of Cattle*

Lisa Panepinto
*On This Borrowed Bike*

George Wallace
*Poppin' Johnny*

---

Three Rooms Press | New York, NY | Current Catalog: www.threeroomspress.com
Three Rooms Press books are distributed by Publishers Group West: www.pgw.com

www.ingramcontent.com/pod-product-compliance
Lightning Source LLC
Chambersburg PA
CBHW031404260825
31493CB00005B/16